DECEPTION

DARK DESIRES ORIGINS BOOK 2

DECEPTION

DARK DESIRES ORIGINS BOOK 2

NINA CROFT

Entangled Publishing, LLC
10940 S Parker Rd
Suite 327
Parker, CO 80134
rights@entangledpublishing.com

Amara is an imprint of Entangled Publishing, LLC.

Edited by Lydia Sharp and Liz Pelletier
Cover design by Covers by Juan
Cover photography from Shutterstock

Manufactured in the United States of America

First Edition November 2020

To Rob, who has promised to explore space with me should the opportunity ever arise!

Chapter One

"Live, for a day will come when you will be happy and bless life."
—Alexandre Dumas, *The Count of Monte Cristo*

Milo blinked his eyes open and frowned.

For a moment, he wasn't sure where he was except in a small, enclosed space that felt like a fucking coffin. He tried to move, but bands held him tight around his chest and head, and every muscle in his body tensed.

He slowed his breathing and forced himself to think. What was the last thing he remembered?

Walking out on a meeting with Rico. After turning down his offer of a place on the fleet leaving a dying Earth and heading for "a new and better world."

Ha—he'd believe that when he saw it. He was guessing more of the same old shit. No way. He'd rather stay on Earth and take his chances.

He'd been leaving the building and then...damned if he could remember.

The light was dim, but he could make out movement through the opaque roof of his tiny prison. Something was happening. A door opened above him, and the restraints *pinged* and released their hold.

As soon as he could move, his right hand reached out for his wand—never far away—and found...nothing.

Fuck.

"You looking for this?"

The voice was familiar, low, with a hint of amusement, and Milo swore again. Aloud this time. He tried to sit up, but something was stuck to his chest—some sort of monitor. He swiped it off, then sat up and swung his legs over the side of the box he'd been lying in. Scrubbing a hand through his short hair, he blinked a few times to clear his vision. He was naked except for a pair of black boxers.

A man—though he used the word loosely—stood in front of him, with Milo's wand in his hand. Tall, olive skin, black hair, eyes so dark brown they were almost black, and a smirk on his face. Ricardo Sanchez. Vampire and—Milo supposed—savior of the supernatural world. He was also Milo's uncle, though no blood relative. A long time ago, and in a faraway place, Rico had been married to Milo's mother's sister. Until she'd been burned at the stake as a witch.

Rico, having spectacularly failed to save his wife's life, had once promised Milo's mother that he would look out for his nephew. Milo had been six years old at the time. He'd never seen his mother again. But centuries later, and against all the odds, Milo was still alive. So he supposed he should be grateful.

He pressed a finger to his eyes. "Where the hell am I?"

Rico grinned. "Guess."

God, he could be annoying. Milo looked around him. They were in what appeared to be a storage facility. In the low light, he could just make out rows and rows of containers similar to the one he'd woken in. Thousands of them. *Cryotubes…* He'd seen pictures on the newsfeeds.

The lids were closed, and a green light glowed on each one. Milo was getting a bad feeling about this.

He concentrated. There was no sense of movement, but all the same he couldn't shift that feeling that everything was about to go to shit.

He'd told Rico "no." He didn't want to go into space. He wanted to keep his feet firmly on the ground. Flying was not his favorite thing—in fact, he hated flying. Why the hell would he voluntarily step foot on a spaceship? Besides, he had things to do on Earth.

The vampire wouldn't have ignored his express wishes. Would he?

Stupid fucking question. "I'm on a spaceship, aren't I?"

"Welcome to the *Trakis Two.*"

Milo blew out his breath. Maybe there was still time to get off. "Tell me we haven't left Earth yet."

"I'd love to, but…"

This was just getting better and better. "Why?"

"I promised your mother I would look after you."

"That was five hundred fucking years ago."

"A thousand, actually."

He went still. He'd been asleep for five hundred years? His mind didn't want to process that information.

When he remained silent, Rico raised Milo's wand. "Abracadabra," he said, waving it between them. Luckily, nothing happened. "Piece of crap."

Milo held out his hand, and for a brief moment he thought Rico was actually going to return the wand. But it seemed his luck had run out. At the last moment, Rico snatched it back.

"On second thought, I'm going to keep this for a while. Never know when it might come in useful." He tucked it down his boot, and Milo gritted his teeth. The wand was a part of him, an extension of his very being. He snarled.

"Who's a grumpy warlock?" Rico teased.

Milo studied him for a moment, trying to decide whether he could take the vampire. Nothing fatal, just one good punch on the nose might make him feel better. Rico watched him, that small smile playing about his lips as though taunting him. The tip of one white fang showed. Milo tensed his muscles.

Then a growl rumbled behind him and he glanced over his shoulder. Two men—and, again, he used the word loosely—stood shoulder to shoulder. He recognized the taller of the two—Dylan, alpha werewolf and an asshole. The second he didn't know, but he was clearly another wolf. *Crap*. No way could he take a vampire and two werewolves. At least not without his wand. He turned back to Rico.

"I don't suppose there's a way to get me home?" Except his home was gone. Even if the Earth had survived, it would have changed beyond imagination after five centuries.

"Not a chance." Rico gave a casual shrug. "Besides, you have a new home now. You'll be pleased to know we have landed on our brave new world."

Would it be any better than the old one? He doubted it.

"And," Rico continued, "as much as I'm enjoying this little family reunion, right now we have more important things to do. Get dressed—there's a bag under the tube—we have a meeting in five minutes. On the bridge." And he was gone.

On the bridge? Hell, this was like something out of *Star Trek*.

Maybe it was all some elaborate practical joke and they were really back on Earth. But Rico wasn't one for practical jokes. Which meant…

He was trying to wrap his head around the fact that Rico had somehow got the jump on him, knocked him out, and he'd been asleep for…five hundred fucking years. And Earth was far, far away. Or maybe didn't exist anymore.

He jumped to his feet. For a second, he thought his legs were going to give way beneath him. He steadied himself with a hand on the cryotube as he heard one of the wolves give a snigger.

Two werewolves he could definitely take. Even without a wand. But then what? Where was he supposed to go?

And he had to admit that he was curious. So he ignored them, bent down, reached beneath the cryotube, and tugged out a bag. Inside, he found the clothes he'd been wearing for that last meeting. He pulled on a pair of jeans, a T-shirt, socks, and boots, and he was ready to go.

Chapter Two

"All human wisdom is contained in these two words—"'Wait and Hope.'"
—Alexandre Dumas, *The Count of Monte Cristo*

Destiny blinked her eyes open, and a grin curved her lips.

She was awake. That could only mean one thing…

The thought filled her with a mingled sense of excitement and dread. In all her twenty-six years before she was put into cryo, she'd never stepped foot outside the laboratory. Now, hopefully, there was a whole world to explore. People to meet.

She lay on her back, and above her, through the opaque canopy, she could vaguely see someone moving. *Doctor Yang.*

Pushing down her impatience, she ran a calming mantra through her mind. Things would happen when the time was right—that's what Dr. Yang always said. Destiny forced her muscles to relax, her heart rate and breathing to slow. Metal bands around her head and chest held her firmly in place, so until the tube opened, she wasn't going anywhere.

After what seemed an age, the door lifted from the

outside and the restraints clicked open. Destiny reached up and peeled the monitors from her chest. Taking a deep breath, she sat up and swung her legs over the side of the cryotube.

Dr. Yang came to stand in front of her, and Destiny automatically held out her arm then sat quietly while the doctor took a blood sample and checked her vitals. She was used to this, and she knew that until it was done, she wouldn't get any answers.

Finally, the doctor nodded. "You're good."

"I feel great." Destiny pushed to her feet but swayed a little, and Dr. Yang extended a hand to steady her, then stepped back, her hand dropping to her side. Dr. Yang had always said she needed to be strong, so Destiny straightened her shoulders and took stock. "Everything is working fine," she said. And it was true, already she was feeling steadier.

She wanted to ask if they had arrived but was scared to, in case they hadn't actually gotten anywhere and maybe the ship was dying, or they were lost somewhere in space, or had broken down. There was so much that could go wrong.

She cleared her throat. "How long?"

Dr. Yang handed her a glass full of a pink protein shake and she took a sip—it tasted of nothing—and swallowed.

"Three hundred and twenty-two years."

Wow.

She forced the next question out. "Are we home?"

Dr. Yang gave one of her rare smiles. "We are. We landed on Trakis Four a week ago."

A week? They'd been here a whole week and she was only just being woken. She bit back her disappointment.

Dr. Yang wore a white lab coat over her ship's uniform of black pants and a red fitted shirt. It was the same thing she always wore when Destiny saw her. She was smaller than Destiny and only came up to her chin, and she had brown skin and golden eyes, slightly slanted in her round face. She'd once told Destiny that her appearance came from the combination of her Jamaican father and Chinese mother.

From the geography books she'd read, Destiny knew that Jamaica had been an island in the Caribbean Sea and China a huge country in East Asia. Both were gone now.

Destiny had no clue who her mother and father had been. All she knew was she had pale skin, blond hair, and blue eyes. But according to Dr. Yang, it wasn't important where you came from—that world no longer existed. What mattered was only what you did with your life. From now on, everyone left alive would have a role to perform.

She stretched her arms above her head—her strength was returning—and looked around. Nothing had changed. The lab was a small, crowded space, about twenty feet across and circular with silver walls. This was the extent of her world. The only existence she'd ever known. She'd never set foot on Earth or seen the sky or breathed fresh air.

Her heart rate kicked up again. "Can I go outside?"

"Not just yet."

A flicker of anger awoke inside her and she stamped it out as fast as it had arisen. Anger would get her nowhere; she'd learned that at a very early age. Learned to bury her fury deep inside until she'd almost convinced herself it was nothing but a bad memory.

"We need time to determine whether the planet is safe," Dr. Yang continued.

"I could help."

Dr. Yang gave another smile, but a small, tight one this time, and the last of Destiny's hope shriveled and died. "You're far too important to risk, Destiny. Be patient. When the time is right."

Then what?

Everyone on the ships had been chosen to ensure that

humanity reached a new world and that they would thrive. Everyone had a part to play, and in an uncertain future, they all had to stick to those parts.

Apparently, Destiny herself had been born to play an important role in the survival of humanity. According to Dr. Yang, she should be proud. And she was. Really, she was, just sometimes—okay most of the time—she wished she knew what that role was. But if she ever asked, then the doctor would get angry and closed off and Destiny wouldn't see her for a long, long time. And then she'd be alone, and she hated to be alone. Dr. Yang was the only person who ever came to the lab.

She sighed. While she would do her duty, and do it with pride, was it so much to ask that she could just live a little first? Breathe the fresh air, feel the wind on her face, the sun on her skin. Was it warm or cold on the new planet? Did it rain? She'd never felt rain or the sun or swum in the sea. Was there even a sea? Or animals? Birds in the sky? The questions were building inside her, yearning to get out.

Dr. Yang turned to go, and Destiny couldn't help herself, she reached out and touched the doctor's arm. "Please. Let me come with you."

Dr. Yang flinched and glared, and Destiny dropped her hand to her side. She held herself very still, but then the tension went out of the other woman.

"Not yet, Destiny. You must be patient."

I don't want to be patient.

Who knew how much time she had? While she had no clue what her role was, she suspected it must be dangerous. Otherwise why not tell her?

"It's just to keep you safe," Dr. Yang said. "You know how important you are. How special. We wouldn't want anything to happen to you. But as soon as we're sure there's no danger, then you can leave the ship."

She turned away, crossed the room, and pressed her hand to the panel and the door opened.

Destiny's eyes pricked, but she stared straight ahead as Dr. Yang stepped out. The door slid shut, and Destiny was left alone. Sinking to the floor, she hugged her knees to her chest and stared at the closed door. She didn't need to try it to know it was locked.

She had a role to play. She was special. Important.

She wasn't a prisoner. They were just keeping her safe.

Chapter Three

"On what slender threads do life and fortune hang…!"
—Alexandre Dumas, *The Count of Monte Cristo*

"Lead the way," Milo said, then followed the werewolves between the rows of cryotubes. All the tubes still contained their sleeping cargo—he could make out their blurred faces through the panels on the upper surface.

While the air smelled slightly stale as if it had been around too long—like five hundred years too long—it was perfectly breathable, though with a faint metallic taint. He saw no one else.

As they reached a set of double doors, they halted, and Dylan pressed his palm to the panel on the wall beside them. The doors slid open, and they entered a corridor, silver curved walls and yellow light. Too bright after the dimness of the cryo-room. He blinked until his eyes adjusted and looked around, although there was little to see, then hurried to catch up with the wolves.

They eventually halted in front of another set of doors.

Dylan opened them in the same way as the others and then waved for Milo to enter.

This was a big circular room with blank screens on the wall all around. The bridge, no doubt. In the center of the room, Rico sat in what Milo presumed was the captain's chair, an impressive array of buttons and panels on the seat arms.

The vampire twirled, then pressed one of the buttons and the screens came to life. Whatever they were showing was dark, and he could make out nothing.

"Welcome to Trakis Two," Rico said, waving his hand at the screens.

"I thought we were on the *Trakis Two*?"

"We are. It was suggested that each planet take the name of the ship that lands on it. Hence, as we are on the *Trakis Two*, that's now also the name of the planet."

Milo stepped closer to one of the screens. "It's pretty dark out there."

"It's always dark out there. Don't you love it? Of course, the other side of the planet is always light."

Milo thought for a moment. "It doesn't rotate on its axis?"

"Clever boy," Rico said. "I knew I was right to wake you. Just the man we need for the job."

Milo thought about pointing out that he was far from a boy. When they'd boarded the ship, he'd been about forty years younger than Rico, an insignificant amount when you considered they had both been close to five hundred years old. Though Rico must be twice that now, presuming he'd been awake since they left Earth.

"What job?" he asked.

"Curb your impatience. We're just waiting on the others." He pressed a different button, then spoke into some sort of comm unit. "Katia, get your ass out of bed and to the bridge now. And bring Logan."

He waved a hand toward a seating area that contained a table with eight chairs. Milo sat down, and Rico took the chair opposite, Dylan the one next to him. Rico reached beneath the table and pulled out a bottle and three glasses. Suddenly, Milo was very thirsty.

After pouring the amber liquid, Rico pushed one glass across the table to Milo. He picked it up and sniffed—it smelled like scotch—then he swallowed it in one go and nearly choked.

"Jesus. What is that stuff?" His throat was on fire.

"Home brew—I had to do something useful while all you lazy bastards were asleep."

"You've been awake the whole time?" Milo rasped.

"Every single day."

He held out his glass, and Rico refilled it. Milo sat back in his chair and studied the vampire. "So, you drugged me and brought me here against my will?"

"You were being stubborn. What was I supposed to do? Leave you to your dreams of revenge until the Earth imploded and you died? Your mother would roll in her grave."

Not possible. As far as he was aware, his mother didn't have a grave. There hadn't been enough left of her to bury. But he'd only been six at the time of her death, so the details were sketchy.

"Do we know what happened to Earth?"

"No clue," Rico said. "The fleet lost contact after a few years."

Damn. He would have liked to know what had become of the planet. And he would really like to know whether a few old acquaintances were really gone for good. Milo had spent most of his life hunting down his father, seeking for a way to destroy him. Not really revenge—whatever Rico said—more a service to the rest of the world. His father was pure evil. But even if the Earth hadn't been destroyed, his father was beyond his reach now. Five hundred years and God knows how many millions of miles beyond his reach.

He blew out his breath. It wouldn't surprise him to discover that Rico had brought him along on this trip for that precise purpose. Rico had long claimed that Milo's obsession with his father was unhealthy, and that if you made your life about revenge, even if you succeeded, you would be left with nothing. And in some ways, he was right. The search had consumed Milo. So what the hell was he supposed to do now?

"Did all the ships make it?" he asked.

"Not all, no."

The plan had been for twenty-four ships to leave the Earth. Each carrying ten thousand Chosen Ones. People selected through a lottery process to ensure the survival of humanity. Except the lottery hadn't been open to everyone—Milo had certainly not received a ticket. So Rico had decided that wasn't really fair and arranged to exchange half the Chosen Ones on the *Trakis Two* for people…or whatever… of his own choosing. Milo didn't know the details, but he suspected it hadn't gone well for the Chosen Ones involved.

A small, slender woman with black hair and green eyes entered the bridge, followed closely by a tall guy with blond hair and strange, almost purple eyes.

Rico waved a hand toward them. "Katia you know, and this is her friend, Sergeant Logan Farrell of the New World Army."

He nodded to Katia as she took a seat next to Rico and her friend took the chair on the other side of her. Katia was a werecat who'd worked for Rico a while back. Milo liked her as much as he liked anyone. Her "friend" appeared to be a fairly new werewolf. A strange combination, though they were obviously a couple. There was a sense of closeness to them.

"There's a New World Army?" he asked.

Katia grabbed a couple of glasses from under the table and poured herself and Logan a drink. "There was," she said. "Logan here is the sole surviving member. The rest were on the *Trakis One* when she dived headfirst into a black hole."

Wow.

He'd missed a lot.

The *Trakis One* had carried Max Beauchamp, the President of the Federation of Nations. Max was supposed to be in charge when they got to the new world. He was no loss—a total asshole. "The *Trakis One* is really gone?"

"Well, there's no coming back from a black hole," Katia said, then downed her drink.

He'd never seen a black hole, but he wouldn't have minded seeing Max Beauchamp sucked into one. His lips twitched.

"I think you're being a little insensitive here," Rico said. "A lot of people died."

A lot of people he didn't know. Why should he care? Hell, he wouldn't care if most of the people he did know were sucked into a black hole. So why worry about a load of people he'd never met and now never would?

"What is he?" Logan Farrell whispered the question to Katia, but Milo caught the words and realized Logan was asking what *he* was.

"Can't you guess?" Rico asked.

Logan shook his head. "Nope. Not a clue."

"Think magic," Rico said.

Logan frowned. "A wizard?"

"Close, but no. He's actually a warlock."

"There's a difference?"

Rico leaned across the table and topped off Milo's glass, which he'd emptied again. "You want to fill him in?"

"No."

"Why is that no surprise?" Rico snorted. "A wizard is a male witch. They're mainly human but get a few powers from making dodgy deals with dodgy people. A warlock, like our friend Milo here, is the offspring of a witch and a demon. Their magic mainly comes from demonic powers." He smirked. "They're usually unfriendly bastards with chips on their shoulders, and Milo is no exception. He doesn't play well with others—except unfortunately, this time he doesn't have much of a choice. Because he owes me."

The words oozed self-satisfaction, and Milo gritted his teeth.

The truth was, once, a long, long time ago, Rico might have saved his life. And he was never going to hear the end of it. "Just tell me what the fuck you want," he growled. "I presume there's something you need me to do."

"Of course. We've been invited to attend a council meeting. On Trakis Four."

"What council?"

"The newly formed Council for the Advancement of Mankind."

He cocked his head. "That sounds completely made up. Is it even a real thing?"

"It is now," Rico said. "With the *Trakis One* gone, there's no one in charge. Some guy called Luther Kinross, on Trakis Four, is making a play for the vacancy, though he's not saying that outright. The thing is—the other ships are going along with him, so right now we don't have a lot of choice."

There was always a choice. "Thanks. But I think I'll pass."

"Not an option, my friend."

Milo sighed. "Why me?"

"Well, we would send Katia and Logan, but Katia was under investigation when the *Trakis One* went down."

This just kept getting more convoluted. "Investigation for what?"

"Working with terrorists to destroy the fleet."

He shot a questioning look toward Katia, and she merely shrugged.

"And there were too many people aware of that," Rico went on. "Besides, Katia and Logan were supposed to be on the *Trakis One* when she dived into the black hole. Sending them now will raise too many questions. So I had a think—and came up with you."

"Why me?" he repeated. "Get to the point."

"Because you are so charming."

"Ha."

"Okay, you're not particularly charming, but there's a reason you were the best Facilitator on Earth. You know how to negotiate. You're level-headed. You can be relied upon not to do anything too stupid. But in the event everything goes to shit, you'll do what's necessary. Plus, you can pass for human—which is clearly going to be a big advantage."

Milo suspected that was the main reason. "And if I do this, then I don't owe you anymore?"

"I wouldn't go as far as to say that—I did save your life at great personal risk. But I would be *very* grateful, and I might even give you your magic stick back." Rico grinned but then his expression quickly turned serious. "Look, we need information. Find out everything you can about this Kinross guy. Whether he's got any reason to think he should be in charge and anything to back it up. And most important—is he any threat to us."

Milo wanted to say *hell no*, but he also wanted his wand back. "I'll think about it."

Rico shook his head. "You didn't want to come on this trip. I get that. But you're here now, so make the best of it. This is a chance for a new start. *Dios*, when you were young, you'd go on and on about changing the world. Making it a place where we wouldn't have to hide what we are, where we could all live out in the open. Free."

"That was a long time ago." He'd been idealistic back then. But the truth was he'd never really let go of that dream, just realized the impossibility of people like him ever being accepted as anything but evil back on Earth. So he'd buried the dream deep. Now it awoke sleepily inside him, nudging at his mind.

"Tell me," Rico murmured, "that you don't still want that world."

A world untainted by religions that claimed they were monsters. "Maybe."

"Well, this is your opportunity. We can make Trakis Two *our* world. Unless this Kinross decides to stick his nose in. So get to Trakis Four and find out what's going on." Rico took a swallow from the bottle and smiled. "And don't worry about being lonely. We're sending Dylan with you."

Christ, no. "I'd rather go alone."

"I'm sure you would. But you can't. They're expecting two representatives, so you're going to have to get over the whole I-want-to-be-alone thing and play nice. It won't be for long. Then you can come back, make your new world, or disappear into the darkness and do whatever the fuck you want."

"That might be the nicest thing anyone's ever said to me."

"Then you really need to get out more—another reason for you to be on this job. Practice your social skills." Rico stood up. "I'm going to make sure your shuttle is ready. Katia and Logan can fill you in on the details of what's been going on and what subjects to avoid."

As Rico crossed the room, Milo called after him. "What about my wand? I might need it."

Rico pursed his lips. "*Dios*, no. You need to be discreet. Which means the last thing we need is you waving a wand around like Harry-fucking-Potter." And he was gone.

Milo sat back and sipped his drink, feeling the warmth

spread through his stomach. He was still finding it hard to get his head around all of this. They'd come five hundred years across space. And he'd been asleep all that time.

But for now, he was on safe ground. At least for the next few minutes. He looked at the others around the table.

"It appears I'm going for a ride in a shuttle with a werewolf." His stomach churned at the thought. "What could possibly go wrong?"

Logan raised his glass and grinned. "You really want us to answer that?"

Definitely not.

Chapter Four

"He was a fine, tall, slim young fellow, with black eyes, and hair as dark as the raven's wing; and his whole appearance bespoke that calmness and resolution peculiar to men accustomed from their cradle to contend with danger."
—Alexandre Dumas, *The Count of Monte Cristo*

Destiny wasn't sure how much time had passed since Doctor Yang left.

She'd spent most of the time reading *The Count of Monte Cristo* on the computer. Doctor Yang had provided her with books she deemed suitable, but they were mainly textbooks that had been used back on Earth. Destiny had studied them diligently and she now had the equivalent education of twenty-eight university degrees in subjects as diverse as Quantum Mechanics to Philosophy. She could also speak fifteen languages fluently.

Unfortunately, Dr. Yang believed fiction to be frivolous and inappropriate. But when she was sixteen, Destiny had found a copy of *The Count of Monte Cristo* buried deep in one of the computer's hard drives. At first, she hadn't even realized it was fiction—she'd never encountered a story before. She'd believed it to be true, historical facts. Eventually she had worked out that it wasn't real, and she'd been utterly fascinated. The story spoke so eloquently of freedom and honor and duty and...love. And a deep craving had awoken inside her for an emotion she hadn't even known existed.

She'd read and reread the book. Especially at times when she was feeling down.

Like now.

The story gave her hope. Even if it wasn't real.

Right now, though, she was running on the treadmill, trying to get rid of her excess energy. She'd been feeling so restless since she'd woken from cryo. Before, when they were traveling through space, there had been nowhere to go—the spaceship had been her whole world and so she'd accepted it. Now she felt trapped. Like a prisoner. Outside of the lab, there was a new world to explore, people to meet, and she wanted to be out there so much her chest ached. So she ran until she was too tired to go any farther, too tired to think, until she could feel her heart pounding, and at least she knew she was alive. And still she kept running.

"Destiny?"

She jumped, then slammed her hand on the control to stop the machine. She hadn't heard Dr. Yang enter, and, breathing hard, she glanced around warily. Her exercise routine had always been carefully monitored and controlled. Today she had exceeded the recommended use of energy and she studied Dr. Yang. Was she annoyed? Would she punish her? But Destiny could tell nothing from the other woman's expression.

She wiped the sweat from her forehead. "I didn't hear you come in."

"No, I could tell." Dr. Yang smiled. "I have good news for

you. You've been cleared to leave the ship."

A grin tugged at her lips and she held them tight together. Dr. Yang didn't like overt expressions of emotion, but inside she was fizzing. "Really?"

"Yes, really. Go shower quickly and collect your things." She handed Destiny a bag. "We're leaving right away."

She jumped off the running machine and hurried to the small bathroom. After stripping off her clothes, she turned the water on to hot. She showered fast then switched to the dryer, bouncing on the balls of her feet as the warm air brushed over her skin. Once dry, she dressed in an identical outfit, pulled on her shoes, then shoved the rest of her things into the bag. Two more identical outfits and a toothbrush. That was all she had.

Dr. Yang was waiting by the external door when she came out.

This was really happening. She was going *outside*.

She held her breath, sure something would occur to stop them from leaving, as Dr. Yang pressed her palm to the panel and the door slid open. Her breaths were coming hard and fast, and she slowed them down, counting to ten with each one. Then she was stepping toward the door and through it. She stopped for a moment and looked around. They were in a wide corridor with silver walls and bright light overhead. She hurried to catch up with Dr. Yang, who was striding purposefully away. As they came around the corner she almost skidded to a halt as a figure came into sight.

A man.

The first she had ever encountered. He was taller even than her, with short black hair and dark brown skin. He didn't slow as he passed her, just nodded, and she followed him with her gaze until he disappeared from sight.

Dr. Yang glanced over her shoulder and frowned. "Hurry up, Destiny."

She shook herself and hurried on.

They came to another doorway. As it slid open, a cacophony of noise hit her ears. She blinked then stepped into a huge, cavernous room filled with things and...*people.* Men and women. Some pale, some with dark skin, others with Asian features like Dr. Yang. More people than she had imagined could exist in one place. At first it seemed like chaos, but as she watched, she noticed they were actually well organized. They carried things out of the room, unloading the ship. Presumably, this was all the equipment and stores that had been brought with them from Earth. Everything they would need to help humanity settle into their new home.

A couple of men in dark green uniforms seemed to be in charge, directing the unloading. They nodded to Dr. Yang but looked at Destiny curiously. She *was* dressed differently. The workers were all in beige jumpsuits, hers was yellow—Dr. Yang had let her pick the color. Yellow was her favorite.

She paused to run her hand over a large metal object. She had no clue what it was, but the metal was cold to the touch.

"Destiny!"

She hurried after Dr. Yang. There was so much to see, but hopefully there would be at least a little time to examine all these new things.

Finally, they reached the doorway. She halted, hovering at the edge of the ramp that separated the ship from the new world. And then she was breathing in the fresh air, filling her lungs. It smelled as she had imagined sunshine would smell. As she'd imagined the color yellow would smell.

She stood and stared.

She blinked at the bright light. There was the sun. Actually, there were two suns. A large yellow—almost white—ball just peering over the horizon and a smaller orange sun higher in the sky. The air was warm, and a light breeze tickled her skin as she held her face up to the sunlight.

It was so beautiful her chest ached.

The ship had landed on a plateau, and before it lay a shimmering lake of blue water, and beyond that a forest of small, stumpy green trees. She turned her head; behind them a steep mountain loomed over the ship. High above, some sort of bird or other flying animal circled lazily in the sky. So free.

How she would love to fly.

A man came up behind her, a large square box in his arms, nearly knocking her over; she stepped to the side, then watched as he carried the box down the ramp and placed it in the back of a large vehicle.

"Come along," Dr. Yang said.

She followed her, but as they stepped off the ramp, Destiny came to an abrupt halt. For the first time in her life she was actually touching the ground. Not a floor, but actual dirt. A tremor ran through her. Then something caught her eye off to the right. A spaceship was coming in to land, small and sleek and silver. Dr. Yang had also stopped.

"Who is that?" Destiny asked, not really expecting an answer, but to her surprise, Dr. Yang spoke.

"They're representatives arriving from the rest of the fleet. There's to be a meeting," she murmured. "That shuttle is from the *Trakis Two*—you can tell by the number on the side."

The shuttle touched down lightly on an area of flat land near the ship. There were already three others parked in a row.

"They all came over on the *Trakis Five*," Dr. Yang continued. "But the ship is remaining in orbit and they're using shuttles to bring them to the planet surface. Come."

The door to the shuttle slid open and two figures emerged. Destiny hesitated.

The first man was dressed similarly to Dr. Yang, though

his shirt was yellow. But it was the second man who held her attention. She couldn't look away.

He was quite possibly the most beautiful thing she had ever seen.

Tall and lean, dressed in blue pants and a black shirt that fitted his form. His hair was short and black, and his silver eyes wandered restlessly over the scene in front of him. A scar ran down his right cheek. He looked wild and free like the bird in the sky, and she took a step toward him as though she were pulled.

The movement must have caught his attention, because he turned slightly, raised his head, and stared straight into her eyes. For a moment their gazes locked. He didn't smile, didn't change his expression in any way, but she felt a connection tug at her. A shiver ran through her and her skin tingled. Her mouth went dry as she hugged her arms around herself, yearning for something, but no clue what. Then the man beside him spoke and he shook his head, breaking the connection, leaving her bereft. They disappeared inside the shuttle, and she stared after them.

"Destiny?"

Dr. Yang was watching her, and she forced herself to smile. "Where are we going?"

"There."

Destiny's gaze followed the direction of the doctor's pointed finger. An island lay in the center of the lake, bustling with activity. Already a building rose out of the flat land. Was this to be her new home? The walls were the same sandy color as the mountain behind them, and there were windows that would look out onto the forest and the mountain. She could imagine the sun streaming into it in the mornings.

Dr. Yang strode across the sandy ground to where a red vehicle waited for them and then opened the door and gestured for Destiny to get in. She climbed inside and the doctor got in beside her.

Clutching her bag on her lap, she stared out the window, then turned and looked behind them. The ship was huge. Her gaze shifted to the much smaller shuttle from the *Trakis Two*, but there was no sign of the man who'd caught her attention.

Would she ever see him again?

She wanted to pack in as much as she could. She would learn to swim in the lake, climb the mountain, lie under the warmth of the suns. Meet the mysterious stranger who made her body shiver and her skin tingle. Maybe learn about love. She'd read about love in *The Count of Monte Cristo* and it was high on her list of things to experience. Also probably at the top of the "never going to happen" list, but she could dream. Even Dr. Yang couldn't stop her from dreaming.

"Have you ever been in love?" she asked.

Dr. Yang frowned. "What are you talking about, Destiny?"

"Nothing."

Then they were moving. And the only world she had ever known grew smaller and smaller behind her. As they reached the water's edge, with a shifting of machinery, they drove straight into the water and toward the land. It took only minutes to cross. She had seen pictures of old-fashioned castles on Earth. This reminded her of that, the tall building surrounded by a moat. For protection, she assumed, but protection against what? What dangers had they found on this brand-new world?

The vehicle pulled up outside the building, and she got out and stood looking around. There were people everywhere, working, building—would she be expected to work, too? Dr. Yang ushered her up a set of stairs and through an open doorway into a wide hall. A man stepped forward and they spoke briefly. She didn't seem happy but finally nodded and came back to Destiny, giving her a tight smile.

"Your room is downstairs."

Oh… She wanted to be high up. She wanted a view. But she knew better than to question the doctor when she had that closed-off, unhappy expression, and she just gave a brief nod.

The man led them through a door, down a set of stairs, through another door. The corridor was narrow and the light dim. He stopped in front of a metal door with a grill in the front. He turned the handle and the door opened. Stepping aside, he gestured for her to enter.

Her feet locked in place, her stomach churning as all the brightness oozed from the day.

The room was dark, and no sunlight reached here under the ground. She looked at Dr. Yang, but her face still held that closed-off expression, and Destiny knew there was no help there.

She clung to her bag and stepped into the darkness. As she entered, an orange light flickered to life. The room was small, maybe ten feet by ten feet. She blinked but held her shoulders stiff until the door closed behind her, and the lock *clicked*. She waited until the sound of footsteps faded, then she sank to the floor.

What have I done wrong?

Chapter Five

"Remember that two-legged tigers and crocodiles are more
dangerous than those that walk on four."
—Alexandre Dumas, *The Count of Monte Cristo*

Elvira Yang blinked as she walked away. She wouldn't let herself feel, but the look on Destiny's face as she stepped into that cell would haunt her forever.

She took a deep breath. She needed to stay strong for a little while longer. Soon this would be over, and she would be free to join her family. All the same, she could try to help. While she'd kept her distance over the years, something about Destiny had always tugged at her. Perhaps because Destiny was her creation. She had molded her. Human, but better than nature could ever create.

She headed up the stairs to the first floor. Here the corridors were wide, and sunlight flooded in through the windows. She knew her way around and went straight to the office. Silas stood outside the door, no doubt protecting his boss from unwelcome visitors. Which didn't include her.

"Can I see him?" she asked.

"I'll check."

She liked Silas. He appeared to be one of those rare things—a decent human being—apart from his total loyalty to Luther Kinross, of course. One day she would ask him where that came from. Luther was larger than life and possessed the art of inspiring loyalty, until you got to know him. Then you realized what a ruthless bastard he really was.

Back on Earth, Luther had been a billionaire, a powerful man who'd appeared to have no urge for the limelight. Instead, he kept to the shadows, happy to control from behind the scenes.

He had interests in a number of fields, and he'd funded her research for many years. Also, one of his companies had had the contract for selecting and training the crews for all the fleet. She presumed that was how he had managed to get her a place.

Here, he was making a more overt bid for power. But then, with the destruction of the *Trakis One,* right now, everything was up for grabs. The *Trakis One* had carried Max Beauchamp, the president of the Federation of Nations and intended leader of the new world. Until his ship had crashed into a black hole. As far as she was concerned, it was no loss to the human race. In the years before their departure from Earth, Beauchamp had put an almost complete ban on any sort of medical research, claiming all resources needed to be focused on the escape plan.

While Luther couldn't have foreseen the black hole, he appeared to have set everything in place for this, including her presence on the *Trakis Four*, years before the fleet even left Earth.

Silas spoke into the comm unit on his wrist and gave her a nod. "You can go on in."

The door slid open, and she stepped into the room. It

was set up like an old-fashioned library from a stately home. Bookshelves with real paper books, a Persian rug on the floor, a big mahogany desk across the far corner. Luther stood at the window, staring down at the planet below, but he turned as she approached.

He was a handsome man with blond hair and sharp blue eyes. Tall, with not an ounce of spare fat on him—he was an ascetic and proud of it. And while he was in his late eighties, he could easily pass for a man in his prime. Thanks to the results of all that research he'd paid for.

"Elvira, how pleasant to see you," he said. "And how is your charge? Is she here?"

"She is."

"Good."

She considered what to say next. She had to be careful; Luther wasn't a man who liked his decisions questioned. "Is it really necessary that she be locked in a cell?"

He pursed his lips. "It seemed a sensible precaution."

"Destiny understands her duty. She's not going anywhere."

He waved her to the upright seat in front of his desk and took the big leather chair opposite, steepled his fingers on the wood, and studied her. She'd become very good at hiding her feelings, and she allowed a small smile to curve her lips, her hands resting loosely on her lap.

"What have you told her?" he asked. "About her *duty*?"

Elvira shrugged. "Not a lot. Just that she has an important role to play in the survival of mankind."

He smiled. "She does indeed."

"She wants to go outside, look around."

"Is that wise?"

She gave another shrug. "I don't see it as a problem. And it will keep her healthy and happy. And that's in all our best interests."

His eyes narrowed as he considered her comment. "You think she might harm herself?"

Destiny was strong, and she was an optimist. She would never kill herself; she would always hope that things would get better. "No, but depression might set in, and that would likely affect her physical well-being."

He gave a small nod. "You may provide her with things to keep her occupied—books—whatever."

"And may she go outside? I'll supervise the trips."

He was quiet for a moment. Had she pushed him too far? Then he smiled. "No, you have important work to do, but I'll arrange for her to spend some time outside. Silas can supervise her."

"Thank you." It was something, she supposed. "Do you plan to meet her?"

He looked thoughtful but then shook his head. "I don't think that would be a good idea." He was probably right, considering Destiny's role. "When will you be ready?" he asked.

"A week, perhaps. Ten days at the most."

"Good." He gave a curt nod. "Thank you for your efforts."

Recognizing the words as a dismissal, she rose to her feet but then hesitated. "I saw the shuttles landing for the meeting."

"And...?"

"The representatives from the *Trakis Two* have arrived, and I wondered whether there was any news of my family. Have they been woken yet? Are they okay?" She surreptitiously rubbed her sweaty palms down her pants.

But he smiled. "I'll talk with the representatives as soon as they arrive and find out what the situation is. However, as you are aware, the Chosen Ones are being woken in batches, so your family might still be in cryo."

She swallowed down her disappointment. "I know. And thank you."

She'd done her best for Destiny. For what it was worth. She'd always known what fate had in store for her charge— but they all had a role to play.

And there was her own family to worry about.

They had to come first.

Chapter Six

"The difference between treason and patriotism is only a matter of dates."
—Alexandre Dumas, *The Count of Monte Cristo*

"You keep watch," Milo said.

They were on their way to the first meeting of the Council for the Advancement of Mankind but had decided on a little detour first.

He wanted to get a look inside the docking bay of the *Trakis Four.*

Their main purpose here was to ascertain exactly what sort of a threat Luther Kinross could be to them.

Milo was impressed with the organization on the planet; already, considerable work had been done. As far as he was aware—though he hadn't been down on the surface of Trakis Two—they hadn't built anything yet. Kinross clearly had a detailed plan and was moving ahead with it. Milo had seen various groups at work around the place, presumably Chosen Ones. Making roads and buildings. The work groups reminded him of prison gangs back on Earth and were supervised by armed guards in dark green jumpsuits.

Where had the guards come from?

Kinross was clearly ready for trouble. But how ready?

They needed to find out what other weapons he had brought with him from Earth. And the most obvious place to start looking was the *Trakis Four*.

"Be quick," Dylan muttered. "We're already late."

Milo nodded and headed up the ramp that led to the docking bay. There was no guard, and the door slid open when he pressed his hand to the panel, so he was unsurprised when he entered the cavernous space only to find it empty, except for the two shuttles parked up against the far curved wall and something that looked like a rocket launcher, which didn't bode well. No weapons, but then Kinross would hardly leave weapons out in the open for anyone to see.

"They've cleared it out," he said to Dylan as he walked back down. "Though there is some sort of rocket launcher—a fucking big one. We have to presume that somewhere there are some fucking big rockets to go with it."

Dylan raised a brow. "Nice."

"Now we need to find out where they've stored them and anything else Kinross brought from Earth."

"After the meeting."

A boat was waiting at the small dock to take them across to the island, and they climbed on board.

"It's like a goddamn castle," Dylan said five minutes later, as the boat docked on the island. "I'm guessing Kinross has delusions of grandeur."

A tall man in a dark green jumpsuit stood at the door. "You need to hand over your weapons," he said.

"Why?" Dylan asked.

"Because there are no weapons allowed in HQ. This is a friendly meeting; you won't need a gun."

"What about yours?" Dylan nodded to the pistol at the man's waist.

The man didn't reply, just stood blocking the entrance.

With a sigh, Milo unstrapped his holster and handed it over. After some grumbling, Dylan did the same.

"Across the hall and through the double doors opposite," the man said, waving them through.

Milo followed the directions and stepped through the doors—then came to a standstill.

The room was huge and round, with a high ceiling and arched windows. A large, circular table took up most of the space, with chairs all around. Most of them were occupied.

"Perhaps you should have put on a uniform," Dylan murmured from beside him. "You know, so you fit in."

Milo glanced down at his jeans and T-shirt. He supposed Dylan was right, though fitting in had never been his strong suit. Most of the people in the room were wearing some variation of the uniform of the crew of the Trakis fleet. Black pants tucked into black boots, and various colors of shirts— depending on their rank and position on the ships. Dylan wore a yellow shirt, which apparently meant he was second-in-command. There were a couple of greens denoting ships' captains. A few blues and more yellows. And most of the people looked old. He and Dylan were the exception.

By his reckoning there should be sixteen representatives in total.

On the trip over, Dylan had brought him up to speed on what had gone on over the past five hundred years. Although twenty-four ships set off from Earth, twelve of them had quickly gone in an entirely different direction and they'd lost contact after a few years. Of the remaining twelve, two additional ships were lost: the *Trakis Eight* and *Nine*. One had hit an asteroid and exploded. The other suffered a life support malfunction and everyone died. Then, of course, the

Trakis Three was blown up and the *Trakis One* had dived into a black hole. That left eight ships. Two representatives from each. He counted—only twelve people around the table. Add in him and Dylan and it looked like the Council for the Advancement of Mankind was two representatives short.

At the far side of the table, there were two vacant seats next to each other, and he and Dylan made their way across the room, his skin twitching as all eyes focused on them.

While the table was round, it was clear who sat at the head. All the chairs were identical, except for one directly opposite where Milo now sat—it was bigger, the back reaching upward like some sort of throne. The man sitting in it was blond with piercing blue eyes. He was also the only other person at the table who was not in uniform.

This must be Luther Kinross, the man responsible for arranging the meeting.

At that moment, Kinross rose to his feet. He was a tall man who exuded a presence. Milo took an instant dislike to him, but that was pretty much normal. He didn't like many people.

"Welcome to Trakis Four and the initial meeting of the Council for the Advancement of Mankind. Thank you for taking the time to attend. I hope we will all find it beneficial. First though, I think we need to take a moment to pray for the tragic loss of the *Trakis One* and all on board. And to that purpose, I will hand you over to Captain Aaron Sekongo of the *Trakis Four*, and the new head of the Church of Everlasting Life."

"Brilliant," Milo muttered. "Have I mentioned I hate the goddamned church?"

"You have."

The man in the seat next to Kinross rose to his feet. Tall, he wore a red shirt, and he had dark brown skin and dark brown eyes.

"Let us pray."

Everyone bowed their heads, except Milo and—he noticed—Kinross. The other man caught his gaze and raised an eyebrow.

Milo let the words wash over him as he worked out a plan of action. They needed to discover where the cargo of the *Trakis Four* was being stored. What, if any, weapons Kinross had access to. He was guessing that if there were weapons then they would likely be stored in this building. So he needed to do a search.

Finally, the prayer ended.

"May God have mercy on their souls," Sekongo said.

"Amen," everyone replied collectively.

Sekongo sat down and Kinross spoke again. "We owe it to all those who lost their lives to make the survival of humanity our priority, so their sacrifice will not have been in vain."

Beside him, Dylan gave a snort of disbelief. "Sacrifice? It was hardly voluntary."

"In these sad times," Kinross continued, "we need to come together and work as a team. We all need to understand our strengths, and our roles, if we're going to succeed."

"And I'm guessing someone needs to be in charge," Dylan murmured from beside him. "And Mr. Kinross no doubt believes he's the man for the job."

Kinross was welcome to it as far as Milo was concerned. He wasn't looking to be in charge of anything. He just wanted to get this job done, return to Trakis Two, and start work on that new world. *His* version of it.

Was it possible? A world where he and others like him didn't have to hide their true natures? Certainly not on this planet, where clearly the Church already had a foothold.

Kinross was still talking. Hopefully Dylan was paying attention, because Milo had tuned the voice out. He wanted to go and have a look around. Part of their job here was to work out exactly what Kinross wanted and whether they were going to at least make the pretense of going along with him. But he suspected Kinross was hardly going to reveal his true endgame at this meeting. They'd have to discover that some other way.

The other—more interesting—part was to determine what, if anything, Kinross was capable of if they refused to play his game.

Who was he exactly? Milo had done some research, but there was very little to be found out about the man. He wasn't crew. He was one of the Chosen Ones, so how had he managed to be woken up and seemingly take charge in the span of four weeks? It must have been well organized. Likely he had Captain Sekongo of the *Trakis Four* on his payroll or at least somehow under his control. Maybe with promises that the Church would play an important role in the leadership of the new colony.

That had presumably taken some detailed planning. So what else had Kinross planned? What did he have to back up his bid for leadership?

Dylan nudged him in the side. "Are you listening to this?"

"No. Give me the highlights."

"He wants confirmation of everything on board the *Trakis Two* so they can evaluate where those items can be most effectively utilized. I'm guessing Rico isn't going to be too happy about that. He's not really into sharing."

"He can always lie."

"Apparently, Kinross has the manifests for all the ships. Where the hell did he get that information?"

Damn. "Likely paid someone for it."

"But how? This must have been arranged even before he left Earth. That's scarily efficient."

Milo had come to the same conclusion. He shook his head, then realized Kinross had stopped talking. Milo glanced across to find his attention, and the rest of the room's, on him and Dylan. Had they heard anything they were saying?

"Is there something you would like to share?" Kinross asked.

God, it was like being back in school, or how he imagined that would be. He'd never actually gone to school—one of the results of being brought up under the guardianship of a vampire. "Not right now," he said. "But if I do, you'll be the first to know."

After that, he tried to pay attention, but there was a lot of stuff about waking up the Chosen Ones...who should be woken and when. Rations and equipment to be handed out. Blah, blah, blah. Work rotas and building schedules.

Milo bit back a yawn. Christ, this was boring. He needed to get the hell out of here. His mind drifted to the woman he'd spotted that morning watching him from the *Trakis Four*.

There had been strength to her features. Short blond hair, strong cheekbones, a wide mouth. She'd been staring at him as though she wanted to jump his bones right then and there. And she was welcome to—after all, he hadn't been laid in over five hundred years.

Maybe he'd look her up. There must be someone who would know who she was. She'd been with a woman in a red shirt. A scientific officer? He could start there.

"What are you smiling about?" Dylan asked.

"Nothing. Interesting meeting."

"Liar." He grinned. "You'll tell me later."

"Actually, I won't."

At that moment everyone around them stood up and started clapping. Hopefully, that signaled the end of the meeting. He stood up as well and clapped so he blended in— no one could say he wasn't making an effort.

"We can go now?" Milo said.

Dylan shook his head. "There's a dinner. Time to get

acquainted with each other. Don't you want to get acquainted with your new friends, Milo?"

"No."

Dylan laughed then broke it off. "Look out, the big man is heading our way."

Kinross came to stand beside him. He shook Dylan's hand and then Milo's. He tried to get a sense of the man, but Kinross wasn't giving anything away.

"Good to meet you," Kinross said. "But I'm interested, Mr....?"

"Call me Milo."

"I'm interested, Milo, as to why you were chosen as the representative for Trakis Two. As you can see"—he waved a hand around the room—"most of the representatives are crew members. Except for yourself."

"And you," Milo felt he had to point out.

Kinross smiled, though his expression was thoughtful. "All the same, I'm interested to know why you're here."

Nosy bastard. "You'll have to ask the captain that."

"Captain Sanchez, I believe? I'm afraid I don't know the man. And I thought I knew all the captains."

No doubt he had a list of them as well. "I'm sure he'd be delighted to talk to you."

Dylan coughed at that, to hide his laughter, and Kinross's eyes sharpened.

"And you, Mr. Kinross," Milo said, "how did you find yourself not only on the council but seemingly in charge?"

The man smiled. "Just luck, I guess."

Milo seriously doubted this man left anything to luck.

"Now, I must talk to the rest of my guests," Kinross said. "Please make yourselves at home."

"Gracious, isn't he?" Dylan said as they watched his retreating back.

"I don't like him," Milo replied.

"I heard you don't like anybody."

"Maybe…" He thought about it but was unable to come up with a name of anyone he truly liked. "I'm going to take a look about the place. See if I can find out what's going on around here. If anyone asks, tell them I came over all faint and had to lie down."

"Okay. I'll have a chat with the captain of the *Trakis Four*. Perhaps he'll talk about Kinross. Don't get caught."

"I'll do my best." The room was filling up. More people in uniform, probably the crew of the *Trakis Four*. And maybe the *Trakis Five*, the ship that had collected them all from their new planets and brought them here.

Kinross was across the room, deep in conversation with a man in a yellow shirt. Off to the side, a woman was watching them. He looked closer and recognized her from that morning, the scientific officer. He glanced around the room but failed to see the blonde anywhere. She hadn't been in uniform, though, so maybe she didn't get an invite.

He nodded to Dylan, then slipped out of the room and back into the front hallway. There was no one in sight, but he didn't want to linger. At one end of the hall, a staircase led upward, and a number of doors exited off the hallway. He tried the closest, and it opened to his touch but led into an empty room. So did the next. The third door he tried was locked. He whispered a spell and the lock clicked open. Without his wand, his magic was limited to simple tricks and glamors, but still sufficient to unlock a door. It opened into a stairwell that led downward, underground.

If Kinross was going to hide any deep dark secrets, or any weapons, underground sounded like an excellent hiding place.

The staircase was narrow, and at the bottom another door led into a corridor, lit with a dull orange glow.

Had they dug the tunnels as they built? He didn't think

so. While the walls were smooth, excavated out of the ocher rock, the place didn't feel as though it had been dug only days ago, but rather, as though it had existed for a long time. Maybe that was why Kinross had built here.

Up ahead, he heard voices and he went still. He turned, but there were voices behind him as well. Looking around, he could see nowhere to hide. He hurried on, the voices getting louder, until he came to a metal door with a grill. He pushed, but it was locked, and he repeated his spell and slipped into the room.

And came to an abrupt halt.

He wasn't alone.

Chapter Seven

"I was delighted to see you again and forgot for the moment that all happiness is fleeting."
—Alexandre Dumas, *The Count of Monte Cristo*

Destiny lay curled up on the bed. She didn't know how much time had passed. Left alone, she'd explored the confines of her new home, which had taken all of thirty seconds. It consisted of this small room and an even smaller bathroom. No shower, just a toilet and a sink.

She was a prisoner. Locked in a cell. But she hadn't done anything wrong.

For a brief moment, rage had woken inside her and risen to the surface. She'd thrown back her head and screamed. It made no difference, though. If anyone had heard, they'd ignored her.

Now the anger had faded and despair tugged at her mind. She tried to banish it. Things were what they were; you had to accept and make the most of them. There was a good reason she was here. It was for her own protection.

I am important.

But that brief interlude in the sunlight had changed everything.

If only she understood things better, then she might find her circumstances easier to accept. Dr. Yang had always said that she wanted to know too much. That she didn't *need* to know everything. She should just accept the way things are.

She squeezed her eyes shut. In her mind she saw the bird flying high. Free. Then she saw the man from the shuttle. His silver eyes staring into hers. She had a flashback to the way he had made her feel. Strange and tingly and as though she might burst into a thousand pieces.

She wanted a chance to explore the feelings growing inside herself. She wasn't naive enough to believe in love at first sight. But she'd felt so alive.

A grating sound at the door made her bolt upright on the bed, her eyes opening.

And there he was. In the dim orange light, he was unmistakable. She stared. Had her brain somehow conjured him up? Was this just her imagination playing tricks with her? She pressed her fingers to her eyes, but he was still there when she opened them again.

He raised a finger to his lips.

Even in her limited experience, she knew what that meant. He wanted her to be quiet, and she clamped her mouth closed on the questions that tried to tumble out. Then he stepped to the side of the door and pressed himself back against the wall.

Now that the immediate shock had faded, she could hear footsteps approaching, boots thudding against the hard floor outside her cell. Lots of boots. Her gaze flashed from the man, to the door, and then back to him. He raised an eyebrow but didn't speak.

Why didn't he want whoever was approaching to know

he was there?

Who was he?

Was he dangerous, or was he the one in danger?

And how had he gotten through the locked door?

A face appeared at the grill; eyes stared into the room, but whoever it was said nothing. She looked back and stayed silent. The face vanished, but more footsteps passed. Her gaze darted around the room, always coming back to the man. Dr. Yang had told her she was here for her own protection. Did this man mean her harm? But if so, he didn't appear to be in any hurry.

"Can you look?" he said. "Tell me what you see?" The words were quietly spoken but still she jumped. Then she got to her feet and crossed the room, peered out between the bars.

"There are men carrying boxes." As she watched, one of them came back in the opposite direction. He wasn't carrying anything. "And they're returning without them."

"What sort of men?"

She glanced at him. "Are there different sorts?"

He shook his head then paused for a second. "What are they wearing?"

"Dark green jumpsuits."

"Are they armed?"

She put her face to the grill and studied one of the passing men. "They have pistols in holsters at their waists. But I can't tell what kind."

"Okay. Well, I guess you've got company until they finish hiding whatever it is they're hiding down here. We might as well get comfortable."

He sank to the floor and sat with his back against the wall and his legs stretched out in front of him. She realized he couldn't be seen down there if anyone looked in through the door.

"You don't want them to know you're here?"

"Hell, no."

"You speak strangely," she said.

He grinned and something inside her warmed. "I've made worse first impressions, so I'll take it." He pulled a metal flask from inside his jacket, unscrewed the top, and held it out to her.

She looked at it distrustfully. Her diet had always been carefully monitored, but now she had the sudden urge to break the rules. Just little ones. She edged closer and took the flask. Their fingers touched and she almost leaped back. But she held her ground, brought the flask to her lips, and took a gulp. Fire filled her mouth, burning down her throat. She choked, squeezed her eyes shut, waited for the pain to stop.

Had he poisoned her?

Dr. Yang would be very upset if she'd allowed herself to be poisoned. That wasn't part of the plan. Not that she knew of, anyway.

"You've killed me," she wheezed.

She heard a chuckle.

He was laughing at her pain? But then the pain was receding, and she opened her eyes. Maybe she wasn't going to die after all. She looked at him curiously, then handed the flask back. He took a deep swallow—so, not poison—and then held it out to her again, one eyebrow raised in challenge.

She took it slowly, raised it to her mouth and swallowed. Not so bad this time, and she smiled. "What is it?"

"Whiskey. Homemade."

She took another sip.

"Hey, be careful with that stuff. It *will* knock you out if you drink too much too fast."

She handed back the flask and perched on the end of the bed—she was feeling a little unsteady now. From here, though, she could safely watch him. She wanted to make the most of this meeting. "Who are you?"

"Milo."

"I saw you this morning, Milo."

"I know," he said. "I caught you staring."

"You're very beautiful."

He laughed. "You're not so bad yourself." He studied her, his head cocked to one side, a frown between his eyes. "You look...familiar. Have we met before? On Earth perhaps?"

"I've never been to Earth."

"Everyone's been to Earth. Or rather comes from Earth."

"Not me. I was born on the *Trakis Four*."

"Really?" He didn't sound as though he believed her. "So what did you do to get locked up down here?"

Nothing! The tips of her ears burned. "You don't like my room?"

"Hell, this isn't a room. It's a cell. A prison, where they lock bad people up so they can't leave."

"Except I'm not bad. And I didn't do anything wrong." If she said it enough, she might convince herself. She waved a hand around her room. "And this is for my protection." *Of course it is.*

"Protection against what?"

She gritted her teeth. "I don't know."

He shook his head again. "You are one strange lady."

"I am?"

"Oh yeah. What's your name, strange lady?"

"I'm Destiny."

"Are you indeed? Pretty name. Do you tell all the men you meet that they're beautiful?"

"You're the first man I've met. Though I did see others on the trip from the ship this morning. But none looked like you."

He grinned. "I'm one of a kind, babe."

"Babe?"

"It's an…endearment. Has no one ever called you babe before?"

She couldn't imagine Dr. Yang calling her anything but Destiny. "No. But I like it."

He was watching her again, brows drawn together as though she wasn't behaving as expected. She had no idea what was expected. How could she? But she wanted him to like her. Maybe she should try to explain. "You're only the second person I've ever talked to in my life."

His eyes widened. They were beautiful eyes, silver rimmed with black, and his lashes were long. "Who's the first?" he said.

"Dr. Yang."

"Is that the woman you were with before?" When she nodded, he said, "Is she the one who locked you up down here? For your own protection?"

"She is." The way he'd said it, though, it sounded all wrong, and the need to defend her guardian surged within her. "Dr. Yang has always taken care of me."

"What about your mother and father? Were they crew on the *Trakis Four*?"

"I don't know." A wave of sadness washed over her. She'd learned about normal family units in her schooling, but she had no clue what had happened to her parents. Or why they'd never taken care of her. Dr. Yang said it wasn't important.

"How old are you?" Milo asked.

Good, something she could easily answer. "I was twenty-six when I went into cryo." She studied him, trying to guess his age, but all she could gauge was that he wasn't elderly. "How old are you?"

"I'm…" An expression she couldn't decipher flashed across his face. "A little older than that."

Though he didn't look old, there was a sense of age about him, as though he'd done things and seen things she couldn't even imagine. She'd bet he had experienced life, had climbed mountains, swum, flown. Made love. At the thought a shiver ran through her. She sighed. The things she wanted to do were building inside her, all mingling with feelings and hopes she just didn't understand.

Her eyes pricked and she pressed her lips tight, looking away and staring at the wall, pulling herself together while she felt like she was falling apart. She wasn't a child to cry for things she couldn't have.

She was a grown woman with an important role to play.

Outside the cell, the footsteps had faded to nothing. The men had gone. She didn't want Milo to leave, but he must have noticed the silence as well. He pushed himself to his feet, then took the couple of steps to the door and peered out.

"They've gone."

She had an urge to beg him to stay just a little while longer. To talk to her—tell her about the world. The old one and the new one. At least she could experience things secondhand. All she knew was she didn't want him to go. Didn't want to be alone.

"Don't go."

He turned to face her, his expression serious. "I have to leave, but you don't have to stay. No one has the right to lock you up like a prisoner and tell you some bullshit about protecting you." He shook his head. "The door is unlocked."

She could be free. All she had to do was step out. "I should go with you?"

"Not with me."

"Why?" She frowned, and he stared at her for a moment before answering, the hard lines of his face softening a little.

"You wouldn't like it with me. I'm not good company, and I work alone."

"Oh." She thought for a moment. "Alone we are nothing. We have to work together for the greater good." That's what

Dr. Yang had always told her.

"More bullshit. *You* might have to. Not me." He glanced at the door again and back to her. "You should really think about leaving."

For a brief moment, she considered the idea, but where would she go? And besides, she didn't want to disappoint Dr. Yang. "I can't. But you could stay. For a little while longer? I don't like being alone."

He shook his head, then took a step closer. "I've never met anyone like you. And I've met a hell of a lot of people."

She hadn't realized how big he was until he was right in front of her, looking down. She peered up at him, mesmerized by his eyes. Reaching out, he rested his hand against her shoulder, and heat seeped through her clothes and into her skin, warmth singing through her body. She swayed toward him, her lashes fluttering closed—

Then something buzzed.

What? Her eyes blinked open.

The noise was coming from the machine on his wrist. He glanced down, then stepped back, his hand falling to his side. He looked at her and turned away, spoke quietly into the machine and then listened. When he turned back, she knew he was leaving. His expression was rueful.

"I have to go."

"I know."

"Look, just..." He ran a hand through his short hair and frowned. "Just don't believe everything you're told."

"Why not?"

He gave an exaggerated sigh. "Because people lie. All the time. To get what they want. I doubt your Dr. Yang is any different. You should get out of here."

"I can't," she said, even though she wanted to. She wanted to get out and stay out this time. But what she wanted didn't matter. "I have my duty."

He snorted and turned away, crossed to the door, but paused and glanced back at her. "Take care of yourself, Destiny."

Then he was gone.

Chapter Eight

*"We are always in a hurry to be happy... for when we have
suffered a long time, we have great difficulty in believing in
good fortune."*
—Alexandre Dumas, *The Count of Monte Cristo*

The door was pushed open from the outside and Destiny
jerked upright.

"Why isn't this door locked?" Dr. Yang's sharp voice
came from the corridor, and Destiny's shoulders slumped.

Had she really thought Milo had come back? Why would
he? He said he liked being alone. But then *he* probably hadn't
spent 95 percent of his life in his own company.

Dr. Yang was talking to someone on the other side of
the door now, but Destiny couldn't catch all the words—
something about the lock being broken.

"Well, get it fixed," Dr. Yang snapped. "Now."

She hadn't slept since Milo had left. Instead, she'd sat
staring at the door, knowing it was unlocked and she could
step outside at any time. The idea had made her almost light-

headed. But as the hours trickled by, she hadn't approached the door. Hadn't walked out.

Was she a coward? No, it wasn't fear that kept her inside.

How could she just walk away from her responsibilities? Whatever Milo had said, she wasn't here because she was a prisoner. She was here because she had accepted her role in life. As they all had to do if humanity were to survive the changes and challenges facing them. And she was proud to be of service in whatever way she could. Not everyone got the chance.

All the same she was aware of her anger simmering close to the surface. Meeting Milo had made her yearn to experience life even more. What harm could it do? At least they could tell her.

Dr. Yang entered the room, her gaze going directly to Destiny.

She squirmed a little. She suspected she was feeling guilty. Up until now, she'd never really done anything to feel guilty about except maybe ask too many questions. Now she had a secret.

Should she tell Dr. Yang about her visitor? The urge to unburden her conscience lasted only a few seconds. Clearly, he hadn't wanted to be found here last night, and she didn't want to get him in trouble. Maybe he would come again.

So instead, she forced a smile. "Good morning." If it even was morning. How was she to tell when she was stuck underground? She blew out her breath; she needed to relax, or Dr. Yang would notice something was wrong. Everything Destiny did was noted and recorded.

"Did you sleep well?"

"In my cell?" The words were out before she could think better of it, and she held her breath waiting for the rebuke.

Dr. Yang shot her a sharp look. "You're being melodramatic, Destiny. It's not a cell, just a safe place for you to stay."

She opened her mouth to ask why she needed a safe place and then she went still. Another figure had entered the room behind Dr. Yang. A man.

He was big, as tall as Milo and broader at the shoulder. He wore a dark green jumpsuit, similar to the men Milo had been hiding from last night, and he had a pistol at his waist. She raised her gaze to his face. He wasn't beautiful like Milo, but he *was* smiling. And, unlike most of Dr. Yang's smiles, his was reflected in his eyes, which were warm and brown. His short hair was brown as well.

"Destiny, this is Silas Wynch. Silas has offered to walk with you for an hour a day so you can get some fresh air and see the new colony."

She'd been staring at the man, and now she turned to Dr. Yang, a smile tugging at her lips. "I can go out?"

"Of course." She sounded annoyed. "I told you—you're not a prisoner. But you're valuable to us and we care about you. Silas will look after you."

She was going out. Even if it was just for an hour. She tightened her lips and held her face still; Dr. Yang didn't like overt signs of emotion. But she was going out. Inside she was fizzing.

Maybe she would see Milo.

She shoved the thought aside. Her future did not include Milo. He'd made that more than clear. Pushing herself to her feet, she nodded to Silas.

"Hello, Mr. Wynch."

"Call me Silas. And it's a nice break to go for a walk with a pretty woman." He held out his hand, and she looked at it for a moment and then stretched out her own slowly. It was engulfed in his bigger one and he shook it vigorously.

She liked Silas. She didn't feel the same giddy sense of excitement Milo induced in her, but that was probably just as well. She was sure Dr. Yang wouldn't appreciate giddiness.

"Can we go *now*?" she asked.

Silas shrugged. "Why not?"

"I will be accompanying you today," Dr. Yang said.

Destiny was almost sorry about that. She sensed that Silas would be far easier to talk to if he were alone. She would certainly find asking questions easier without Dr. Yang's disapproving presence—and she had so many questions she wanted to ask. But maybe tomorrow they would be alone.

Sitting on the edge of the bed, she pulled on her boots and she was ready to go.

Dr. Yang led the way and she followed, with Silas walking behind her. As they exited the cell, she glanced down the corridor where had they had been carrying the boxes last night. What was in them? What had Milo been doing down here? Obviously, he wasn't supposed to be there, because otherwise, he wouldn't have had to hide.

She could see nothing except the corridor leading away and no chance to investigate further as Dr. Yang was already striding in the opposite direction. Destiny hurried to catch up, following her up the stairs and through the doorway into the wide-open hallway with its windows and sunlight. She stood for a moment, looking around. Today there were more people, all moving with purpose. This was life. Things happening.

"You look like you've never seen people before," Silas said, coming up beside her.

"I haven't. Not really. Well, only yesterday when we came from the ship. It's wonderful."

He was looking at her in an odd way. Pretty much as Milo had looked at her last night.

Ahead of them, Dr. Yang came to a halt. She'd likely realized she was leaving them behind. She turned around and frowned. "Come along. We don't have time to waste."

Beside her, Silas grinned. "Hey, cut us some slack, Elvira. This is supposed to be fun."

The frown deepened, which came as no surprise. Dr. Yang believed fun was frivolous. Destiny waited for her to make a comment, but she just turned and walked away. She looked at Silas. He shrugged and they followed.

Out into the bright sunshine.

And she stopped again, just for a brief moment, and raised her face to the sunlight.

There wasn't a cloud in the sky. It was blue shading to violet. She'd seen pictures of the skies on Earth and this was different. So beautiful her chest ached.

This time, instead of the hybrid vehicle they had come in yesterday, they walked to a small dock where a boat was tied up. Silas jumped on board, then helped Dr. Yang, who stepped carefully onto the boat. Then he held out his hand to Destiny. She took it, he tugged, and she jumped, landing on the swaying deck. She fell against him and pressed her hand to his chest to steady herself.

"Destiny!"

She pulled back at Dr. Yang's stern tone but could feel the smile on her face. This *was* fun.

Silas let her go then moved to the front of the boat and the engine purred to life. And they were moving, first backward, then they turned and moved gently forward. He looked at her and smiled.

"You want to go for a ride?" he asked.

Oh yes!

As she nodded, he pushed a lever forward, and they were flying across the water.

Chapter Nine

"God is always the last resource."
—Alexandre Dumas, *The Count of Monte Cristo*

Milo sat at the top of the ramp of the shuttle. Not far away, just off to the left, a group of men and women were working on the road that led to the island. They were supervised by more men in the dark green jumpsuits he'd come to recognize designated them as Kinross's soldiers.

The guards were all armed. The workers wore beige jumpsuits, and most of them didn't look happy. One, a small, wiry guy with Asian features, dropped the sack he was carrying and turned to the nearest guard.

"I demand to see who is in charge. I should not be doing this work. I paid good money for my place. I didn't sign up for this."

"You want to eat," the guard said, "then you work. No work. No food. We all have to pull our weight in the new world."

Destiny had said something similar the night before.

About duty and pulling together. Milo didn't agree with it any more now than he had then.

"Sanctimonious bastard," Dylan muttered, dropping down to sit beside him. He took a swallow from the flask in his hand—Rico had sent them with a good supply of whiskey—and handed it to Milo.

He took a swig, then picked up his knife and the piece of wood he was whittling. Earlier that morning, he'd taken a trip to the forest on the other side of the lake. The trees here were different than on Earth—unsurprisingly—so he didn't recognize any of the species. But they were trees, and it felt like wood. He'd selected a strong, straight sapling, felling it with his knife.

Much of his power back on Earth had been tied to the Earth elements. Air, earth, water, fire, and he used his wand to magnify and channel those powers, to focus them. He had no idea how the powers would transition to this new world. But he could sense an innate magic in the place. While Rico had failed to return his wand, Milo was hoping that if he made a new one out of local wood, it would work here. He had an idea that before this was over, he would be thankful for a bit of magic.

He and Dylan were silent until the road crew moved away, but Milo knew it wouldn't last. Dylan was a pack animal and he liked to talk.

"So did you find anything last night?" Dylan asked.

"A little. There are tunnels beneath the main building. Looks like they've been there a long time—not something new. Kinross is storing something down there. I couldn't get a look at what, but I'd imagine some sort of weapons. Among other things. I need to take another look." He thought about Destiny. Locked in a cell for her own protection. And the really tragic thing was she believed that nonsense.

She'd said she was born on the *Trakis Four*. He hadn't

heard of anyone else born during the trip from Earth. Which didn't mean it hadn't happened.

"Have you heard of anyone born on the ships since the fleet left Earth?" he asked Dylan.

"No. It would be against fleet regulations. Why do you ask?"

"No reason."

She was a mystery. He liked mysteries. And there was something so appealing about her, as though she were a blank canvas that had never been marked. She'd told him that she'd never met anyone else. No one but the doctor who was in charge of her. How could that have been? Why had she never encountered any of the other crew members? Clearly, she had been kept isolated. But why?

Maybe she'd been sick, though she looked healthy now, and besides, that wouldn't explain why she was locked in a cell beneath Luther Kinross's castle.

That's what it reminded him of—a castle.

"What did you think of our new friend, Luther?" Dylan asked.

"Total dickhead."

"But a dickhead with an agenda. And he's well prepared. He must have had things in place before the fleet left Earth to be able to take over this smoothly. My guess is the crew of the *Trakis Four* are on his payroll, and he had some sort of mercenary army on board."

"The guys in green."

"Yeah. They're the only people armed right now. Well, except us."

While they had surrendered the guns they'd carried the previous night—guns which hadn't been returned—they had more weapons on board the shuttle. Weapons and booze. At least Rico had gotten the supplies right. "Things seem peaceable right now," Milo said.

"I doubt that will last. Most of the Chosen Ones weren't exactly chosen. They paid for their places and they didn't come cheap. These guys were players back on Earth. They're not going to be happy getting downgraded to manual laborers."

Dylan had a point. But they were hardly in a position to comment—hadn't they done the same thing? Bought their places on the *Trakis Two*, with little or no thought to the thousands of people whose futures they had stolen. Though he supposed by that point the real Chosen Ones had likely already been replaced by the paying customers. So there was perhaps a little justice. But it did make you think about just what they were populating the new world with. The cream of humanity.

Ha.

"What are you up to?" Dylan asked.

"Nothing."

He peered a little closer. "You're making a wand? Cool." He sat down next to Milo, elbows resting on his knees. "What's the deal between you and Rico, anyway? Is he really your uncle?"

Milo wasn't going there. It was none of Dylan's business. "There is no deal."

"Come on. I saw the way the two of you were together. There's history."

None he wanted to share, so he just shrugged.

"And was Rico right? Do you think we should come out in the open about what we are?"

"Why not? You don't think humans are ready to accept us?" Actually, he was pretty sure the ones on Trakis Four were nowhere near ready.

Dylan considered the question. "Maybe you—you're like Harry bloody Potter, and even us werewolves have a chance—hey, we can be sort of cute and furry."

He'd seen Dylan's wolf form, and "cute" it was not.

"But vampires?" Dylan continued. "I'm not so sure. Humans are their prey. That's never going to change, and most people won't be too comfortable with that."

"There have always been humans more than willing to voluntarily feed a vampire. They don't need to kill to feed on them."

"Maybe they don't *need* to. That doesn't mean they don't *want* to."

"Well," Milo said, "they'll just have to learn a little restraint."

"Ha. Tell that to Uncle Rico."

"I have. Numerous times." He thought about the sort of world he would like to live in. Free from prejudice and fear. "Just imagine…a world where we can be open about what we are. Where we don't have to hide in the shadows. There's so much of our nature that's shrouded in mystery. We come out in the open and we have a chance to explore that, find out who and what we really are. Are we truly evil as the Church says?"

"Well, if Kinross has his way, then you're shit out of luck. The Church is going to spread like a pestilence across the universe. I figure he sees it as one more way to control the people."

"Then we'd better make sure Kinross never gets near Trakis Two."

Dylan shook his head. "I don't think that's going to be so simple. I think Kinross has his eye on the whole system. So if you want your own brave new world then we'd better come up with a plan to stop him in his tracks."

Milo was saved from replying as his attention was pulled toward the water. A boat was speeding around the lake. Dylan grabbed a pair of binocs and watched for a moment.

"That's the woman you were eye-fucking yesterday morning when we landed."

"No, I wasn't." But he grabbed the binocs and peered at the boat. It took a moment to come into focus. There was Destiny. No longer a prisoner.

She was laughing up at the man beside her, the big guy in green who'd been in charge of taking their weapons last night. He was driving the boat. Without thinking, Milo got to his feet. He took a moment to place his new wand-in-progress safely in the shuttle, then strode down the ramp, Dylan close behind him. The boat was heading toward the small dock now, and he stopped a short distance away.

He didn't know her or what she would do. There was a chance she might just point him out and tell her new friend that he'd been nosing around below ground last night. Milo was pretty certain that would only lead to him getting locked in Destiny's old cell.

As the boat pulled up at the dock, she looked around in wonder—much as she had looked at him last night—as though she had never seen anything like him in her life before. She tilted her face up to the sun and closed her eyes.

When she opened them, she looked straight at him. She started to smile and then stopped abruptly. Bright girl. She wasn't going to give him away, after all.

He watched as they climbed out of the boat and walked in the opposite direction—she had a great ass. She glanced back over her shoulder. He winked and she grinned, then hurried away.

• • •

Elvira had never seen Destiny so animated.

She'd always been a happy child, content with the confines of her existence. It was only later that she'd grown dissatisfied with the answers she received and the restrictions to her life. Elvira had been careful with the information she had given, but Destiny was intelligent, too intelligent maybe. She was quite aware that her life wasn't in any way "normal."

As she'd grown older, she'd also grown introspective, quiet, holding the questions inside. Because she'd learned quickly that she wouldn't get any answers.

That was partly the reason why Elvira had placed her in cryo when she had, because the questions had been getting too hard to ignore. But also because the time had been right for Elvira. She'd completed what she'd been brought on board the *Trakis Four* to achieve. She had more than paid for her ticket. And she was getting old; she was eighty-five, and if she wanted to live to see her children grow up then she had to go into cryo herself. And no way could Destiny remain awake without her. So she had gone to sleep as well.

Maybe she should never have woken her. Just left her in cryo until she was required. But somehow, she hadn't been able to do that. She'd given herself all sorts of reasons as to why—that she needed to wake her to check she was functioning optimally, that there had been no damage from the cryo. But really it was the little voice inside her whispering *it's not fair*.

She exhaled. Since when was life fair? She wasn't that naive.

Destiny was bouncing, laughing at something Silas said, thrumming with life.

Had she done the right thing?

At that moment, Destiny turned to glance over her shoulder and stopped, her eyes widening. Elvira followed her gaze. Two men stood a few feet away, watching them. There was a hint of familiarity, but she couldn't work out where she had seen them before. Both were tall, broad at the shoulders and lean everywhere else. Elvira had always considered herself beyond the lure of sexual attraction, but they were... stunning. Both dark haired, the one in front wore the yellow shirt of a second-in-command. He had golden eyes and an amused smile.

The other wore blue jeans and a black T-shirt, and the black ink of tattoos trailed down his arm—she hadn't seen ink in a long time. And he wore some sort of amulet on a chain around his neck. He had mesmerizing silver eyes that were narrowed on Destiny, a frown between the dark slash of his brows. She turned back to look at Destiny, who was still staring at the man, but she must have sensed Elvira's gaze as she glanced toward her then hurried after Silas.

Elvira looked back at the silver-eyed man. He was still watching Destiny but seemed to sense Elvira's interest and turned his attention to her. For a second, she froze. There was something slightly threatening in his expression, his nostrils flaring. As his gaze met hers, she remembered where she had seen them before. They'd been landing yesterday as she and Destiny had left the ship. Destiny must have seen them then.

They'd arrived on the shuttle from the *Trakis Two*.

For a second, she hesitated, then called out to Silas. "I'll catch up with you later."

She walked toward the two men. As she approached, the man in jeans turned to his companion and spoke quietly; the other shrugged but strode away.

Elvira stopped in front of him. He towered above her and she had to look a long way up, while an inner voice whispered to walk away. To be patient. Luther had told her that he would find out about her family. And she trusted him. Didn't she?

But this man had come from the *Trakis Two*. He would obviously have contacts there. And she wasn't doing anything wrong asking about her family.

A shiver ran through her as she forced herself to hold his gaze. There was something almost inhuman about him. She shook away the thought. She was being fanciful.

"I'm Dr. Elvira Yang. I was third Scientific Officer on the

Trakis Four." She offered her hand. For a few seconds, he just stared at it, then a smile curved his lips and he reached out and shook her hand.

"Milo Velazquez. How can I help you, Dr. Yang?"

She licked her lips. She was nervous and almost didn't recognize the emotion. What was there to be nervous about? Nothing. "I have family on the *Trakis Two*," she said. "My daughters. I was wondering if they'd been woken yet."

"I wouldn't know. I'm not part of the crew."

"But could you find out?"

He studied her for a minute, and she couldn't read what was going through his mind. Finally, he gave a brief nod. "I'll ask the captain."

The tight band around her chest loosened. "Thank you. And you needn't mention this to anyone else."

He raised an eyebrow. "Why would I?"

"No reason." She forced a smile; she'd never been good with gratitude. "It's just…I know I should be patient but…"

"But it's been five hundred years."

"Yes."

He gestured toward where a group of Chosen Ones, dressed in beige jumpsuits and supervised by three armed men in green uniforms, were digging foundations for a new structure. "Do you know what they're building?"

She'd seen the plans in Luther's office. "A church."

She wasn't a big fan of the Church. In the years before they had left Earth, the traditional religions had faded in popularity to be replaced by the expanding Church of Everlasting Life, which had seemed to appear out of nowhere. Saffira Lourdes, their founder, had quickly become one of the president's most trusted advisers. Elvira had met her once. She'd been an interesting woman, but an odd leader for a religious cult. The new church had frowned upon any research into genetic modification, and Elvira's own work had ground to a halt. Until she had been approached by Luther.

"Christ," he muttered. "Just what we need in the brave new world. Same old crap."

A smile tugged at her lips. "You're not a member, Mr. Velazquez?"

"No. Not a member. Not a believer. And call me Milo."

"Captain Sekongo of the *Trakis Four* was a designated member of the Church." All the crew rotations had at least one designated member, supposedly to care for the spiritual health of the crew. "He's high up in their hierarchy, and he's all set to take control now that Saffira Lourdes is out of the picture. I also believe he's a friend of Mr. Kinross." Likely he had offered the support of his congregation in exchange for their new church.

"So is Kinross a member?"

Somehow, she doubted it. "I'm not really sure. You'll have to ask him."

"I'll do that." He was silent for a moment, but she was quite aware he had other questions. "The guards," he said. "Where do they come from?"

"What do you mean?"

"Are they Chosen Ones? Or was there a military force on the *Trakis Four*?"

She could feel a frown pulling her brows together. She thought about Silas. He was obviously ex-military, but he was also a friend of Luther's. It was clear that they'd had some sort of connection back on Earth. So how had Silas gotten a place on the fleet? Had he won the lottery and just happened to end up on the same ship as his old friend Luther Kinross? It seemed highly unlikely. It was more probable that Luther had somehow procured him a place. But whose had he taken? And what of the others? She tried to count up how many guards she'd seen around the place, but she hadn't been paying that much attention. Plenty, though.

Who had been left back on Earth so Luther could have his army on hand when he arrived in their new world?

She shook her head to clear the thoughts. "I have no idea who they are," she said. "Well, thank you. You'll let me know if you find out anything about my children?"

"Of course."

She turned to go. Destiny and Silas were almost out of sight, and it made her a little nervous. She didn't think it was a good idea for them to get too friendly. She wasn't sure how much Luther had told Silas about Destiny, but from his reaction to her, she was guessing not a lot.

"Tell me." Elvira paused at the sound of Milo's voice behind her. She turned reluctantly. "The blond woman." He waved a hand to where Destiny was standing in the distance with Silas. "Who is she?"

"She's nobody," she said dismissively and then hurried away. The familiar pain churned in her gut. Pain she wasn't ready to analyze and certainly not give a name to.

She'd done what she had to.

Chapter Ten

"Ah," said the jailer, "do not always brood over what is impossible, or you will be mad in a fortnight."
—Alexandre Dumas, *The Count of Monte Cristo*

The walls were closing in on her. The ceiling pressing down. Her mind was being compressed and a scream built up inside her.

Destiny had thought going outside would help. Instead it had only increased her restlessness.

Why? Why was she locked up in here?

She remembered Milo asking her what she'd done wrong. And she still didn't know.

She sat cross-legged on the floor, staring at the door. Then leaped to her feet and took the two strides across the room, tugged on the handle. Nothing happened. Of course it didn't, because she was locked in here like a zoo animal—she'd read about zoos back on Earth and couldn't believe they'd existed. That animals had been locked up. Except here she was, just as helpless.

No, not helpless. She gritted her teeth, then drew back her fist and punched the rock wall.

Ouch!

The pain brought her back to herself. Resting her forehead against the grill in the door, she forced her breathing to slow, then ran a calming mantra through her mind.

We exist for the greater good. I must not question. When the time is right all will be revealed. I am at peace with my world.

Over and over again until a measure of calm returned.

They all had a role to play in this new world. This was hers. She didn't need to understand why; she just had to do her duty, as they all did. Milo was wrong. They had to all work together for the good of humanity.

Should she have told Dr. Yang about her visitor?

Maybe. But it would have gotten Milo into trouble, that much she knew. Probably they would lock him up as well, and she couldn't bear that.

The outing that morning had been wonderful, though. She'd liked Silas, loved the fresh air, the sun on her face. Then she'd felt a prickling on her skin, a sense of someone watching her, and when she'd turned, the whole world had come into focus and then narrowed on that one point. There he was.

Milo had such a sense of power and life to him. An aura glowing around him. She'd found herself smiling and had to clamp her lips together in case she gave him away. He'd watched her in return, one dark eyebrow raised. And she'd forced herself to look in the opposite direction. Then Dr. Yang had gone to talk to him and that had given her the perfect excuse to ask Silas who he was. Very casually, of course. She'd been careful not to reveal that they'd met or how. She was learning subterfuge. Did that make her a bad person?

Silas had said Milo was one of the representatives from

Trakis Two, but other than that he didn't know. Apparently, he was a bit of a mystery. Not a crew member like the other representatives. She was working out who everyone was. The crew members wore a uniform of black pants, black boots, and a shirt, different colors for different roles—Dr. Yang's was red because she was a scientific officer. Then there were the workers. They wore jumpsuits like hers, but beige. And most of them did not seem happy. She'd seen an argument break out; the man had thrown down his tools and demanded to see who was in charge. He'd been marched off somewhere.

Then there were the men like Silas. They wore green jumpsuits and carried weapons.

Lastly, there was her and there was Milo. Both different. Her in her yellow jumpsuit and Milo in his blue pants and black, tight-fitting shirt. She liked that they had something in common.

Even if she was never going to see him again.

Because she was locked in a *cell*.

An idea had been building in her mind since she'd gotten back from the trip outdoors. Silas had promised her that he would be back tomorrow to take her out again. How difficult would it be to slip away from him then? She was fast. She'd just have to pick her moment. Maybe when they were close to the forest she could disappear into the trees. She wouldn't go for long, just a few days or even hours. She could climb the mountain, paddle in the lake. Explore this new world. Maybe visit Milo in his shuttle. Once the idea entered her mind, she couldn't get it out again.

A faint banging sound drifted down the corridor, and she lifted her head to listen. Then it was gone. Maybe just her imagination.

She backed away from the door until the cot bed hit the back of her legs, and she sank down. Resting her head in her hands, she tried to clear her mind and gain some measure of peace and acceptance.

At the sound of running footsteps, her head shot up. She didn't have time to move as the locked door was suddenly flung open from the outside and Milo appeared.

Again? Was he in trouble?

His eyes widened as he caught sight of her.

Destiny jumped to her feet, just as another man appeared behind him, and she stopped her forward momentum. He was as tall as Milo, with dark hair and golden eyes. He wore a crew uniform with a yellow shirt. This must be the same man she'd seen him with before, but from a distance. Her gaze shifted between the two of them as they moved farther into the room and the door closed behind them. Milo turned briefly, pressed his hand to the door, and it closed. He moved to the right of the door while his partner moved to the left, and they both pressed their backs against the wall. Milo raised his finger to his lips, and she clamped her mouth closed, while excitement fizzed inside her and words welled up in her throat. They were definitely in some sort of trouble.

"This was a really bad idea," the stranger said.

"Yeah," Milo growled, "and let's not forget that it was *your* fucking really bad idea. Now shut up."

They did. Both of them going still.

Destiny sat back down and clasped her hands on her lap. She could hear more people in the corridor now. The sound of several running boots. She held her breath, but they didn't slow, just kept going straight past her cell. She waited until the sound had disappeared in the distance and then waited some more. Her gaze flicked between the two men, then to the door, and back to Milo. He grinned, and she felt a smile tugging at her own lips.

"So here we are again," Milo murmured.

"I didn't think you'd come back."

"Neither did I. Just can't stay away." One corner of his

mouth tugged upward, as if he might smile, but then it quickly dropped again. "Actually, I didn't think you would be here."

She frowned. "Where else would I be?"

"Outside. With your new friend."

It took her a moment to realize he meant Silas. Was Silas her friend? He'd been nice to her, but she suspected friendship was more than that. "He's not my friend. He's my..." She searched her mind for a suitable word. "...my bodyguard."

"Why do you need a bodyguard?"

She shrugged.

"Is someone going to introduce me?" the second man asked.

Milo grunted. "I'd rather not."

The man ignored Milo, stepped toward her, and held out his hand. "I'm Dylan. I saw you yesterday when we landed."

She took his hand. "I'm Destiny."

"Of course you are." He shook and held on. There was a strange energy to him that shivered across her skin. Different from Milo. But also different from the other humans she had met. She glanced at Milo; he was practically growling at Dylan, who then grinned and let go of her hand. "Pretty name. So what did you do to get locked up down here?"

She cast an accusing glance at Milo. Did everyone think she was some sort of criminal? "Nothing," she said. "I'm here for my own safety."

"And is there a particular reason you wouldn't be safe?"

"There must be. Otherwise I wouldn't be locked up down here." She gave them both a pointed look. "What are *you two* doing down here?"

"We thought we'd take a look at what was in those boxes they were bringing in last night," Milo said.

"Why?"

"Because we're nosy bastards," Dylan replied. "Unfortunately, they've posted a guard, who wasn't there yesterday. I don't think they were too happy to see us here. Though hopefully, they didn't get a good look." He stepped toward the door, peered through the grill. "I can't see anything." Opening the door, he leaned his head out, then back in quickly. "There are guards at the end of the corridor. No getting out that way."

Milo sighed and ran a hand through his hair. "Looks like we'll just have to wait it out."

Destiny bit back a smile; they would have to stay a while. Being locked away wasn't so bad when you had company.

Dylan leaned back against the wall and shoved his hands in his pockets, while Milo paced the confines of the small room.

"Tell us about yourself," Dylan said. He seemed to be uncomfortable with silence.

"Oh no. I'm boring." But that didn't mean she didn't want to talk. "Tell me about Trakis Two. What's it like? What are the people like? Is it the same as here? What's it like flying on a shuttle? When do—"

"Whoa," Dylan said, smiling. "Slowly. One question at a time."

"Sorry. It's just that I want to know…everything."

"Hmm. Well, Trakis Two is different from this planet."

"How?"

"It doesn't spin on its axis like most planets. So there's no day and night. Half the planet is dark and half is light."

"Interesting. I wouldn't like to live in the dark, though. I like the sunlight."

"Pity you're stuck down here then," Milo muttered.

"I know, but we all have our roles to play, and this is mine."

He shook his head. "Except you have no clue what that role is."

"When the time is right, I'll know."

"And what if you don't like it? What if you decide it's not a role you actually want to play?"

She bristled. "I'll do my duty. As we all need to."

"Not me."

"Anyway," Dylan continued. "I've not been down to the surface of Trakis Two yet, so I don't personally know what it's like. But Rico says it's okay, nice temperature, good air, everything we'll need."

"Rico?"

"He's the captain of the *Trakis Two*."

"Is he nice?" she asked.

Dylan sniggered.

"No. He's not nice," Milo replied. "He's— *Shhh*." He broke off, going entirely still. "They're coming back."

Without saying another word, he and Dylan moved to either side of the door again. She could hear the others now, the booted feet coming back more slowly this time.

She stood where she was, uncertain of what to do. She didn't want them to get caught. While she wasn't sure what would happen if they did, she sensed nothing good. And she didn't want them to go, either. For a few minutes, just talking to them, she'd felt so alive. Like she imagined a real person with a normal life would feel. She wanted more of that.

She waited for the footsteps to pass, but instead, they slowed and stopped in front of the door. A face peered in through the grill and she stood very still, not even blinking. The face backed away, then she heard the door rattle as they tried it. But it was locked again—how did Milo do that? Would they go?

"Holy crap," Dylan whispered. "Any ideas?"

"No good ones," Milo said.

"I figure even a bad one will do right now."

Milo reached out and touched the lock lightly, whispered a word. "That will hold them, but not for long." He glanced around the room as if searching for some way out, but there was nothing. Nowhere to go. She could have told them *that*.

The guard was rattling at the door again. He was talking to someone, but she couldn't make out the words.

Milo blew out his breath. "This is a really bad idea." As he spoke, he pulled a stick from where it had been tucked into his belt. About two feet long, slender, the wood was dark brown and polished. It looked like an extension of his arm.

"Oh no," Dylan said. "That is a really, *really* bad idea."

"You want to stay?" Milo asked.

Dylan looked as though he was debating the idea. He glanced to the door, then at Milo, and back to her. "I guess this is goodbye. Nice meeting you, Destiny." He reached out and rested his hand on Milo's arm.

They were leaving.

Don't go.

The words echoed in her head and some invisible force pushed her forward. She stretched out her hand, and her fingertips touched Milo's chest just as he raised the stick into the air and muttered a word.

Then a loud roar filled her ears and crimson light flashed in front of her eyes and the world was spinning.

Then everything went black.

Chapter Eleven

When Milo opened his eyes, his first thought was—the new wand hadn't worked. Damn. Why? Everything had seemed to happen just as it should.

But it *couldn't* have worked, because Destiny still stood right in front of him and bringing her along hadn't been part of the spell.

He lowered his wand. Different world and different wand, he reminded himself. No wonder the results were also different.

Destiny was standing right in front of him, her arm outstretched, her fingers touching his chest. Her blue eyes were wide and staring, her mouth open. That was the first inkling that while the spell might not have had completely the right results, something had certainly happened.

"Where the hell are we?" Dylan asked from beside him.

Milo at last forced his gaze from Destiny and looked around.

They were no longer in the cell. And if he listened carefully, he couldn't hear the sound of approaching feet. All good so far. Except for the bit about not knowing where they were. And the bit about how Destiny seemed to have come along for the ride.

"I have no clue," he murmured.

"Well, that sucks."

"Do you want me to try and take us back?" He'd meant the question sarcastically, but Dylan actually considered it for a moment.

Then he shook his head. "God only knows where we'd end up."

"What happened?" Destiny asked. "We were in the cell…" She peered around her. "And now we're not." She blinked a couple of times. "How?"

"Teleportation," Dylan said, his expression completely serious.

Milo snorted. They weren't supposed to bring attention to themselves. The use of magic in front of "normals" was completely prohibited. They'd had strict instructions from Rico not to do anything that might make people look in their direction. This was definitely one of those things. But if Rico hadn't pinched his wand, then he might have had more control, and Destiny would still be back in her cell, everything left in place as they'd found it.

Of course they also would have just vanished in front of her eyes, but she had no witnesses and likely no one would believe her.

He briefly considered trying another spell to send her back to where she had come from. But right now, he had no clue where he actually was, so, as Dylan had aptly pointed out, who knew where she would turn up? He tucked the wand back into his belt, counting himself lucky he'd managed to get them somewhere undetected, and all in one piece.

"Teleportation?" Destiny asked. She scrunched up her nose. "Is that possible? I've not heard of it before."

"It's a prototype the scientific officer on the *Trakis Two* developed," Dylan replied. "Not in general use and not entirely reliable."

Hey, Dylan was good at this making-stuff-up thing. He'd sounded totally plausible.

"Which is why we don't know exactly where we are," Dylan finished.

"Wow," Destiny said. "That's almost like magic."

"Yeah. Almost."

Milo looked around again. If he had to hazard a guess, he would say that they were still underground, in some sort of big chamber. High above them, he could see a patch of star-strewn sky through a hole in the roof. The night was clear, and the stars gave sufficient light to see.

There was no way out through the top, though. At least not without magic, and he wasn't willing to risk that again until he'd made a few tweaks to his new wand. The walls were sheer rock and the ceiling at least five hundred feet above their heads. No, they were going to need another way out.

Dylan pulled a flashlight from his pocket and waved it around the room. There were a number of openings that led off from the chamber. It was just a matter of deciding which one to take. He closed his eyes and tried to orientate himself. Back on Earth it would have been easy, he could lock into the ley lines that crisscrossed the land and pinpoint his exact location.

Not here.

There was nothing. Okay, maybe a low level buzz of magic somewhere, but nothing he could latch on to.

He opened his eyes, found both Destiny and Dylan staring at him. He shrugged, and said, "I just needed a moment to think." Then he headed off to the nearest tunnel entrance. He peered into the darkness but could make out nothing. Dylan came up behind him and waved the flashlight down the tunnel. Smooth, curved ocher walls that looked like they'd been gouged out of the ground with some sort of machine.

Could there be other intelligent life forms on the planet? It hadn't occurred to him before now. On the surface, there was no sign of any form of civilization. There were definitely indigenous life forms; he'd seen bird-like creatures in the sky, though so far, he hadn't come face-to-face with any animal life.

Maybe the tunnels had been made by some sort of giant worm.

Or maybe there had been intelligent life forms, but something had wiped them out.

Though he would have expected to have come across some sort of evidence on the surface.

"What are we going to do about her?" Dylan said quietly.

By her, he presumed Dylan meant Destiny. And right now, he had no clue. She was still standing in the same spot but turning slowly to look around herself. Then she stood still and tilted her head, staring up at the sky high above them. She reached up as though to touch the stars.

A smile tugged at his lips as he watched her. There was something so...ingenuous about her. A sense of wonder in everything around her. Most of the "people" he mixed with were somewhat jaded. Hell, he was probably the most jaded of all.

"You like her," Dylan murmured.

"No, I don't."

"You're smiling. Not sure I've ever seen that before. Makes me a little uneasy."

"Fuck off."

"I would if I had any clue which way to fuck off to," Dylan said. "But that doesn't answer my question. What do we do with her? Can you send her back?"

He shook his head. "I won't risk it."

"Probably for the best. Right now, I think we're still in the clear. No one actually saw us. But if she goes back, then we're blown, and that would not be a good thing. Kinross isn't going to be too happy about us nosing around."

"We could say we got lost."

"You think he'll believe that?"

He rubbed a hand over the scar on his cheek. "Maybe it's not a problem. Destiny won't tell if we ask her not to."

"Who is she anyway?" Dylan glanced at her. "Why is she a prisoner?"

"She told me she was born on the *Trakis Four*. She doesn't know who she is, but she believes she has a mysterious duty to perform and they're keeping her safe in that cell until she can do it."

"Bizarre."

Definitely. "I suppose we could— Wait, *shh*." It was very faint, but in the distance, he could hear the sound of feet. A lot of feet, heading in their direction from down the tunnel. "Turn off the flashlight," he said.

Dylan turned it off and they stood for a moment. "Time to get the hell out of here."

At least that decided for them which way they should go. Not this way. He glanced around and spotted another tunnel, almost opposite where they stood. That looked as good as any.

He hurried back to where Destiny waited.

"We have to go," he told her. "But you don't need to come with us. We can leave you here and your friends will find you."

She chewed on her lower lip, her gaze darting between the two of them. Was she thinking about her duty? She was clearly torn. She looked back up at the stars.

He realized he didn't want to leave her here, and he wasn't

sure why. He hardly knew her. She wasn't his responsibility. He didn't do responsible. But he hated the idea of her being caged in that cell.

"Come on, Milo," Dylan said. "We need to get the hell out of here."

He was right. Their hunters were only minutes away.

"Can I go with you for a little while and then come back?" Destiny asked.

"Of course. You can do whatever you like." At least she could if she came with them. If she didn't, then no doubt she'd be locked up again.

She cast a glance toward the tunnel, where the sound of approaching people was growing louder. Then she smiled and it lit up her face. "Take me with you."

In that moment, he had a premonition that he was perhaps making a huge mistake. A mistake that would ripple down and change everything. But also in that moment, he couldn't see how.

He grabbed her hand. "Let's go."

Chapter Twelve

"If you wish to discover the guilty person, first find out to whom the crime might be useful."
—Alexandre Dumas, *The Count of Monte Cristo*

A knock sounded on the door. Luther glanced up from his work then swiped the control panel to show the camera view of the corridor. Silas stood outside the door. Luther swiped again, and the door clicked to unlock. Once it opened, Silas stepped into the room. He crossed the space and sank into the chair opposite.

Luther grinned. "You're a mind reader. I need some help."

Silas raised an eyebrow. "You do?"

"Yes. I need a title. I was thinking…Leader?"

Silas shook his head. "A little on the nose perhaps."

"Commander in chief?"

"Sounds too military. We don't want to scare people."

"Not yet, anyway. How about President?"

"Too many bad connotations," Silas replied.

Probably right. Nobody wanted to be grouped together with President Max Beauchamp. The guy had been a fuckwit. Secretly, Luther really liked the title of king. He'd had a fascination with King Arthur from when he was a child growing up in a high-rise council flat in Glasgow. But he didn't think it would go down too well. The last monarchy in the UK had hardly been role models.

"God?" Silas suggested.

Luther laughed. "That might upset the Church." Not that he'd usually give a shit, but right now he needed the Church of Everlasting Life on his side, however much he might dislike the idea. They had a lot of influence. At some point in the not-too-distant future, he was expecting a level of unrest. Right now, the troublemakers were quietly disappearing. But there were way too many Chosen Ones with an inflated sense of self-worth. All that talk before they left Earth about being the future of humanity. It had gone to their heads.

"Prime Minister?" Silas said.

"Hmm." He considered it. He liked it actually. Still had a few negative connections, though. "How about First Minister?" He grinned. First Minister of the New World. "You can be Second Minister if you like." After all, what was the point of being in charge if you couldn't spread a little love around? "Well, that's one thing off the to-do list. I'll make the announcement tomorrow. So, is there something you need?"

"A couple of things," Silas said. "We're getting some aggro from the labor groups. It's all very well making the troublemakers disappear, but there's just too many of them. It's going to interfere with the schedule."

He suspected the main issue was that many of the Chosen Ones hadn't exactly been chosen. They'd likely paid for their places. He, more than anybody, knew how easy that was. All you'd needed was money and connections, and there had been plenty of people with those. Likely many of the people building his castle had been billionaires back on earth. The thought made him smile but didn't solve the problem. "How about children?"

"Children? Won't that be seen as a little unethical?"

If Silas had one flaw, it was a tendency to be too...nice. "I'm not suggesting we use babies. Say between the ages of twelve and sixteen. Old enough to work, young enough to be malleable."

Silas didn't appear convinced, but he shrugged. "I'll look into it."

"You said a couple of things? What's the other?"

"I just wanted to give you a heads up. The woman, Destiny, has disappeared."

At first the words made no sense, and he had to remind himself of who Destiny was. Then his jaw clenched. "What do you mean she's disappeared? She was in a locked cell, underground, with no windows. How the hell could she disappear?"

"We have no clue."

Luther got to his feet. He paced the length of his office and then back again to stand in front of Silas, who appeared entirely too unconcerned, considering. Though Silas had no idea of Destiny's role. Luther hadn't shared that with anyone except Elvira Yang. And he would have to decide what to do about that when the woman was of no further use.

"Could someone have helped her?" But who? She knew no one except for Dr. Yang and Silas. He trusted Silas with his life and Dr. Yang had too much at stake.

"We don't know," Silas said.

"Hell, is there anything you do fucking know?"

Silas ignored his show of bad temper. He was used to him. Luther took a deep, calming breath. Where could she go? She was alone on a strange world. She'd maybe just noticed that some imbecile had left the door unlocked and wandered off.

She would come back when she got hungry. But who the hell had left the door open? "Tell me what happened."

"We had an alert earlier this evening. One of the new sensor alarms went off down on the lower level. A patrol was sent to investigate but found nothing untoward. While they were down there, they checked on Destiny and found she was gone. The door to her cell was locked, but she wasn't inside."

"How the hell is that possible?"

"Again—no clue. Obviously, no one is owning up to anything. They've started searching, but the place is a warren. We hadn't realized how extensive the tunnels are."

He frowned. "Man-made?"

Silas grinned. "Unlikely *man*-made. But not natural, that's for sure."

Had someone betrayed him? But who? No. It was just a stupid mistake. Someone had left the door unlocked. Destiny had left and closed it behind her. She'd come back on her own. Or Silas's men would find her. He had everything under control.

Luther rubbed at his chest, felt the familiar ache, a twinge in his arm. Closing his eyes, he breathed deeply. In. Out. Until the tightness left him and he could breathe easily again.

"I want you to take lead on this, Silas. You need to get her back. And soon."

Silas frowned. "Why? Who is she? Why is she so important? Do you have a thing with this woman?"

"No. Of course not. And it doesn't matter, because you don't need to know. But take whatever resources you require and find her."

"You want her alive?"

"Hell yes, I want her alive." He took another deep breath. "I need her back. That's all *you* need to know."

Silas raised an eyebrow. "Okay. I'll go look for her." He turned and headed to the door. "I liked her, you know.

Destiny, I mean. She's a bit of a cookie, but she's a nice woman." And he left.

Luther hadn't needed to hear that. He didn't need to know how *nice* Destiny was.

He crossed to the window and stood staring down at his new kingdom.

The building work was going on even after dark, under the flare of solar-powered flashlights. His people all laboring away. They were building something good here. Something worthwhile. And everyone had their roles to play. His was to provide the vision, others to build it. Destiny had her own role, and Dr. Yang had assured him she was compliant.

Where the hell was she?

Chapter Thirteen

"…joy takes a strange effect at times, it seems to oppress us almost the same as sorrow."
—Alexandre Dumas, *The Count of Monte Cristo*

Destiny was on the point of exploding, and she hugged her arms around herself as though she could hold all the excitement inside. But she couldn't.

She'd never felt anything like this.

Unruly emotions bubbled up inside her and a big grin kept trying to escape. No doubt Dr. Yang would have taken one look at her and given her something to calm her down. But Dr. Yang wasn't here.

Milo was. And his friend Dylan, who, while not having quite the same effect of twisting up her insides as Milo did, was still very exciting.

But thoughts of Dr. Yang did sober her a little. Dr. Yang had given her everything and all she had asked in return was obedience. Destiny was going against everything she had been brought up to believe in. She *would* go back, but first she just wanted a little time to explore these new feelings. What would that matter?

"Which way?" Dylan asked, dragging her from her thoughts.

"That way," Milo replied. "You go first—your eyesight is better." And then they were off and running.

For a moment, she stood rooted to the spot. Then she took a deep breath and leaped after them. And with that one leap forward, something shifted inside her, as though she was shedding a huge weight that had been dragging her down.

This freedom might not be forever, but it was for now, and she was going to savor every second until she went back.

Dylan disappeared into one of the tunnels, Milo close behind him, and she followed into the darkness. For a second, she slowed; while there was no light in the tunnel, she could hear them moving fast ahead of her. Putting her hand out in front of her, so she wouldn't crash into anything, she followed as fast as she could. But they were getting away from her. Clearly more confident in the dark than she was, and their legs were longer. She increased her speed, but then hit a wall as the tunnel turned a corner and she tripped and fell, banging her head as she went down. *Ouch!* She couldn't hear them anymore and panic engulfed her. She wanted to call out but was scared someone else might be in earshot, though the sound of their pursuers had faded. She heard…nothing.

She was alone. She was used to that.

But she didn't want to be alone anymore. A sob rose up inside her and she swallowed it down.

Then footsteps sounded ahead of her and a light flashed in the darkness. She pushed herself up, and she was kneeling when Milo appeared. He stopped in front of her, the flashlight playing over her, and she blinked.

"Taking a rest?" he asked.

"I fell."

He shook his head, but then without saying anything further, he reached down, gripped his hands around her waist, and lifted her from the floor. A second later, she was flung over his shoulder. A hand clamped on her bottom, and a squeak escaped her mouth, and then they were moving.

This time he kept the flashlight on, but she couldn't see much because she was upside down and her face was pressed against his back. So she closed her eyes and just concentrated on the strange sensations rushing through her body. The hand on her bottom was having a weird effect—she was guessing some manifestation of sexual desire. She was trying to analyze the sensation; she was hot and achy and little tingles were running from his palm all over the rest of her body, settling between her legs and in her breasts. Strange and not unpleasant. He increased his speed and she bounced, and his hand squeezed, and heat flooded her.

She scrabbled for something to hold on to but couldn't get a grip, and in the end, she wrapped her arms around his waist, closed her eyes, and held on tight. Finally, he slowed and came to a standstill. He stood for a moment, not breathing hard despite the sprint while carrying her.

He placed her on her feet. She stood for a moment, getting her balance, and then looked around her. They were in another cavern, though this one was more of just a widening of the tunnel, the same dark yellow-orange walls, a low ceiling, and no opening to the outside world. She could almost feel the weight of rock pressing down on her.

Dylan was leaning against the wall, arms folded across his chest. "What kept you?" he asked.

"I fell," she said, defensive. "Milo carried me."

"So I saw. Quite the knight in shining armor, isn't he?"

"Piss off, Dylan."

She'd read about them in her history books. "Are there still knights in armor?" she said.

"No, of course there aren't." Dylan frowned. "Don't you know anything?"

She sniffed. "I know lots of things. I know…" She tried to think of the most impressive things. "I know Einstein's theory of relativity. I know how genetic modification works, I know all the kings and queens of England, and the presidents of the Unites States. I know—"

"Enough," Dylan snapped, though he was smiling. "I get the point."

"Leave her alone," Milo said. "She's spent her life on a spaceship. Give her a break."

She smiled at him, and he scowled. What had she done wrong now? She had no clue how to behave in these situations. "Can you teach me to be normal?" she said.

Dylan choked.

"Us teach you?" Milo snorted. "We'd have to be normal to be able to do that. Normal is vastly overrated anyway." He looked around. "Seems like we've lost our followers, but I still have no clue where the hell we are."

"Let's keep going in the same direction," Dylan suggested. "If we don't come across a way out in…say an hour, we turn around and head back, and hopefully they'll have stopped looking for us."

"Why are they looking for you?" Destiny asked.

"Well, they obviously don't want anyone to know what they're hiding under Luther's brand-new castle."

"Luther?"

"Luther Kinross. He's our Lord and Master."

She frowned, trying to remember if Dr. Yang had ever mentioned this Luther. But she couldn't recall anything. "What about President Beauchamp?"

"Disappeared into a black hole."

Her eyes widened. "Really?"

"Yup. Along with the whole of the *Trakis One*." Dylan

studied her for a moment. "Where have you been?"

Locked in a lab and then locked in a cell. But she didn't say the words because they sounded a little…disloyal. And she owed Dr. Yang everything. So she just gave a shrug. "I was in cryo until only a few days ago and I haven't caught up on everything yet. Where do we go next?"

She wanted to go everywhere, see all there was to see. And she wanted Milo to teach her everything he knew. *Everything.*

"I reckon we've come about half a mile due north," he said. "Which means, right now, we're under the lake."

Destiny glanced up at the ceiling, imagining all that water on top of them.

"And if we keep going in the same direction," Milo continued, "then hopefully there will be some way out of this tunnel system on the other side."

"That will be the opposite side to where the encampment is," Dylan pointed out.

"Not a bad thing. Away from prying eyes. With luck, they won't suspect it was us down there, otherwise we're fucked."

She tried to recall where she'd seen, or heard, that word before—certainly not from Dr. Yang. "Getting fucked is a bad thing?" she said.

Dylan laughed, but Milo just blinked at her. "In this instance? Yes."

"And what do we do with our new friend?" Dylan asked, waving a hand in her direction.

Destiny held her breath, waiting for Milo's answer. He wouldn't send her back, would he? She had every intention of going back. Of course she did, just not yet. A day or two. Just to look around. To maybe climb the mountain and swim in the lake. To lie under the sun and watch the birds fly overhead.

"She can't come back to our shuttle," Milo said. "I imagine someone will be searching for her." He cast her a look, his eyes narrowed as if trying to work out who or what she was.

"I won't be a nuisance," she said. "I can sleep in the tunnels. I don't need much."

He stared a moment longer, then gave a shrug. "Let's get out of here first and then we'll decide."

She beamed him a smile and he shook his head. Was he regretting letting her come along? Probably.

"Who do you think made these tunnels?" Dylan asked. "They're not natural. If you look closely you can see the machine marks. And no way could Kinross have done this in the time he's been here. And why would he, anyway?"

"I'm thinking aliens." Milo grinned. "Are you thinking aliens?"

"Hell, yeah." They both glanced around. "Do you think they're still here?" Dylan asked.

"Invisible aliens? Or maybe they're just shy."

"According to Dr. Yang," Destiny offered, "there is a less than 0.001 percent chance of encountering an intelligent alien life form here."

"Killjoy," Dylan muttered.

He clearly didn't like her comment, though she wasn't sure why. Were all people this hard to understand, or just men? She'd never had this problem with Dr. Yang.

"Maybe they were visitors not indigenous to the planet," Milo suggested. "And now they've gone back to wherever they came from."

"Or perhaps they're waiting around the corner, with laser guns to blast us."

"Maybe we shouldn't—" Destiny started, but she stopped when Milo rolled his eyes. "What did I miss?"

"He has a wild imagination, that's all," Milo said. "Let's keep going."

Dylan headed off down the tunnel opposite the one they

had come out of. Milo looked at her. "Are you okay to walk?"

Did he want to carry her again? Certainly, part of *her* wanted him to. The sensation of being held had been...nice. But she also didn't want to be a burden. She needed to appear strong and capable. The last thing she wanted was to give him any excuse to leave her behind or send her back, thinking she was weak and needed protection.

She stood up straight and gave him a bright smile. "I'm good." And of course she was. There was light this time, Milo had kept the flashlight on, and they were walking, not running in the dark.

Dylan had already disappeared from sight and Milo gave her a last look then followed.

It was strange. She had the feeling that out of the two of them, Dylan was the "nicer" person. There was something not so "nice" about Milo, even though she enjoyed his company, but she couldn't work out what it was. A darkness behind his eyes. A coldness. At the same time, she sensed that it was only because of Milo that she was still with them. If it was up to Dylan, then she guessed she'd have been back in her cell or abandoned or worse. But for some reason, Milo was okay with her coming along. She wouldn't go so far as to say he actually wanted her there, but he wasn't totally averse to the idea, either. The thought widened her smile and put a skip in her step as she followed him.

She liked watching him move. She'd never seen an animal up close, not even a mouse, but he reminded her of what she would have imagined a big wild cat—a lion or maybe a tiger—would have moved like, all smooth, easy grace and coiled energy. Ready to pounce. A shiver ran through her. She really was feeling a little strange.

Dr. Yang had told her there were animal fetuses in cryo on board the *Trakis Four*. They would be woken up and brought to full-term growth if the conditions were right. One day, there might be lions roaming the forests. Or wolves. She'd love to see a real, live wolf. Maybe there was something similar already in the forests. Silas had told her that they were going to set up teams to explore the planet, make an inventory of any indigenous creatures. She would love to be part of that.

Milo glanced over his shoulder and slowed down so she could catch up. The tunnel was wide enough to walk side by side now. "You okay?" he asked.

She nodded. "I was just wondering if there were any wolves in the forest."

He raised a brow and glanced up ahead, toward Dylan. He'd stopped at a point where the tunnel branched out and was clearly waiting for them. "I hope not," Milo said, lowering his voice. "Dylan is afraid of wolves."

"He is?" She couldn't imagine Dylan being afraid of anything.

"He got bitten by one back on Earth, now he's terrified of the things."

"Poor Dylan."

"Why am I poor?" he asked as they stopped beside him.

"Milo told me you'd been bitten by a wolf. That must have been awful."

Dylan's eyes narrowed as he turned his attention to Milo.

"He was just trying to explain why you're afraid of wolves," she hurried on. Maybe Milo had been out of line telling her that. Or maybe Dylan was ashamed of his fear.

Dylan shook his head and then grinned. "Yeah, scared shitless. I have nightmares about Little Red Riding Hood."

"What's that?"

"A storybook from back on Earth. A fairy tale. You know what one of them is, don't you?"

"They're not true. And they're frivolous. Not serious reading. Dr. Yang told me."

"Your Dr. Yang does sound like a real killjoy."

She'd never heard of the word before tonight, but she could guess what it meant and her lips twitched, suppressing a smile. Yes, if there was any joy then she had a feeling Dr. Yang would kill it dead.

"I've read *The Count of Monte Cristo*," she said. "About a hundred times. It was the only storybook I had."

"We'll have to get you some reading material," Dylan went on. "Some really, really frivolous stories. Some fairy tales and"—he glanced at Milo with a sly grin—"some romance."

"Romance?"

"Didn't Dr. Yang tell you about romance?"

She shook her head, then smiled. "Though she did give me a manual on human reproduction. But she said it was a little archaic and that test tubes were much better for fertilization. I was born in a birthing bag. Apparently, it's much more hygienic and safer. She believes most reproduction will be carried out that way in the new world. We need to carefully monitor the genetic combinations of new humans because the gene pool is so much smaller now."

"Definitely a killjoy," Dylan muttered. "And you"—he waved a hand at Milo—"have your work cut out." He cast a glance at Destiny. "Though it might be worth it. "

"Piss off," Milo said.

She was totally lost now. The more time she spent with them, the more she realized that she was lacking so much knowledge. In some ways she knew a lot—she could quote quantum physics theories—but about people and what made them work, she understood nothing. A niggle of disloyalty told her that it was because of Dr. Yang. She'd clearly controlled the information she allowed Destiny to see.

What gave her the right?

A flicker of anger burned to life deep inside her, but she snuffed it out.

There were no doubt good reasons. She had to believe that.

"So which way, now," Milo asked.

She stared down the two tunnels. They both looked identical.

Dylan stood in front of the first and, closing his eyes, he breathed in deeply. He opened his eyes and moved to the next tunnel, repeating the process. What was he doing? She sniffed the air and could sense nothing but a vague musty smell.

"This one," Dylan said, waving to the second tunnel. "The air is fresher, and it looks like there's a slight incline, so hopefully it's heading up to ground level."

"Let's go then."

They fell in behind Dylan, walking side by side again. Which was nice. She cast Milo a quick glance; he was staring straight ahead but turned as if sensing her gaze. "You understand we're going to have to leave you when we get to the surface." He paused, then continued. "That is if you still want to stay out. I'm sure we can organize something if you've decided you want to go back."

She shook her head. "No. Not yet. And I'll be okay. I'm used to being alone." Though she hoped they wouldn't abandon her completely. She needed food. Already, she was experiencing the first pangs of hunger. She'd missed dinner.

"So I gather. One of us will come back as soon as it's safe and bring you some food and other stuff."

"The stories," she said. "Will you bring them?"

He grinned. "We'll load you up an ebook with every story I can get hold of. Including '"Little Red Riding Hood."'

A shiver of excitement ran through her, quickly followed by a feeling of unease. "Why?" she asked. "Why are you being nice to me?"

"Damned if I know."

They were climbing now, not steeply but steadily, rising toward the surface of the planet.

Beside her Milo came to a halt. "Look." After switching off the flashlight, he waved a hand ahead of him. Without the light, the tunnels were in darkness, but ahead of them she could make out a patch of not quite so dark. A figure silhouetted against it—Dylan.

They hurried up to join him and stood at the entrance to the tunnels, staring out. They were in some sort of forest. She'd seen trees when Silas had taken her around the lake that morning. That's where they must be, but the trees were thick, and she could make out nothing but more trees. Through the leafy canopy above their heads she caught glimpses of the star-strewn sky. A fat, heavy moon hanging low provided most of the light—just a dim yellow glow. She'd never been outside at night before. It was beautiful and gave her a sense of freedom, of possibilities, she'd never experienced before.

Milo stepped farther out, and she followed as if glued to his side. They would leave her soon. He turned slowly around. "There," he said. "That must be the light from the buildings."

She could see it now, a faint radiance through the trees.

"It's going to be a long walk," Dylan said.

"Can't you teleport again?" Destiny asked. For that matter, couldn't they teleport her inside their shuttle so she could go with them?

"No!" They both spoke in unison.

"It's really just a prototype," Milo said. "Very dangerous. Emergencies only. No, you stay here, and we'll come back as quickly as we can. You'll be okay?"

"Of course. I told you, I'm good at being on my own."

"Stay close to the tunnels, don't wander off. We don't know what else is here. There could be predators. In fact, Dylan, give her your gun."

"Really? You think that's a good idea?" But he was

already unstrapping the belt from his waist. He moved toward her and wrapped it around her waist then buckled it in the front. "You know how to use it?" he asked.

"No." Of course she didn't know how to use it. She had a strange idea that Dr. Yang would not approve of her carrying a weapon. The thought made her smile.

"All you do," Dylan said, taking the pistol from the holster and placing it in her hand, wrapping her fingers around it, "is aim and squeeze the trigger."

"But don't unless it's an emergency," Milo added, "because likely, they'll hear the shot from headquarters."

She looked at the weapon in her hand and frowned. She'd read about weapons. She didn't like the idea at all. "I couldn't kill anything," she said.

"If it's an animal, then just aim over its head or to the side. The noise should be enough to frighten it away. If it's a person…" He gave a shrug. "You must decide for yourself."

She forced a smile. "Thank you. I'll be fine."

"Then we'll be off." He pushed the flashlight into the loop on her belt. "So you can see where you're going. Now we must go show our faces so people don't think we're hiding."

She nodded but her chin wobbled.

Dylan patted her arm. "Don't worry, I'll look after him for you," he said.

Milo rolled his eyes but then gave her a nod and turned to go.

Destiny held herself very still as they walked away, disappearing into the forest and leaving her alone in the dark night. *Free.*

Chapter Fourteen

"How did I escape? With difficulty. How did I plan this moment? With pleasure."
—Alexandre Dumas, *The Count of Monte Cristo*

Destiny stood for a while after they'd vanished. The night was warm, but she hugged her arms around herself.

They'd promised to come back.

But would they?

What did she really know about them? Nothing.

Finally she moved, turning full circle. Behind her lay the entrance to the tunnels, and she fixed that in her mind—if she got lost then Milo might never find her. Directly ahead was the glow of light from the buildings on the island. She walked toward it, taking a direct route through the trees. They were not much taller than her, with thick trunks, the bark silvery in the dim light. The leaves were small and pale green. She'd read books about the flora and fauna of Earth, but she didn't recognize these. Though that wasn't unexpected. This wasn't Earth.

She walked for a few minutes until she came to the edge of the trees and ahead of her was the lake, silky smooth without a ripple, a reflection of the yellow moon in the still water. This was the widest part of the lake and no sound managed to cross the space between her and the buildings on the island.

Were they looking for her?

Was Dr. Yang worried? She felt a pang of guilt at that, but only for a little while. She moved out of the trees and across the stretch of gray sand. At the water's edge she hunkered down and trailed her hand in the water. It was cool but not cold and she waggled her fingers.

A sharp pain shot from her fingertip and she reared up, falling back on her bottom. Something had bitten her. She stared at her fingertip and could make out the shape of teeth indented in her skin. No blood, though, as the skin wasn't broken. She edged closer again and stared into the water. Silvery round bodies of some sort of water animal swam just below the surface. More like a fish, she decided.

Lowering her finger again, she watched as the fish swam around it. Maybe she'd frightened them more than they had her. She held her breath as one nudged her hand with a silver snout.

Good.

She wanted to swim in the lake—though maybe not tonight—so better to make friends than enemies.

Standing up, she wiped her hand down her pants, then with one last look at the island, she turned and headed back the way she had come. She found the tunnel entrance with ease but was reluctant to go back. Instead, she sat cross-legged on the ground. Closing her eyes, she just listened. At first, she thought everything was silent, but the longer she sat, the more she noticed the subtle sounds of the forest. A rustle in the undergrowth, the faint cry of some bird high above her, a leaf dropping from a nearby tree.

A sense of peace washed through her.

Her mind cleared of all the tension she hadn't even known was there. And as her mind cleared, she became aware of the anger buried deep down and rarely acknowledged.

What made Dr. Yang in charge of her? Who gave her the right to lock her in a cell and keep her a prisoner? To punish her when she behaved in a manner the other woman didn't like?

Were some people born to lead and others to follow?

At some fundamental level, she didn't believe that.

Was it because Dr. Yang had brought her up? In human society, did that give her the right to decide the course of Destiny's whole life? Surely there came a time when you should be free of the constraints to which you were born. When you made decisions based on what you knew and what you'd learned. When you earned the right to be independent.

Though she did believe that everyone needed to work for the greater good. For society as a whole. It was the only way they could survive. And if she had a pivotal role in that—whatever it might be—then she would do her duty, as everyone else did theirs.

But that was tomorrow, or the day after, or…

She jumped to her feet. This was her time to explore; she could figure the rest out later. She'd maybe leave the forest for daylight—she really didn't want to have to shoot at anything. Instead, she headed back into the cave system.

Once inside, she stood for a while in the darkness, listening for any sounds that might indicate someone had followed them. There was nothing but silence, and she pulled the flashlight from her belt and flicked it on. She headed back the way they had come, but when she came to the first junction where they had headed upward, she took the other tunnel, which led her deeper underground.

Why had these tunnels been built? Had people lived down here? Had they been hiding?

The tunnel widened, and she came to another junction. Again, she took the tunnel heading farther down, making a mental note so she could find her way back. She stopped again and listened, but she was still alone.

After a while, the tunnel widened into a huge cavern, similar to the one they had teleported into, except without the hole in the roof, so there was no natural light coming in.

Parked in the center of the cavern was a spaceship.

Her feet stopped moving as she stared up at it.

It looked nothing like the ugly bulk of the *Trakis Four*. The ship that had brought them from Earth was about a quarter of a mile long, shaped like a bullet, and a dull khaki-gray color. This was smaller, though not as small as the shuttle that Milo had flown in on.

The ship was shaped like a horseshoe from back on Earth—she'd seen pictures—and was black and silver and sleek and beautiful. Some sort of script she couldn't read was written along one side—the letters like nothing she had ever seen. The ship's name?

Where had she come from?

Was she part of the fleet?

But Dr. Yang had told her all about the fleet, and all the ships were identical.

Was there intelligent life on the planet after all? If so, why had they remained hidden?

Or was this ship from other visitors? Like the *Trakis Four*.

She walked slowly toward it, her heart hammering, as she waited for someone or something to appear. She wasn't sure whether she wanted that or not. What would they be like? Would they be able to communicate?

Why did she always have so many questions and no

answers?

The ship was probably about a hundred and fifty feet in length, forty feet wide, and twenty feet high. Not a colony ship then, unless the colonists were really small. She walked all the way around it. At the front, high up, was some sort of glass window, but she couldn't see in.

Stepping closer, she reached out a hand and touched the side. The metal was cool under her palm.

Nothing happened.

She backed away a little and sank to the sandy floor and just...stared.

"Hello?" she called out.

Again, nothing happened.

She jumped back up to her feet and studied the ship. There was no sign of a door or any way inside. She moved closer and knocked on the side. "Is anyone there?"

There was some sort of rectangular panel on the side of the ship. Similar to what opened the doors on the *Trakis Four* but bigger.

She touched her hand to it lightly. Then harder, pressing her palm flat against the metal. For a second, nothing happened yet again. But then a shudder ran through the ship and the side directly above her shimmered, lines forming in the shape of a door. Heart racing, she stepped back as it slid open and a ramp appeared, leading upward into the ship.

Should I?

Shouldn't I?

This could be dangerous, but really, she didn't have any choice. She had questions that needed answers. Her feet moved of their own volition, and she took her first step upward.

Chapter Fifteen

*"We frequently pass so near to happiness without seeing,
without regarding it, or if we do see and regard it, yet without
recognizing it."*
—Alexandre Dumas, *The Count of Monte Cristo*

The first of the suns was just rising, taking the chill from the cool air as Milo made his way around the edge of the lake. The circumference was around ten miles, but the morning was pleasant.

The dawn light was orange. Later, the second sun would rise and that was a bright white light, but for now the world was bathed in a muted golden glow.

Pretty.

This was apparently spring. The days were shorter than on Earth, approximately twenty hours, but the years were longer, around five hundred days, though the scientists were still working this out. The planet made an elliptical orbit around both suns and traveled approximately 1.5 billion miles in that orbit. He'd been doing his homework and reading all the comms that came in from the scientific team, which was run by Dr. Elvira Yang. And that reminded him—he had yet to chase up her family on the *Trakis Two*. Though after talking with Dylan, he had an inkling he was not going to have good news for the doctor.

Each crew member had been allocated three cryotubes for family members. But unfortunately for Dr. Yang, in some cases, someone had tampered with the tubes before they left Earth and changed the crew family for someone else. They weren't sure how extensive the sabotage was or who was responsible. Maybe Dr Yang's family was all tucked up safe on the *Trakis Two,* but he wouldn't bet on it.

As soon as he got back to the shuttle, he would contact Rico. Without the boost from the shuttle's systems, the comm units they wore only functioned locally and wouldn't reach the *Trakis Two*.

From what he could gather, Dr. Yang had considerable influence—or that was what the gossip said, according to Dylan who'd been making friends or at least trying to gather some information. It wouldn't hurt to get a few people on their side. He would leave that to Dylan. He was better at it than Milo.

Dylan was trying to find out more about who Kinross was. What was his background? How did he come to have so much power? But so far no one was talking. Maybe no one knew.

Milo had a duffel bag slung over his shoulder filled with goodies for Destiny. Food and drink and an ereader.

He hadn't wanted to venture out before light. Last night Dylan had shifted form on the way back; he could see better and scent better as a wolf. They hadn't encountered anything larger than a small bird, but Dylan had claimed there were signs of bigger things out here in the forest. Though he'd also said there was no evidence of anything in the tunnels, so

Destiny should have been safe.

A meeting of the council was scheduled for later that morning, so he had to get back and to the island by then. They didn't want to give anyone reason to suspect them of being anything other than good, conscientious representatives.

Would Destiny even be here?

Maybe she'd taken fright and headed back to the safety of her cozy little cell.

He didn't like that idea and had no clue why.

He didn't want to care. His one disastrous venture into love had left him wary of the emotion. And that was the understatement of the century—of the millennium actually. He ran a hand over the raised weal that curled around his throat and extended down over his left shoulder, just touching his heart as though to remind him that love could definitely leave you burned and scarred.

Anyway, why was he thinking of love?

Destiny intrigued him—that was all. She was just so... different. And he wanted to know why. She was also sexy as hell, and while he might have given up on love, he still enjoyed sex, and it had been a long time for him even without considering all the years he'd spent in cryo.

Destiny had a life plan. She was going back to do her duty to mankind. In which case, why not have a little fun before she returned? Except he had a strange idea that it might not be so easy to let her go.

He had no intention of staying on this shithole of a planet longer than necessary. Kinross was bad enough, but add in the church and this was no place he wanted to be. And as Destiny's "duty" seemed to be tied to Trakis Four in some way, it was clear they were not destined to be close. Not even on the same planet.

He was probably just suffering from some sort of withdrawal symptoms due to five hundred years in cryo. Rico had said it could have some funny side effects; he just hadn't gone into details.

Maybe it would be better if Destiny had returned to her cell, then he could get back to concentrating on the job he was here to do. Find out what Luther Kinross was up to and whether he had the means to exert any influence over Trakis Two.

When he emerged from the trees, she was sitting cross-legged in front of the tunnel entrance as though waiting for him. She leaped to her feet, a huge, beaming smile on her face.

Someone was pleased to see him at least. And that caused a mixture of happiness and guilt. He was guessing Destiny didn't have many friends, only Dr. Yang, and he had a suspicion that the scientist did not have Destiny's ultimate well-being on her agenda.

Just what was Destiny's mysterious destiny?

She ran toward him and halted. A flicker of uncertainty crossed her face, then she shook her head and reached out, grabbing his hand. "Come. Come with me. There's something you *have* to see."

"Hey, slow down." But her enthusiasm was infectious, and he allowed her to pull him along. She dragged him to the cave entrance and then inside. What had she found?

The light disappeared as they hurried down the tunnel and she switched on the flashlight and played it across the walls. As they came to the first junction, she took the opposite tunnel from the one they had come along last night, then another. She turned off the flashlight and drew him the last feet in utter darkness, then the light flashed on again.

"Holy shit," he muttered.

It was a spaceship.

And not one of theirs.

He tugged free of Destiny's hand and walked around the

sleek black and silver vessel. She was like something out of a science-fiction movie. He came back to stand beside her. "There's nobody here?"

"No."

"They could be inside." Were they watching them, even now? Fucking aliens. Jesus.

"No." She took his hand again, slid her fingers into his, and tugged him forward. When they reached the ship, she placed her free hand on a panel at the side. A moment later a door appeared, then a ramp, and the door slid open.

What the hell?

How long had it been here? Where had it come from?

Even though they'd been in space five hundred years and were God knows how many miles from Earth, he'd never actually expected to encounter aliens. "Should we go in?" Hell, of course they should.

"I've been inside," Destiny said. "There's no one there."

He felt a stab of disappointment at that, mixed with a smidgen of jealousy. She'd already been inside. Was that bravery or stupidity to head into the unknown all alone without backup? Maybe a little of both.

She dropped his hand and headed up the ramp, and he hurried to catch up. The doorway was a little bigger than he would expect. The aliens had maybe been larger than humans.

The inside appeared to be in darkness, but as Destiny stepped through the doorway, lights flickered on. They were in some sort of hold, a little like the docking bay on the Trakis ships but much smaller. Probably to store stuff, but the space was empty now except for a vehicle parked against the far wall. His fingers itched with the urge to go see what it did, whether he could turn it on. But Destiny was already heading in the opposite direction. She walked up a ramp and stopped at a door at the top and raised her hand.

"Can I?" he said.

She turned to him with a smile. "Of course."

She moved aside and he pressed his palm to the panel. The door slid open with a quiet *whoosh*.

So how did it work? Would they open to any pressure? Was it heat? Touch? Shape?

He could feel a grin tugging at his mouth. This was really fucking cool.

Destiny was heading off again down a corridor. She'd clearly already been exploring and knew where she was going. A few feet on, she came to another door. This one opened onto what he presumed was the bridge. At this end, it was approximately ten feet wide, but broadened to around thirty feet at the front, where there was a clear window that looked out into the darkness of the cavern. Beneath that was a bank of consoles, smooth and featureless, and in front of them, two huge chairs. It looked like the aliens were humanoid but definitely larger than the average human. Two more chairs sat on either side of the room, with their own smaller consoles with screens above, blank at the moment.

Destiny sat down in one of the chairs at the front—it dwarfed her—and pressed her palm to the smooth console in front of her. It flickered to life and turned into some sort of control panel.

"I didn't dare press anything else in case I—"

"Took off?" He could imagine that would be quite worrying. His stomach lurched—he *really* didn't like flying. All the same, his fingers were itching again. He sat in the seat beside her and stared at the console. There was a big red button in the center, and then lots of other controls. But he had no clue what any of it did.

"I searched the whole ship," Destiny said. "There's nobody alive and no dead bodies." She sounded almost disappointed. "What do you think happened to them? The people who flew her. Where did they go? Why would they leave this behind?"

He shrugged. They would probably never know. "You spent the night in here?" he asked. "All alone?"

"I'm used to being alone." She shrugged. "There are cabins with beds. They must have been a lot like us. But bigger." Her stomach rumbled. "Sorry. I don't suppose you have anything to eat."

He got the satchel from his shoulder and dug inside, pulled out the box of food he'd brought with him. "I didn't know what you'd like, so I brought some of everything." He handed it to her, and she tugged off the lid and peered inside.

She selected a chocolate muffin and nibbled on the corner. "This is so good," she mumbled. "Dr. Yang says that sweet things are not healthy. But it's delicious."

Dr. Yang was definitely a killjoy.

She finished the muffin and took out a piece of cheese. Ate it. Then a bread roll. And another. Where was she packing all of that? Finally, she sat back. He handed her a bottle of water and she unscrewed the top and drank deeply.

"Thank you."

"So what now?" he asked. "Are you going to stick around here and work out how to fly this thing? Then head off into space?"

She shook her head.

He'd been teasing, but she looked so serious, now he really wondered. "What *do* you want to do, Destiny?"

She shifted in her seat so she was facing him. "I don't know." She bit her lip. "I should go back, but I don't want to, at least not just yet. I mean I will eventually, but first, I want to…" She shrugged. "I don't even know what I want to do. Just that there has to be more than what I've already done. That's pathetic, isn't it?"

"Not at all. I think it's understandable considering your

crappy upbringing." At the same time, she was unlike anyone he had ever met. Unspoiled. He had an urge to find out why. To discover what had made her this way. Where she had come from. What she tasted like when he kissed her—

—*And* stop that train of thought right there.

He was attracted to her, he could admit that much, but kissing her was a bad idea. He needed to keep talking, get his mind off things he had no business thinking.

"So tell me about yourself."

"Okay." She settled into her seat. "I was born on the *Trakis Four* in the year 2224. I don't know who my parents were. Dr. Yang said it wasn't important, but I would still like to know. I never met them. I never met anyone except Dr. Yang."

That was seriously odd. "What about the crew of the *Trakis Four*?"

"Dr. Yang said everyone else was asleep."

"Then she was lying. All the ships had crews awake. Up to thirty-four crew members at any one time." Except the *Trakis Two*. Rico had kept the crew to a minimum. He had apparently spent the first rotation learning everything he could. After that, he'd only woken up whoever was essential.

Her nose wrinkled and a line formed between her brows. "Why would she tell me they were asleep? Dr. Yang says that lying is a sin."

Obviously, only for everyone else. For some reason, she hadn't wanted Destiny to meet the rest of the crew. Or them to meet her. But why? "Maybe we could ask her one day. So where did you live?"

"In the laboratory. It was okay. I had my own space. And a gym so I could exercise. But I was lonely. Often I wouldn't see Dr. Yang for weeks at a time. And sometimes…"

"What?"

"Sometimes my head felt like it would explode with everything I wanted to know. But Dr. Yang would get angry if I asked questions, and I would be punished. And I wouldn't see her for a long time. So I learned not to ask."

He was beginning to dislike Dr. Yang. A lot. Maybe he'd make her vanish in a puff of smoke. He was pretty sure his new wand would do that much magic.

"Did she tell you anything?"

"Of course. She gave me lots of things to read and study, and she told me about the exodus from Earth. About how the planet was dying and that the survival of humanity was in our hands. She said that I was important and had a role to play when we reached the new world. That I would help the whole of humanity."

"But she didn't tell you what the role would be?"

She shook her head. "Just that I would know when the time was right. And I must be patient. And I tried to be. I really did. But sometimes…I think I must not be a good person, because I just wanted to know everything. Right now." She blinked a couple of times. "Dr. Yang would be very angry with me."

"No doubt." He hoped she was *really* pissed. The bitch. He had a mind to comm Rico and tell him to find Yang's family and…what? Eat them? "But does that matter?" he asked.

She frowned again as she thought that through. "She brought me up. She's done everything for me. I owe her my life."

"She kept you a prisoner and you owe her nothing."

Her eyes widened at his angry tone. "Are they looking for me?"

Clearly, she was changing the subject. "I don't know yet. If they are, they're doing it quietly and under the radar so far."

"What does that mean?"

"It's an old Earth saying. It means they don't want anyone

to see them. We're going to headquarters for a meeting this morning, so we'll keep our ears open."

"Your ears can close?"

He shook his head. "It's just a figure of speech." He had to leave, and he didn't want to go. Reaching into the satchel, he pulled out the digital ereader. He'd loaded it up with all the books from the entertainment archive on the shuttle.

"This is for you. A present." He pressed the button to open the reader. "It's fully charged and should last a few days. But one of us will be back tonight." Though he was damned if he was going to allow Dylan to come here alone.

She stared at the ereader, her hand sweeping across the screen. "There are so many."

"There should be reviews and rankings to help you choose," he said. "They're split into fiction and nonfiction. Just make sure you know the difference." Christ, if she read them and believed they were true, God knows what she would think of the human race. "Some are facts and some are made up."

"Why do people make them up? Is it like lies?"

A little like lies, he supposed. "Not lies, no, because everyone knows they're not true. Stories are for entertainment, but they're also a way for people to try and make sense of the world around them."

"Oh."

He stood up and looked down at her; she was running her finger over the titles. "I have to go. Do you want to show me the way out of here?"

"Of course." She jumped to her feet. "Thank you for the food and...and everything."

"Thanks for the spaceship." Something occurred to him. "Don't press any more buttons until we find out a little more about this thing." He didn't want her disappearing into space. Or blowing herself up. Or...

A look of regret flashed across her face, but she nodded. "Okay."

She was good at doing what she was told. That should make him happy. Instead, he had the urge to shake her, and that triggered a sense of unease somewhere deep inside. It didn't matter. All that mattered was that she didn't give them away. Then in a couple of weeks they could return to Trakis Two with the information they needed to move forward. Maybe Destiny would have gotten over the duty thing by then and could come with them…

He led the way out of the spaceship, down the ramp. The door shut behind them. They didn't speak in the tunnels, but as they came out into the forest, he turned to her. "You can still go back," he said and had no clue why.

"I will. Just not yet." She smiled. "I want to read my books."

It wasn't the answer he desired and again he wasn't sure why. But something drove him on and he stepped closer to her, so close they could touch. A voice inside his head reminded him that this was not a good idea.

But he ignored it this time, because he'd been wanting to do this since he'd first seen her.

He reached out and she went instantly still. They were so close she had to tilt her head to look into his eyes, and a little line formed between her arched brows as if she wasn't quite sure what to expect. Hell, he had no clue what to expect, either.

She inched even closer. Her eyes were wide, not with fear but with anticipation. She glowed. And he lowered his mouth to hers.

Chapter Sixteen

"…remember that what has once been done may be done again."
—Alexandre Dumas, *The Count of Monte Cristo*

This was a kiss.

Destiny held herself very still. If she moved, he might stop, and she really didn't want that to happen.

His face was so close now that she had to shut her eyes, and then his mouth touched hers. Pressed against hers, his lips were warm and hard. His fingers were in her hair, cupping her skull, tilting her back. Her heart rate picked up and tingles ran across her skin. It was very…interesting.

Too soon, he backed off, and her eyes flashed open. Was that it? She wanted more. He was watching her, his silver eyes half closed.

"Open your mouth, Destiny," he murmured, a faint tinge of amusement in his voice. His thumb stroked her lower lip and her mouth dropped open. "Are you always so obedient?" he asked.

"Yes."

He chuckled. "I'll have to remember that." Then he was coming close again and this time she kept her eyes—and her mouth—open. She didn't want to miss any of this. She felt as though she was poised on the edge of something momentous, something life changing, and that it might be snatched away from her at any second.

He paused, so close she could feel his warm breath against her skin. "You have to breathe," he said.

She gulped in air and then his mouth was on hers, his lips parted. They fitted together perfectly. Then his tongue filled her mouth, and the shock of it pulled her back and away from him. She swallowed, eyes wide, staring at him.

"You want me to stop?"

"No." She shook her head. "Is this what normal people do?"

"I don't think there's anything normal about this. The question is: do you like it?"

She frowned. "I'm not sure. It makes me feel..." A shiver ran through her. "I don't know." She wasn't sure how to put it into words that would make sense. It made her feel like the world might spin out of control at any moment.

"Do you want to find out?" he asked. "All you have to do is ask."

And now she felt as if she were standing on the edge of a precipice and she could back away, or she could jump. She knew then that if she said no, he would stop, and he would turn around and walk away. And she also knew, with a certainty she had never felt before, that she didn't want that. She wanted to jump, she wanted to fly.

"Show me."

His nostrils flared, his eyes narrowed, and his mouth curved into a small smile. His finger stroked down over her cheek, along her chin, leaving a trail of sensation.

This time she lifted her chin and moved toward him, touching her mouth to his, parting her lips, and her tongue slowly slid into the warm cavern of his mouth. He went still, and then a shudder ran through him. For a moment, he tensed, and she was sure he was going to pull away, then his hands tightened, holding her against him and his tongue moved against hers and it was really very strange.

She closed her eyes and concentrated on analyzing what she was feeling. It was all so new and different and... unhygienic? She was sure Dr. Yang wouldn't approve.

His tongue stroked along hers, then the roof of her mouth. He retreated and she heard the words. "Stop thinking, Destiny?"

So she did, because she'd told the truth—she was obedient. She felt the first flicker of rebellion, but now was not the time to rebel. She cleared her mind, and he was back, and she welcomed him, and heat stole over her body. Her hands came up without conscious thought and she mirrored his actions. Threading her fingers through his short, silky hair, she pulled him harder against her, thrusting her tongue into his mouth, tasting him...sharpness and spice. The heat sank down through her body, settling in her breasts and her belly and between her legs. She pushed herself closer to him, needing something but not sure what. With his mouth still on hers, his hands slid down her back and pulled her against him. Something hard stabbed her in the belly.

She didn't want him to stop, so she pressed herself closer. He went still. His hands were on her bottom and he squeezed once and then let her go. Part of her wanted to protest, but more of her needed time to assimilate this new interaction.

What had just happened? Was this *really* what normal people did? But then he'd said nothing about this was normal.

She raised a hand to her face, touched her lower lip; it was swollen and sensitive. Then she forced her gaze upward to find him watching her out of narrowed eyes. "What was that?" she asked.

"That, Destiny, I believe was your first kiss."

She blinked. "Will there be more?"

"Christ knows." Then he turned around and was gone.

Chapter Seventeen

"Learning does not make one learned: there are those who have knowledge and those who have understanding. The first requires memory and the second philosophy."
—Alexandre Dumas, *The Count of Monte Cristo*

In hindsight maybe kissing Destiny hadn't been the most sensible of decisions. Though at the time it had seemed the only thing to do. He'd been thinking about it since that first sight of her, which was maybe a good enough reason to stay the fuck away. But he had kissed her, and it had been on his mind ever since, playing havoc with his concentration.

Dylan prodded him in the side. "Have you heard a word I've said?"

"Nope."

"Got better things to think about?"

Hell, yeah. She'd tasted sweet and hot and that mixture of innocence and curiosity was a huge turn-on.

Maybe he just needed to get laid and he'd stop thinking about Destiny's kisses. There were a few women around, likely looking for suitable mates to start populating the planet with a new generation of humanity. Except he wasn't human, so he didn't qualify, but they didn't need to know that.

"This has the potential to be a complete clusterfuck," Dylan said.

He sighed. "What has?"

"Our new friend, Destiny. She's trouble."

After the pointless meeting, they'd wasted a few hours trying to hack into Luther Kinross's computer system. When it became clear that neither of them had the skills to do that, they'd spent the rest of the afternoon wandering around the colony, talking, watching, having a drink at the bar that had popped up in the collection of buildings forming along the edge of the lakeshore. The customers comprised the guards and the crews and the representatives. So far, he hadn't seen any of the "workers" except when they were working. No doubt they were being kept somewhere "for their own safety." Just like Destiny.

From the talk they had picked up, it had become clear that, while it was not being publicized, there was an intense search going on to find her. Everyone was being questioned. Had they seen a blonde woman in a yellow jumpsuit? Milo had asked who she was but hadn't got an answer. Just that she was ill and needed medical attention.

Could it be true?

Destiny had said she was in the cell for her own protection. She didn't look ill, though, and he figured it was just an excuse. So who was she really?

"If they find her and they find out we got her out of that cell, then my guess is we'll be well and truly fucked."

"Then we'd better make sure they don't find her."

"Maybe we shouldn't take the risk. Maybe we should... dispose of her."

Hell no.

He kept the words in but paused and turned to look at the other man, trying to gauge the seriousness of the suggestion. He was pretty sure Dylan had killed plenty of people in his time. Why should Destiny be any different? Except she was. And that thought almost made him tell Dylan to go ahead. Get rid of her before she became a problem. But he couldn't do it.

"No."

"I'm just putting it out there as an option," Dylan said. "And since when did you get so squeamish?"

"I'm not being squeamish." Well, maybe just a little. Those big, trusting blue eyes. He couldn't bear to think of the light going out in them. She was so full of life. And he was in trouble.

"You want into her pants. I've seen the way you look at her."

"No, you haven't."

Dylan ignored him. "It's sweet really. If a little inconvenient."

"Fuck off."

Dylan snickered. "And we need to address the problem. Before it becomes a bigger problem. Uncle Rico won't be happy if you mess up because you've got the hots for a pretty little blonde bit."

Milo moved quickly, lunging forward and flattening Dylan against the tree behind him, a hand across his throat. "Which part of 'fuck off' don't you understand?"

Dylan grinned, though his eyes flashed feral and a growl rumbled in his throat. Milo was sure he could take the wolf, though Dylan was alpha and stronger than most. Maybe a good fight was what he needed. If he wasn't going to get a good fuck.

For a second, he stared into the other man's face and saw the wolf stir behind his eyes, but the grin remained in place and Milo released his hold and stepped back. "Asshole," he muttered, then shoved his hands in his pockets and walked on. "We'll talk to her. She won't give us away." At least he didn't think so. "And I can put up a few concealment spells, so if they do search this side of the lake, they won't find her." His magic should be good enough for that, though it was a little...unpredictable at the moment. The next bit he wasn't so happy about, but it was sensible. "And we stay away for a few days. Stay where we're supposed to be and visible. Do what we're supposed to, and we find out what's hidden beneath Luther's castle."

"Okay. Sounds like a plan."

His eyes narrowed. That had been way too easy. "Would you have killed her?" he asked.

Dylan chuckled. He had a really annoying sense of humor. "Nah. Just wanted to see your reaction. Actually, I like her. If you don't want her then I might just make a play myself."

He was such a tosser. "I wouldn't do that if I was you." The words actually sounded quite reasonable.

"Why?"

"Because I'll turn you into a fucking toad."

Dylan laughed again.

Ha ha. He was so funny. "It's not a joke."

They arrived at the entrance to the tunnels and came to a halt. He'd been expecting Destiny to be waiting and something tightened inside him. Maybe she was at the spaceship. He hadn't told Dylan about that—he was going to let Destiny show him.

He took a step toward the entrance, but Dylan stopped him with a tap on his arm. He nodded his head toward the trees. Milo looked closer and there she was, sitting with her back against a large boulder, concentrating on the ereader in her hands, seemingly totally oblivious to their presence.

Dylan tiptoed up and grabbed the device. She gave a squeak and looked around, her eyes flashing past Dylan and settling on him. They were wide and wary. And she bit her lip.

"So what has got you so engrossed?" Dylan asked, glancing at the screen. A smile spread across his face and he looked at Milo and winked. "*Fifty Shades of Grey*."

"She's reading Fifty Shades of wanking Grey?"

"Hey, it's educational and one of the bestselling books of the twenty-first century."

Milo hadn't actually read the book, but he'd heard enough about it. Some sort of BDSM crap. He cast the other man a dirty look, then turned to study Destiny. She was watching him, her eyes wide and her lips turned up in a smile.

"You kissed me," she said. "And I felt strange. But now I know what it was. Desire."

Behind them Dylan sniggered.

Milo had been feeling a little strange himself. His dick twitched at the memory.

Her smile widened. "I like reading. It is very educational. Thank you, both of you." She held her hand out to Dylan. "Can I have my reader back? I want to finish my book."

Dylan handed it to her. She gave a regretful look at the screen and then closed it off and slid the reader into her back pocket.

"What else have you read?" Milo asked.

"*Brave New World*. I enjoyed it. And *Harry Potter*. I want to meet a wizard."

"It's not true, Destiny. Wizards don't really exist."

Dylan sniggered again. Milo ignored him.

"I know. I think I understand what stories are better now. Not truth, but also not lies. I think there is some small truth in all of them. Anyway, I also read *A Brief History of Time* by Stephen Hawking, which was interesting. And *The Collected*

Poems of W. B. Yeats."

"You read fast," Milo said.

"Do I?"

"It would take Dylan a year to read that many words," Milo said, "and he still wouldn't understand half of them."

She turned to look at Dylan. "Really?"

"A slight exaggeration. But you definitely read faster than the average human. So what did you think about them?"

She frowned, then nibbled on her lower lip. A new habit? "I don't know. It's too…much. Too much information. I need to think about it. Get it straight in my mind. It's all jumbling up and…" She gave a small shrug. "It's different than what I thought the world was. Different from what Dr. Yang told me." She gave another shrug. "Why didn't she tell me the truth? There's so much more than…"

"Duty?"

"I don't know. I need to think. Read some more. Maybe there isn't more in the end. Maybe duty is the same as honor and that's what's important."

"*I could not love thee, dear, so much, Lov'd I not Honour more,*" Dylan murmured.

"What's that?"

"A poem by Robert Lovelace," Milo replied.

"I don't understand love yet. But I will. The answer is there."

"Well, don't expect to find it in *Fifty Shades of Grey.*"

She studied him. "I think you should kiss me again. I think desire and love are connected and I need to understand."

"A word of warning," Dylan said. "I suspect our friend Milo here might be okay with the desire part, but I'm pretty sure he doesn't do love. You'd be better off with me if you're wanting to experiment. Don't you want to kiss *me*, Destiny?"

She looked at him, her head cocked on one side, a slightly puzzled smile on her lips. "No."

Milo chuckled but decided that was plenty of talk about love and desire. He was supposed to be keeping his distance. "We've brought some food," he said to change the subject. "Let's eat."

She sank to the ground and leaned against the boulder. Milo sat across from her, and Dylan stayed on his feet, keeping watch though Milo thought they were safe right then. He rummaged in his backpack and brought out some containers of food. Vegetable curry and bread. And donuts.

She took a spoonful of curry and closed her eyes, concentrating on the taste he guessed. "This is good." Opening her eyes, she smiled at him. "So what have you two been up to?"

There was no reason not to tell her. She already knew they were looking into what Kinross was planning. "Wasting our time trying to hack into Luther Kinross's computer system," he said.

"And failing," Dylan added.

"Why do you need to get into his computer system?"

"We just want to know what his plans are," Milo replied. "And how he intends to implement those plans. Right now, he's not sharing much of anything."

"Like Dr. Yang not sharing my role," Destiny said, a small frown between her brows. "Maybe you'll know when the time is right."

"And who decides that?" Dylan snapped. "I'm betting on Luther fucking Kinross. But who put him in charge?"

Destiny's frown deepened. "I don't know."

"Me neither. But this is my life, and no asshole, self-imposed dictator is going to tell me how to live it."

Destiny finished the curry and then examined the donuts. They had pink icing and sprinkles. "So pretty." She took a bite and her tongue swiped over her lips and heat shot to Milo's groin. He wanted to kiss her again and a hell of a lot more. And teach her what desire was. Dylan was right—he didn't do love.

Destiny popped the last of the donut in her mouth, wiped her hands down her pants, then glanced between him and Dylan. "Would you like me to help? I'm good with computers."

"Why not? You can't be worse than the two of us." Milo reached into his pack and pulled out a tablet computer. He swiped it on and then handed it to her. She stared at it for a few seconds and then her fingers started moving.

"What are you doing?" Dylan asked.

"Looking for signals. I think your Mr. Kinross likes to be in control. He would want to be able to access all the other computers. Which means his system must be sending and receiving signals."

"And have you found any?" Dylan asked after a few minutes of silence.

She glanced up and grinned. "Of course. I told you I'm good. I'm just tracing the signals back to where they came from." She tapped the screen. "This seems to be the main hub. Everything goes through here. Kinross's Castle."

Milo snorted. "The man has delusions of grandeur. But can you get in?"

"Give me a second." Her fingers were flying again. "I'm in. Though there are some areas I can't access. I'm sorry." She handed him the tablet and picked up another donut.

"Don't be," Milo said. "You've gotten much further than us." He scanned down the information on the screen. "There's a big section here called Stellar Recruitment. Does that mean anything to you?" he asked Dylan.

Dylan moved to stand behind him so he could see the screen. "It was the company that organized the recruitment and training of the ships' crews."

"And can you guess who owns it?"

"Kinross? Well, that explains a lot. It would have given him access to the ships before they left Earth. He would have been able to put his own people in place."

"And access to the crew families. You think that was Kinross?"

Dylan shrugged. "It makes sense."

"There's a whole load of information here. Manifests for all the ships. Crew details. And guess who's got a big red flag next to his name. Captain Ricardo Sanchez of the *Trakis Two*."

"That's not good. But again, it makes sense if Kinross was in charge of recruiting the crew members."

"Is it useful?" Destiny asked.

"Very."

"I'm glad."

Milo guessed she liked being useful. Otherwise why would she want to return to a situation where she was a virtual prisoner? To perform a mysterious role that she knew next to nothing about. It seemed crazy to him. "Do you want to go back, Destiny?"

She thought about her answer. "I want to do my duty. But just not yet." She glanced away for a moment and he could almost see the thoughts warring in her head. Dr. Yang had done a real number on her. Brainwashing her into this role-to-play crap. "I have lots of books still to read and I don't think Dr. Yang would approve of *Fifty Shades*. And I have six more Harry Potter books. And the Bible and so many more. But I *will* go back."

"If you do, you can't tell them about me and Dylan."

"You'd be in trouble?"

"Big trouble."

"I should lie?"

"We'll go back to Trakis Two at some point. After that, it won't matter. So maybe just stay with us until then. And you can finish your books and maybe we can get you some more."

"Can you get me books on how spaceships work?" she asked.

He didn't think there were many books on that particular subject, but maybe there would be engineering manuals on the *Trakis Two*. "I'll see what I can do."

"Thank you. And yes, I'll stay here until it's safe for you. I don't want any harm to come to you and Dylan. You're my friends. I've never had any friends before."

Christ, that made him feel shitty. He didn't want her for a friend. He wanted to be her... He shook away the thoughts and pushed himself to his feet. "If you hear anything or see anything in the forest then go hide in the tunnels. I'm going to put a cloaking device on the entrance.

"What's a cloaking device?"

"It's a prototype. New."

"Like the teleporter?"

It took him a moment to realize she meant when he'd magicked them out of her cell. "Just like the teleporter." He caught Dylan's gaze as he spoke.

"Liar," the other man silently mouthed.

Yeah. Time to change the subject. Again.

"We need to get back and analyze this information. But first, let's go show Dylan your spaceship."

Chapter Eighteen

"When you compare the sorrows of real life to the pleasures of the imaginary one, you will never want to live again, only to dream forever."
—Alexandre Dumas, *The Count of Monte Cristo*

Destiny raised her head and listened. She'd been engrossed in her book, but she'd just reached the end—again—and now the outside world intruded.

Had there been a noise? She concentrated and picked up the sound, analyzed it. Booted feet. For a moment her heart lifted. It'd been two days since she had seen Milo and Dylan. She'd missed them, but at the same time, she'd needed these days alone.

So much information to assimilate.

She loved reading. Sometimes she thought she could stay here in the forest forever, read all the books and then start over again.

Other times, she wanted Milo back—she wanted to test out her newly developed skills. She was learning how humans behaved. Except there were so many possibilities. She needed to work out just what sort of person she was and then she would know how to act.

Then she listened closely. There were more than two people headed her way. So unlikely to be Milo and Dylan. Milo had told her it was vitally important that no one else know where she was, and she didn't want to get them into trouble. When she wasn't reading, she spent most of her time wondering what Milo was up to. How was his investigation into Kinross going? Had they been telling the truth—all they wanted was to discover Kinross's plans? Or was there more? She suspected the latter. She'd learned a lot about secrets and lies since she'd been reading. It wasn't only bad people who kept secrets and then lied about them.

Though she'd never believe Milo was bad.

The feet were getting closer. Time to go. She rose silently, quickly checking the area in case she had left anything that might signal her presence. For a moment, she considered giving herself up. But only for a moment. Something told her she would not see the outside of her cell again if she went back now, and she wasn't ready. So she slipped through the trees and headed for the entrance to the tunnels.

There was nothing to see. Milo's cloaking device had made the entrance vanish, so it appeared to be no more than an extension of the forest.

She ducked inside, then turned so she could peer out, holding her breath as a group of four men appeared. All in green jumpsuits. All with weapons holstered at their waists. Dr. Yang had said they were coming to a brave new world. So why did these men need weapons? Who were they going to shoot?

Would they shoot *her* if they found her?

No. She was important. Of course they wouldn't shoot her. But she suspected they would use the weapons to force her to return if she didn't want to go. She pressed herself back against the wall, but the men gave no indication that they could see her. They appeared quite relaxed, talking among themselves, though she couldn't make out the words. Finally, they passed the entrance and disappeared from her view. She sank down and sat with her back leaning against the wall.

Why had Dr. Yang told her so little? What hadn't she wanted Destiny to know? Was it something bad? Was it too much to ask that she just be told what the future held in store for her? Even if it wasn't good, she could cope, especially if it was instrumental in the survival of mankind. She wanted to do her part. She just wished she knew what it was.

Maybe she should write her own story. Milo had told her that stories helped people understand the world around them. So maybe if she wrote her own, then she would understand the meaning of life.

Forty-two.

The number popped up into her head. She'd just finished *The Hitchhiker's Guide to the Galaxy.* It was one of her favorites. If she could choose a future, she would love to travel around the universe, visiting new places and meeting alien civilizations. With Milo as her copilot.

Maybe she would write that story.

Would it be a romance?

Milo had said he didn't do romance.

Did he do sex?

She'd known about sex before. In theory. Dr. Yang had provided her with books about the human reproductive process. Those books had never made her squirm. At least she knew her body's reactions were "normal" when Milo kissed her.

Even if he didn't do romance, if she asked him nicely, would he kiss her again?

. . .

"Go right in," Silas said, and leaned past her to push open the door.

Elvira hesitated and spoke quietly. "How is he?"

"Pissed," he replied, opening the door and ushering her inside.

As far as she was aware, there was still no sign of Destiny. She'd vanished off the face of the planet. From a locked cell. How could that even happen?

Taking a deep breath, she stepped through the door and into Luther's office. He was standing by the window, hands in his pockets, staring down, tension in every inch of his body.

It wasn't good for him, but she clamped her lips closed on the words. She didn't think he would appreciate them right now.

He turned, ignoring her, and spoke to Silas. "Anything?"

"No."

"Damn." Now he turned his attention to Elvira, his eyes cold as ice. She shivered. "How the hell did you let this happen?" he asked.

She wanted to point out that it wasn't *her* cell that Destiny had escaped from. That maybe if they'd treated Destiny better—as she'd suggested—then she might not have done her vanishing act. Except that didn't make sense. How had she disappeared? It was like magic. She was a scientist—she needed a rational explanation.

"She must have had help," Luther said, and his tone held more than a hint of accusation.

"No one even knew of her existence except you, me, and Silas. Who would help her and why?" She glanced at Silas. He'd gotten on very well with Destiny the other day. "Did she say anything to you? Did she mention anyone else?"

He shook his head. "Nobody."

"Maybe your security isn't as good as you thought," she said. "Or maybe you have enemies."

"But why would they take Destiny?" Silas asked. "Why is she so important?"

"It doesn't concern you," Luther snapped. He glared at Elvira. "Could your records have been compromised?"

"Absolutely not. They're on a closed system."

"So there's no reason for anyone to take her. Which means she wandered off on her own. Someone left the door unlocked and she just walked out. And I want the name of whoever is responsible."

She wanted to say it wasn't possible. Mainly because it *had* happened the night before Destiny had disappeared, and Elvira had given the guards a reprimand, which she was sure would have ensured no one repeated the error. But she kept her mouth closed because she didn't have an alternative theory.

"Now she's wandering around the goddamn planet, starving to death. Or she's been eaten by some predator we haven't discovered yet." Luther took a deep breath, and Elvira could see him pulling himself together. Part of her liked to see him like this. Except she had a feeling that he held her responsible, and if Destiny wasn't found then she would pay. Or her family would pay. Probably both.

"What's happening with the search?" Luther asked.

"The drones are ready," Silas said. "And we've called off the foot searchers. It will be easier for the drones to home in on anything of interest if we know there's no one else out there."

"Then go do it. Find her."

As Silas turned to go, Elvira made to follow him. "Wait," Luther snapped.

She didn't want to wait. Luther felt unpredictable like this, as though he might explode at any moment and she didn't want to be around if that happened. She licked her lips, then stopped herself.

Don't show any weakness.

Luther took a step toward her, pointed a finger at her chest, his eyes narrowed to slits. For a moment, he looked truly evil, and her breath caught in her throat. She held herself very still.

"Know this," he hissed, his face close to hers, "if we don't find her, then I'll make sure you never see your family again."

"You can't do that, you can't—"

"You don't know what I can and can't do."

He rubbed at his left arm and her gaze locked in on the movement. "Are you feeling all right?" she asked.

His eyes narrowed. "No I'm not feeling all-fucking-right."

Maybe that would be the answer. If he died—

"I can see your mind working, but don't even think it. Take my word—if I die, you'll never see your daughters again. I have people on the *Trakis Two* who have orders to switch off their life support systems. They'll suffocate in their tubes. Do you understand?"

Her mind went blank. She stood unmoving, unthinking, concentrating on the warm breeze from the open window teasing her skin. This couldn't be happening. Not when she had come so far. Done so much.

Unfortunately, she did understand, and she wanted to scream that it wasn't fair. Instead, she swallowed the sharp, bitter taste that rose in her throat. "This is not my fault."

"Do you think I give a fuck?" Spittle frothed on his lips. She'd never seen him like this. He'd always been so controlled. He wiped his forehead; it gleamed with a sheen of sweat and his face was pale and blotchy. He gritted his teeth. "Understand?"

She nodded just as he clasped a fist over his heart and crashed to his knees.

Elvira leaped into action, dropping down beside him. "Oh God. Don't die. Please don't die!"

Chapter Nineteen

"For all evils there are two remedies — time and silence."
—Alexandre Dumas, *The Count of Monte Cristo*

What was she reading now?

Had she finished *Fifty Shades*? Milo had never been into bondage or any of that kinky stuff. What if she liked the idea?

Anyway, it didn't matter. Milo had already decided he was backing off. No more kissing. And definitely no kinky stuff. She was obviously totally naive, had no experience; the decent thing was to leave her alone. Except he couldn't stop thinking about her, what she'd feel like beneath him, or on top of him. What she'd taste like.

Maybe he'd be doing her a favor if he showed her how good ordinary sex could be. Though he had an idea there would be nothing ordinary about sex with Destiny.

All the same, he wasn't going there.

"You know," Dylan said. "You need to get your head straight—"

"My head is straight."

"Ha. And you seriously need to get laid and stop thinking about Destiny. She's way too nice for you."

True. "I'm not thinking about Destiny."

"Liar."

They were on their way to yet another committee meeting. The whole committee thing was doing his head in. Whoever had said a committee was a life form with four or more legs and no brain had been spot on. Nothing ever came of the meetings. No decisions were ever made. He presumed Luther had already decided the answers and they were just going through the motions.

"I don't like it here," Dylan said. "I want away from this bloody place, and back home. So we need to finish what we came to do. And find out how much of a threat Luther Kinross actually is. What are the repercussions of telling the dickhead to fuck off?"

Milo was betting rather serious. Kinross was obviously a planner. He would have foreseen that not everyone would be happy accepting him as leader. Especially as he couldn't have predicted the end of the *Trakis One* and President Max Beauchamp diving headfirst into a black hole. Max had had an army on board the *Trakis One,* so Kinross must have had a plan to overcome that. But while they'd learned a lot from Kinross's computer system, they hadn't found any information on the weapons. Or about Destiny's role. Presumably that data was stored in the parts she hadn't been able to access. "I'll go have another look in the tunnels tonight. My cloaking spell seems to be working. I can get in and out without anyone seeing. We'll find out what he's hiding down there, though I have a suspicion we're not going to like it."

Luther was too confident and too well prepared. He likely had something hidden away to back that up. Some sort of weapons? But something big enough to be a threat to them on another planet? They needed to know the details. And decide how they could neutralize any threat. "Maybe we should just take the bastard out," Milo suggested.

Luther was always guarded, but between the two of them, he was sure it could be done. And they could take out that miserable bitch, Dr. Yang, as well. That would get rid of the threat to Destiny. And with a bit of luck, no one else would have a clue about her "role" and she would be free to do what she liked. Perhaps she could come back to Trakis Two with them. Live among the monsters in his new world where they no longer hid what they were. What would she think of him then?

"Maybe we should," Dylan said, pulling him out of his daydream. "But let's find out a few facts first."

They were headed toward Camelot, which was how everyone referred to Luther's headquarters—they'd be crowning him fucking King any day now. Everyone loved him. Or pretended to.

Dylan came to a halt as they passed a building site on the edge of the lake. "Do you see anything wrong with this picture?" he asked.

Milo studied the building site. It was swarming with workers in beige jumpsuits, guarded by the usual armed green-clad soldiers. He looked closer and his eyes narrowed. "They're children."

"Or all very short people," Dylan said.

A little girl, she looked no more than twelve, was shoveling sand into a bucket. She had a round face and silky black hair, Chinese, at a guess. Tears made tracks through the layer of dust on her face, and her lower lip was caught between her teeth. She kept casting wary glances at the nearest soldier.

"Am I the only one who thinks there's something not quite right with this?" Dylan asked.

"No. So much for the brave new world. Child fucking labor. And why? There are plenty of adults still in cryo. Why not wake them up?"

"I heard a rumor that they were causing problems. Demanding their rights. Maybe Luther thought children would be easier to handle."

"Let's kill him."

His muscles tightened as his gaze settled on a tall man in a red shirt, with dark brown skin and dark eyes, who was standing off to the side, surveying the scene, a small smile on his smug bastard face. Milo recognized him as Aaron Sekongo, the captain of the *Trakis Four* and also the designated member of the Church of Everlasting Life. A double tosser. He'd led the prayers at that first meeting.

Without giving himself time to accept that it was a bad idea, Milo strode across the few feet between them and stopped, facing the other man. He forced a smile to his face, though his teeth were gritted, and his hands fisted at his side. "What's going on?" he asked, in what he thought was a pleasant tone.

The man looked at Milo and the smile slid from his face. His eyes narrowed and his hand went to the cross pinned to his chest. He cleared his throat. "They are building the new Church. Soon my congregation will have a place to pray."

"And you're okay with this?" Milo waved a hand to encompass the children.

"With what?"

"They're fucking children."

"This has been cleared by Mr. Kinross and they are *God's* children, doing God's work. What could be wrong?"

Jesus, another asshole to add to the might-have-to-kill list. He took a step closer and then halted as he felt Dylan's hand on his arm. Milo cast him a glance and Dylan's eyes widened. He turned slightly so the other man wouldn't hear. "You might want to stand down," Dylan murmured. "There's steam coming out of your ears, your eyes have gone red, and the poor man is clutching his cross like you're the Antichrist. Low profile, remember."

Milo took a deep breath and forced his muscles to relax. "God's work," he said. "Of course it's a worthy cause. And it will no doubt be character building for the little children."

Captain Sekongo nodded, but his eyes shifted away. "If you're heading to the meeting, then it's been canceled." He addressed his words to Dylan. "Luther is indisposed."

Permanently, with a bit of luck.

The man obviously decided it was time to go. He gave a wary nod, then turned away and headed for Camelot.

"You know," Dylan said, "sometimes it's possible to forget what you are. This isn't one of them."

"I hate the fucking goddamn Church."

"You sound just like your Uncle Rico."

"Piss off." But he'd grown up hearing those words. Rico also hated the Church, but then the Church had been responsible for burning Rico's wife at the stake, so the sentiment was understandable. Milo's hand went to the scar that snaked its way down the side of his throat, rubbing at the raised edges. His own reasons were pretty good as well. Bastards. "Let's go."

"You know, you're a nice guy for a demon," Dylan said as they walked away.

"Half-demon. And no, I'm not. Don't tell me you liked that any more than I did."

"No. It leaves a nasty taste in my mouth. This whole setup does. As I mentioned. I'm ready to head home."

"Well that's not happening today. But it looks like we have some free time. What should we do now?"

"Let's go see Destiny."

Back at the shuttle, Milo went to the food dispenser and loaded up with food he thought she might like. She clearly had a sweet tooth. So chocolate? More donuts?

As they were about to leave, the comm system beeped and Rico's face appeared on the screen. "Anyone home?"

Milo crossed the room and accepted the call.

"I've sent those engineering books you asked for," Rico said. "Sardi sorted them out. What are they for?"

"Milo's girlfriend," Dylan said over his shoulder.

"Fuck off," he muttered.

"Milo has a girlfriend?"

"He's in love," Dylan continued, sending himself straight to the top of Milo's might-have-to-kill list. "With this really odd woman. Nice though. And seriously hot."

"Really?" Rico looked intrigued. But then, he was quite aware of Milo's aversion to anything even remotely resembling love. He'd been there for Milo's first and last disastrous relationship. Had front row seats to how well that had turned out. Once again, his hand moved instinctively to rub at the scar on his neck. Then wished he hadn't as Rico's gaze homed in on the gesture.

"No, not fucking really," Milo said. "What do you want?"

"Just checking in. And sending your girlfriend's books."

Milo growled.

Rico grinned. "And I've got some news on those people you asked me to look up."

Dr. Yang's family. Maybe he could get some leverage and get the woman off Destiny's case. "And?"

"They're dead. At least they're not where they're supposed to be. I presume you're up-to-date on what happened with the recent murder investigation and the dead crew members' families?"

He was aware that some of them had been changed for other people. Initially they'd believed their places had been sold to the highest bidder. It was amazing what people had been willing to pay to get off the dying Earth. Now, though, it seemed more likely they'd been substituted for people of

Kinross's choosing.

"I hadn't gotten around to checking out the rest of the crew families," Rico said. "Didn't seem a priority with the *Trakis One* gone. Turns out your Dr. Yang's ten-year-old daughter is six-foot-tall and has a beard. I woke the man up and with a little persuasion, he told me that he's in the employ of your new best friend, Luther Kinross."

Why did that come as no surprise?

Milo was betting there was a whole army spread throughout the fleet. How easy to just not wake up the crew members, and they'd never be aware that their loved ones had been dumped to make way for Kinross's soldiers.

"A mercenary?" he asked.

"Well, he called himself a soldier of the New World Defense Force. Sounds better, I suppose. We checked the rest of the crew families on board and it's the same story. There are eight ships left, thirty crew members per ship, three family members per crew, and ten rotations. That's a good number of soldiers."

"What did you do with them?"

Rico shrugged. "Left them asleep for now." He gave a feral smile, showing the tip of one sharp, white fang. "I'll leave them for when I'm feeling hungry."

Milo shook his head but didn't comment. They'd taken their chances and lost.

"What are your plans now?" Rico asked. "When are you coming back? There's only a small window if you want to return via the shuttle."

At this time, the planets' trajectories meant that Trakis Two and Trakis Four were relatively close together and just approaching the point where they were the closest they ever were. After that, the distance would increase and soon would be out of the range of the shuttles. At that point, they would need to get a lift back. And if things got messy with Kinross, that might not be an easy thing to organize.

"Right now, we're taking chocolates and other goodies to Milo's girlfriend," Dylan said. "Hey, we're prioritizing. Then later tonight, Milo is going to take a look and see what Kinross is hiding under his castle."

Rico's brow rose. "He has a castle?"

"Yeah, it's called Camelot and it has turrets and a round table and everything."

"Sounds like I'd better start practicing my curtsy. Okay. Let me know what you find. We need to understand just how much of a pain in the arse this guy is going to be." The screen went blank.

So Dr. Yang's family were no more, but he wasn't going to jump in and tell her...just yet.

First, he had to find out how he could best use that information.

Chapter Twenty

"If it is one's lot to be cast among fools, one must learn foolishness."
—Alexandre Dumas, *The Count of Monte Cristo*

Destiny had stayed inside the tunnels since she'd seen the men. She didn't want them to find her. Not now. Not yet. She'd curled up in one of the big chairs on the bridge of her spaceship and read.

She'd read *Escape Route*, a mystery written just before the fleet had left Earth, and then she went back to romance: *It Had to Be You* by Susan Elizabeth Phillips. And she'd lost herself in the words and the magic, when she heard someone call her name.

"Destiny."

Recognizing Milo's voice, she jumped to her feet and hurried out and down the ramp. He stood at the bottom with Dylan beside him and she felt suddenly shy. She'd been reading too much sex!

He held out a bag. "Food." As she opened it, the scent of

sugar and other delicious things wafted out and her stomach rumbled. He also handed her a small flash drive. "Books on how spaceships work," he said. "Just don't press any buttons you're not sure of."

"Thank you." Her fingers itched to go back and press some.

"What have you been up to?" he asked.

"I saw some men but I hid, and they didn't see me. Then I stayed inside after that."

"There's no one around now. You want to go for a walk?"

With Milo? *Oh yes.* She nodded, placed her bag of food on the floor, then delved inside and picked out a donut.

"I'm going to stay and look around a bit," Dylan said. "Let you two lovebirds have some alone time."

Lovebirds? She blinked, then glanced at Milo. He was scowling at Dylan, but that didn't stop her heart tripping a beat.

They walked side by side out of the tunnels and into the forest.

"Did Dr. Yang ever talk to you about her family?" Milo asked as they skirted the edge of the lake. The air was warm and the second of the suns was just hovering on the edge of the horizon, so the light was golden. She swallowed her last bite of donut, licking the sugar from her lips. "No, not really."

"She didn't mention she had three daughters aboard the *Trakis Two*?"

For some reason, a flash of hurt swept through her. Dr. Yang had shared nothing of her real life with her. Though really, that came as no surprise. From the books she had read, Destiny could see that Dr. Yang had never treated her as even a normal human being, had never shown any warmth, certainly never treated her as a daughter. Sometimes, despite the fact that they looked nothing like each other, Destiny had dreamed that Dr. Yang was actually her mother and would one day admit it and tell her she loved her and… And what? She hadn't been able to come up with an "and what" back then and she certainly couldn't now.

What she did know was that the doctor had been manipulative and…cruel. There, she'd admitted it to herself. Dr. Yang had been cruel. Not vindictive, but cold and heartless to a lonely child. Maybe that's just the way she was. Except now it seemed she had real daughters. Waiting for her on the *Trakis Two*. Had she cuddled them when they were babies, sang them to sleep, played with them, hugged them when they were scared and lonely? All the things she hadn't done with Destiny.

Her eyes pricked and she blinked and pressed her hands to them. She'd been pretty emotional lately. She suspected it was due to an overload of too many fictional emotions. From a life with no inkling that such things were normal, she was being flooded by feelings. She'd been emotionally repressed and now she was in no way prepared to cope with them. She cried at books—even the ones that were supposed to be funny.

"Hey," Milo said, "are you all right?"

She nodded and then sniffed to prove she was lying. "I just accepted that Dr. Yang never really loved me." She sniffed again. "I actually think sometimes she hated me. And I have no clue why. And she was all I had. All I *have* really." She flashed a glance at his face, analyzed his expression. He looked worried. He was probably scared she was going to break down or something. She'd read that a lot of men didn't like emotional scenes.

"You have me and Dylan," he said.

She stopped then and turned to look at him, her eyes narrowing. "Have I? For how long?"

She knew now that they were up to something. She'd suspected it from that first night when Milo had hidden in her cell. Then Milo himself had confirmed it and the books she had read since had given her the contexts to understand a little more about what was going on.

He looked at her sharply. "Why do you say that?"

"You were right about stories. They help you make sense of the world and I can see more clearly now. You think there's something hidden beneath the tunnels. That's what you were looking for that night when you hid in my cell. And I think that when you've found what you're looking for, then you'll leave." After all, he'd told her they would return to Trakis Two at some point. "What do you think is down there?"

He shrugged. "Weapons. We need to find out what are the possible consequences if we go our separate ways. Will he be able to enforce his…wishes on us when we're on a different planet? Or can we just ignore him?"

He would go, and she couldn't follow. Because however cold Dr. Yang had been to her, there was still the fact that Destiny had a role to play. She couldn't abandon that without knowing more. And to know more, she would have to go back.

She cast a sideways glance at Milo. He was so beautiful he made her chest ache. She wanted him. If she had to go back, then wasn't it only fair that she got to experience life—and love—first? Even if that love wasn't returned. That was all she had ever really wanted. She stopped walking and turned to face him. He was watching her warily, and she gave in to temptation and reached out and stroked her finger down the scar on his cheek. Then rested her hand against his chest, feeling the thud of his heart beneath her palm.

"I'd like you to kiss me again," she said.

His eyes narrowed. "Not a good idea."

"Why?"

"Because you want more than I'm willing to give."

"You don't know what I want." Anger flashed through

her and then was gone. "How can you know, when *I* don't know what I want?"

"Right now, you need a friend."

"With benefits?"

He snorted. "What have you been reading?"

"It doesn't matter." She started walking again. "I have a feeling that things are going to go horribly wrong. I don't know how or why, but I just want to experience as much as I can before that happens. Don't worry, I don't expect you to fall in love with me or anything. I don't think I'm very lovable. But would it be so hard to *make* love to me?"

She heard him swear under his breath and peered back at him. He was running his hands through his hair. "You deserve more."

She stopped again and swung around to face him, hands on her hips, eyes glaring. "Why? What makes me so special? And what if I don't want more?" She just wanted sex for goodness' sake. Men were supposed to jump at the chance. What the hell was wrong with her? "Maybe Dylan would make love to me if I asked him nicely."

"Don't even go there."

Ha. He didn't want her, but he didn't want anyone else to have her either. "Am I so...unappealing?"

"No." He gritted his teeth. "I told you—I don't do relationships."

"And I'm not asking for one. I don't do relationships, either. I just want sex." Gosh, she sounded...whiny. And desperate. How to make a man run in the opposite direction. She needed to read more books.

"Jesus. I—" He paused and raised his head, his eyes narrowing. Then he moved fast, lunging for her and shoving her to the ground, landing on top of her, and then they were rolling down a short bank. They came to an abrupt stop at the bottom, with Milo on top of her.

"What—?"

"Shhh," he muttered.

She listened and could hear it now, a soft whirring sound that was coming closer.

He shifted his body so he covered her completely and she closed her eyes and held her breath. She had no clue what was happening, but at least it had gotten Milo on top of her. She lay unmoving, her brain processing the feel of his hard body on hers. Burrowing her face in his shoulder, she breathed in, her nostrils filling with the hot spicy scent of him. Intoxicating. She might have swooned if she hadn't already been flat on her back.

She wasn't sure how long they lay there, but long after, the whirring had passed them by and faded to nothing. Milo pushed himself up on his elbows. The position brought his lower body harder against hers, and a wave of elation washed through her as she felt the hardness of his erection pressing into her thigh.

He wanted her. And he could have her. She pushed her hips against him then blinked and gazed up into his silver eyes. They narrowed on her, wandering over her face, settling on her lips, which she parted slightly.

"Fuck it," he muttered and lowered his head and kissed her.

His mouth was hard, his lips firm, his tongue hot as it pushed inside, filling her. Heat flooded her body, tingles racing across her skin and settling in her belly, between her thighs, her nipples. His mouth left hers and she wanted to scream at him not to stop. Never to stop. Before she could get the words out, he was kissing the side of her neck, his teeth grazing her skin, then nipping and licking and her nipples tightened, pressing against the material of her jumpsuit.

The pressure eased as he lowered the zipper, freeing her breasts and for a moment he stared down at her, his gaze hot, intent. He parted the material and she felt the air on her bare skin, her nipples tightening further until they were hard little peaks. He kissed first one, then the other, and her spine arched as pleasure shot through her.

He stroked one with his tongue and then sucked it into his mouth and suckled her, and it was better than she had ever imagined. She needed him, his big hands on her and she writhed beneath him, trying to get closer, to show him what she needed.

He bit down on the taut peak, then soothed it with his tongue.

"You are so beautiful," he murmured, one hand cupping her breast, framing it for his kisses.

He lowered the zipper farther, kissing her belly, and she went still. She suspected where he was heading and didn't want to do anything to stop him. Nothing. She even stopped breathing. The pressure was building and building inside her. She was hovering on the edge of her first ever orgasm. Just a little more. A whimper escaped her lips.

"Am I interrupting?" A voice spoke from above them and Milo stopped his kisses. He rested his forehead against her belly for a long moment. Then he raised his head.

"Fucking goddamn Dylan," he snarled.

She wanted to scream in denial, but he was already pulling away from her.

Chapter Twenty-One

"Every man has a devouring passion in his heart, as every fruit has its worm."
—Alexandre Dumas, *The Count of Monte Cristo*

Her face was flushed, her eyes wide. She'd been so close; he'd felt the tension building inside her. He'd wanted to give her that pleasure. Maybe he should just tell Dylan to fuck off.

But the moment had passed.

Saved by the werewolf.

What had happened to "just friends"?

He'd told himself he could do friends. Just keep his dick in his pants and his hands and mouth to himself and they should be okay. All he had to do was avoid temptation. That hadn't worked as planned.

There had been a lot of women over the years. He liked women, they liked him, but he never stayed with the same one for long or allowed them to get close. And he was always clear up front and told them there was no chance of more. He didn't do relationships.

Just as he'd told Destiny.

Relationships always ended badly.

Except Destiny was different. He had no clue why, but she tugged at something deep inside him that he'd thought shut away forever. And that was so not good.

She was right, soon he would leave—he had to. There was no way he could stay on Trakis Four with Luther Kinross and the Church stirring up all the old prejudices. He didn't want to hide any longer.

And Destiny would stay because she had a duty to do. He knew all about people he cared about and duty. It always came first. His mother's had been revenge, and she'd left him to follow that course even though she had known it would mean her death. Maria's duty had been her God and saving Milo's soul.

So no, he wouldn't allow himself to care. And he'd make sure Destiny didn't care, either.

But his dick ached, and he stayed where he was while he got his unruly body under control. Finally he rolled off her and onto his back.

They were at the bottom of the small bank where he'd pushed her when he'd identified the drone.

Had they been seen? He didn't think so. There had been no pause in the drone's speed or direction. If it had picked them up, it would have come in closer for a better visual.

He sat up, hands resting on his knees, breathing deeply, while he decided whether to rip the werewolf's throat out. Beside him, Destiny was tugging the sides of her jumpsuit together, pulling up the zipper with fingers that trembled slightly.

"You want me to go away again?" Dylan asked.

Yes. "No."

He blew out his breath, then got to his feet and held out a hand to Destiny. Her lower lip quivered, but she placed her palm in his and he pulled her to her feet. Her nipples were clearly visible against the thin material of her jumpsuit and he could almost scent her desire on the air.

She ran her hands down her sides and cleared her throat. Licked her lips and heat shot through him—was she doing it on purpose? Just what had she been reading? He was so fucked.

"I came to warn you there are drones in the area," Dylan said, and pushed his hands into his pockets as he glanced between the two of them.

"I know. We spotted one." He waved his free hand around the area. "Hence the hiding place."

Dylan smirked. "Ahh. So that's what you were doing down there. Hiding from the drone?"

Milo tugged her up the bank. She still hadn't said a word. "We'd better get back to the tunnels." She was hardly inconspicuous in that bright yellow outfit. They should get her some different clothes.

He held her hand all the way back, as though she might vanish. They'd sent hunting drones to find her. They must really want her back. And he wasn't quite ready to let her go.

She wanted sex.

Stop thinking with your dick!

Even from the short conversation they'd had tonight—before they'd gotten sidetracked—he could see that she had changed beyond belief from the woman they had taken from the cell. All her life, she'd been kept in total ignorance of the world around her, denied any normal human interaction. Now reading had opened her world and she was soaking up all the vicarious experiences and rebuilding her world almost from scratch. Dr. Yang had a lot to answer for.

They headed back to the spaceship. The suns had gone down. Dylan led them through the dark forest, though he looked back once or twice, his gaze resting on where Milo still held her hand. Destiny was quiet, and when they reached the bridge, she tugged free of his hold and sat in the pilot's seat, then loaded her new books onto her ereader and was soon engrossed. Or at least pretended to be.

He stood at the back with Dylan. They needed to talk, and he didn't want Destiny to hear.

"The drone had to be looking for her," Dylan said. "They clearly want her back. But what for? I don't get it."

"Neither do I. We could ask some questions, but that might alert them to the fact that we know of Destiny's existence."

But maybe he could somehow get the information from Dr. Yang. He could tell her that he had news about her family. That he could get them awakened and brought here—which would of course be a lie, but he didn't feel as though he owed that bitch anything.

First, he needed to find out what was beneath Camelot. If there were weapons that could be a threat to Trakis Two, then they needed to work out a plan to destroy them and get the hell away from here.

"But perhaps it could work in our favor," Dylan said. "We could use her as a trade if things get iffy and we need to make a fast getaway."

Milo bit back his instinctive response, which was *no way.* After all, Destiny had already told him that she planned to go back. That she planned to perform her mysterious duty. And to hell with him. A familiar wave of bitterness washed over him. "Maybe," was all he said.

"In the meantime, I'll fix her up a locator device that will give some warning if there are drones anywhere near. I'll come back with you now, pick up some stuff from the shuttle, and bring it back tonight. Otherwise she'll be stuck in the tunnels."

Dylan was being…kind. Not a trait you expected from an

alpha werewolf. "You like her, don't you?"

He shrugged. "And what about you? You hardly strike me as the hand-holding type. It's sweet really, but perhaps you need to keep a little distance."

No point in arguing with that, so he didn't answer at all. "We need to go."

He headed back to where Destiny sat, her head stuck in her ereader. She didn't even look up as he came to a halt in front of her, just stared at the screen, her lower lip caught between her teeth. Playing hard to get. He was going to start vetting her reading material. But he was finding this new emerging Destiny too intriguing. He cleared his throat and heard Dylan laugh behind him. She glanced up, eyes widening. "Yes?"

"We have to leave."

"Okay." She turned her attention back to her book. She was clearly not happy with him. Hell, he wasn't happy with himself.

As he turned to go, she jumped to her feet and reached out a hand and rested it on his arm. "Be careful, Milo. Those men have guns." She turned to Dylan. "And you look after him."

Dylan grunted. "I think he can look after himself."

He parted with Dylan at the looming bulk of the *Trakis Four* and headed to the lake. He took one of the boats and crossed the small body of water, tying up on the other side. The first thing he noticed was the large number of soldiers about the area. They'd been out searching for Destiny, now they must have been replaced by the drones. The skin of his back prickled.

There were guards in the large hallway, and he recognized

the man who had been out with Destiny. Silas Wynch, Kinross's second-in-command, although not in any formal sense of the word. Milo crossed to him.

"How is Mr. Kinross?" he asked.

The other man's eyes narrowed. "Why do you ask?"

He shrugged. "I spoke with Captain Sekongo earlier. He said Kinross was indisposed."

"He's fine."

Hmm. The man wasn't very chatty. "There seem to be a lot of…soldiers around."

"So?"

"I'm just curious. I wasn't aware there was a military presence on any of the ships other than the *Trakis One*."

Another shrug. "I wouldn't know about that."

"What would you know about?"

"That you and your friend ask a lot of questions."

"Is that a problem?"

"It depends what you do with the answers. But there's no place for going your own way on Trakis Four. We work as a team."

"It's my way or the highway," Milo murmured.

Amusement flashed in the other man's eyes. "Something like that."

"Well, give my regards to Kinross."

"I will."

He turned to go. It was unlikely he was going to get into the tunnels from this direction tonight. Were they suspicious? Likely they were suspicious about everything. Instead, he would find the route back from Destiny's end of the tunnels. Maybe they needed to spend some time mapping out the place.

But when he left the castle, he was aware of someone following him, and they weren't trying to hide. Maybe Wynch was sending him a message.

We're watching you.

His tail followed him back to the shuttle, two men in the green uniforms of Kinross's private army. Dylan wasn't there; he must have already gone back to Destiny. Milo should have felt happier about that. He didn't.

He sat in the doorway of the shuttle and raised a hand at his watchers. Looked like they were in place for the duration.

Heading back inside, he got a bowl of water and sat cross-legged on the floor in front of it. Scrying was a method he had often used successfully on Earth when he'd wanted a glimpse of some possible future. He wasn't sure how it would work here, but it was worth a try. Swirling his finger in the water, he concentrated, trying to see what was to come.

But although the water darkened, went opaque, it refused to give up any secrets.

Chapter Twenty-Two

"I am hungry, feed me; I am bored, amuse me."
—Alexandre Dumas, *The Count of Monte Cristo*

Destiny decided that she wasn't going to think about Milo right now. She wanted him too much, and she couldn't see clearly. But his hands and his mouth had felt so good.

Concentrate on something else.

While she didn't want to be fickle, she actually found it quite easy to not think about him once she started reading. The books were fascinating. Spaceships were just as interesting as romance, and she soon lost herself in the world of quantum physics. And power drives, solar and wind power. The books included the engineering specs for the Trakis fleet. The life support, the power supplies, speeds…the controls.

She came to the end of the book and studied the console in front of her. While obviously this ship was much smaller than the Trakis ships, she suspected that they functioned on the same principles. Whoever had left this ship behind was humanoid. Who had they been? What had happened to them?

Maybe she would find a ship's log.

There was a big red button in the center of the console. She bit her lip.

Should I?

She was still staring at the button, her hand reaching out slowly…

What's the worst that could happen?

Her mind flooded with a whole lot of possibilities. She inched a little closer, then went still as someone called out to her.

Dylan this time.

It was probably for the best; she wasn't ready to face Milo again just yet. He wanted her, she was sure of it, but he was wary, so she had to find a way to let him know he could have her, and she wouldn't be a nuisance—she hoped. She knew what she wanted; she just wasn't sure how to get it yet. Before she spoke to him again, she needed to work out a strategy. She'd do some more research and maybe Dylan could help with that. Plus, she liked Dylan, maybe because she could relax more with him. He didn't make her go all shivery and tongue-tied and…needy.

Dylan appeared in the doorway and tossed her a black duffel bag.

"What is it?" she asked.

"More food and clothes. I stole them from some woman's cryotube on the *Trakis Four*. She looked to be about the same size as you."

"But stealing is wrong."

"So are a lot of other things, sweetheart, but needs must. You're like a beacon wandering around the forest in that yellow outfit."

"That thing we hid from in the forest—"

"The drone."

She nodded. "Yes, the drone. Was it looking for me?"

"I can't think of anyone else it could have been looking for."

"And will the two of you be in trouble if they find out you were helping me?"

"Definitely. So best they don't find out. Which means you stay out of trouble. Here, I've got something else for you." He reached into his pocket and pulled out a silver bracelet. "Put this on your arm," he said, handing it to her. "It will flash and beep if there's a drone anywhere within a mile of you. If that happens, you get under cover. Back here if you can. If not, just somewhere you're out of sight."

She slipped the bracelet on her wrist and raised her arm. It was pretty. "Thank you."

Dylan propped himself against the console, crossed his arms over his chest, and studied her. So she studied him back. He was as handsome as Milo. They were both tall, with broad shoulders and lean hips. His hair was longer, and his eyes a beautiful dark gold.

"Like what you see?" he said, the amusement clear in his tone.

"Yes."

"But not as much as you like our friend, Milo."

"No."

He laughed. "At least you're honest. But unrequited love is tough, and you've picked a hard case to crack there. The man is clearly terrified of commitment."

She sniffed. "I don't love him. I have no intention of falling in love with anyone. I told him I just wanted him for sex."

Dylan's lips twitched. "Maybe he was offended."

Had she been wrong? Every hint and indication had told her that Milo was one of those heroes who was scared of commitment. The ones with the serious trust issues. She had no clue why, and she really wanted to know, but somehow doubted he would share. But maybe she had read him all wrong. What did she know? Nothing apart from what she had read in what she suspected were some seriously trivial books.

"Don't look so worried," Dylan said. "I was joking."

"I don't really understand humor yet. But I thought all men wanted sex."

"You should have picked me, darling. Then we'd be fucking hard and dirty right now."

"Oh." She considered the idea. Trying to imagine kissing Dylan. But it wasn't going to happen. She wrinkled her nose. "I don't think so."

He laughed again. "I'd be hurt," he said, "except I think Milo has it right. You are trouble."

"I don't mean to be."

"Some women are just born that way. But persevere with him. I suspect he's not too far from his breaking point."

A smile tugged at her lips. "Really?" Though she didn't want to actually *break* him.

"I have to head back," Dylan said. "There are some people I need to see. But we'll be back tomorrow. Are you going to sleep?"

"I might go for a walk first now that I have my bracelet. Or a run. Or a swim. I've always wanted to swim. I need some exercise and some fresh air."

He studied her for a moment. Was he going to tell her to stay inside? Would she take any notice? But he just nodded to the bag. "Perhaps not the swim. Not alone. We don't know what might be in the water. And get changed first and keep an eye on that alarm. Don't be caught out."

"I won't."

She waited until he disappeared and then emptied the bag onto the chair. There were blue jeans like Milo wore and a couple of dark, silky tank tops. She kicked off her boots and stripped off the jumpsuit and pulled on the new clothes. They fit perfectly.

She gave the red button a last look and then headed out. As she walked down the ramp, a dog barked somewhere close by and she stopped. She'd seen pictures and films of dogs, but she hadn't known there were any on the planet.

She moved cautiously forward as it barked again. As she reached the entrance to the outside, she saw it and stared. It was huge, black and shaggy, with golden eyes. Much bigger than she'd imagined a dog would be. Its head was almost level with her shoulder. It sat on its haunches, head cocked on one side, tongue hanging out. It didn't look vicious. As she slowly approached, it lay down and then rolled over on its back, waving its paws in the air, and she grinned.

Crouching down beside it, she reached out with a tentative hand and rubbed the soft, silky fur of its—his, she could see that now—belly and he whined softly. Then rolled onto his feet and shook himself. He walked away, and she felt a moment of regret, then he looked back over his shoulder, gave a small yip. He wanted her to follow and she hurried after him.

They walked side by side through the trees until they came to the edge of the forest and onto the sandy beach of the lake. Everything was quiet and dark, just the starlight to guide them. Then he started a slow lope along the edge of the water, and she broke into a run to keep up. Then they were running on the hard-packed sand. She'd missed running, the stretch of her muscles, the quickening of her heart, and this was so much better than on a treadmill. He sped up and she was racing flat-out until her lungs burned and her legs ached, and she felt so good.

"Stop," she called out.

The dog glanced back and then halted. He gave her a considering look, and she could swear she saw intelligence in his eyes. Then he turned and headed straight for the water. And he pounced, submerging under the surface and then coming up, swimming along parallel to the edge.

Longing filled her. She glanced down at her jeans. She didn't want to get them wet. She stripped them off, leaving her in panties and tank top and then she moved slowly to the water. She dipped in a toe. It was chilly but not too cold. She stepped in, then looked up and found her new friend watching her as he trod water a few feet away. She waded in until she was knee deep. Then, taking a deep breath, she dived into the water. As her head went under, she panicked for a second. Then she pulled with her arms and kicked with her legs and she was swimming.

She broke the surface and laughed.

Something nudged her in the side and she panicked again, twisting around to find the dog swimming circles around her.

Reaching down with her toes, she found she could stand, the water only came up to her shoulders and she stood almost submerged. Then she kicked back and lay faceup, floating, staring up at the countless pinpricks of stars in the sky.

She didn't know how long she lay, letting the water carry her. Then the dog nudged her again and she turned and half swam, half waded to shore.

The dog licked her thigh and gave her a sly look and then turned and headed into the forest.

"Good night," she called after him. "And thank you."

Gazing across the water she experienced a moment of real happiness. Gone in a flash. How much longer did she have before her freedom was nothing but a memory? And duty was her life.

Chapter Twenty-Three

*"In every country where independence has taken the place
of liberty, the first desire of a manly heart is to possess a
weapon which at once renders him capable of defense or
attack, and, by rendering its owner fearsome, makes him
feared."*
—Alexandre Dumas, *The Count of Monte Cristo*

What the hell?

Milo's muscles locked tight, his eyes widening as he stepped into the chamber with the alien spaceship and came to a halt. The ramp was up and bright white lights lit up the underside. A loud whirring filled the air, like a giant drone. And as he stood staring, it slowly lifted from the ground.

The whole thing seemed to vibrate. In fact the air in the cavern throbbed.

Then the lights went out and it dropped suddenly, hitting the sandy floor of the cavern with a *thud*.

He ran toward it, then stopped a few feet away. The door opened and the ramp appeared. He couldn't make his feet move forward. What if he went up there and the thing took off again?

What the hell had she pressed?

After what seemed an age, Destiny appeared at the top of the ramp and the tension oozed out of him. She was grinning widely, her eyes lit up with excitement.

"You pressed a button, didn't you?" he asked, eyes narrowing on her.

She hurried down the ramp and stopped just in front of him. "A big red one. But I was sure that it would be okay."

"How sure?"

She shrugged. "Fifty-fifty. Do you want to come in and have a go? I turned it off pretty fast, but we could try for longer next time. A whole lot of things flashed up. There was a screen and when I swiped my hand over it that's when we went up. Then down. It was easy."

He shuddered. "I hate flying."

She patted his arm. "Maybe you need to face your fears, Milo. Get over them."

Why did he suspect she wasn't only talking about flying? "Another day, perhaps." Like never. She was dressed differently, in blue jeans that fitted her perfectly and a dark blue tank top that skimmed her breasts and matched her eyes. "You've got some new clothes."

She twirled. "Dylan brought them for me. He stole them. But he said sometimes stealing is all right."

"How long did he stay?" he asked, trying not to sound suspicious.

Dylan had turned up at dawn, smelling of sex and looking very self-satisfied. He'd thrown himself into bed, muttering something about the tech officer from the *Trakis Four*. A pretty redhead if Milo remembered rightly. But maybe that had just been a ruse to throw him off the scent, and he'd actually spent the night with Destiny. Taking advantage of the fact that Milo was doing the honorable thing.

"Not long," she replied. "He said he had people to see."

"Good. He's a bad influence. You want to explore the tunnels with me?"

His stalkers had gone by the time he'd gotten up that morning and he'd made sure he wasn't being followed before heading around the lake. Unfortunately, he didn't think there was a chance of him doing anything unnoticed in Camelot from now on. They had clearly gone into high alert after Destiny had disappeared.

He didn't think they suspected him or Dylan of anything specific as yet, but the fact was, they stood out as different. However hard they tried to fit in—and he was the first to acknowledge that he hadn't tried *that* hard—they were different. They asked a lot of questions.

Which all meant he needed an alternative route back to the tunnels close to Destiny's cell. He wasn't sure how far he had transported them when he had done the spell, but likely the tunnels were all interconnected.

"Yes please," Destiny said. "Why are we exploring?"

"I want to see if I can find out what they were hiding that first night we met."

"Oh. An adventure. And a mystery."

He handed her a bag of fresh donuts.

"Do we need a torch?" she asked, biting into one and then licking the sugar from her lips, while watching him out of lowered lashes.

"No." He forced himself to turn away, then stood for a moment orientating himself and working out which direction they needed to head in. Finally, he selected a tunnel. "That way." He pulled his wand from his belt as he walked toward the darkness of the tunnel. Destiny fell into step beside him.

"That looks like a wand. Like Harry Potter."

"It's just a…sort of torch." He raised it up and murmured

a word under his breath and a bright white light shone out. He blinked. Too bright—nothing worked as expected here—and he murmured again and the light dimmed. "Let's go."

"Did you find any useful information in Mr. Kinross's computer system?" she asked as they walked.

"Some, but not the stuff we really need. We do know that he has detailed information on all the ships, the people on them, and what they brought with them from Earth. And we know he has an army at his disposal."

"The men in the green jumpsuits with the weapons. But where did they come from? I read about the Chosen Ones and who was given places on the ships and there was no mention of an army."

He paused for a moment as he came to a crossroads. He could go left or right. "That way," Destiny said, pointing left.

They headed off again. "Kinross set things up before he ever left Earth. Put his own people in place." He thought for a moment. Should he tell her about the crew members? Specifically about Dr. Yang's family. Maybe she could give him some insight into how best to use the information. "He switched over the crew member families and replaced them with his own men."

She stopped and turned to look at him. "That's wicked."

"Yep." Perhaps he wouldn't mention how he'd gotten his own place on the fleet. Though he hadn't had a lot of say in the matter—Rico had knocked him out and given him no choice.

"All of them?" Destiny asked.

"We don't know for sure. But all of them on the *Trakis Two.*"

She blinked, processing that information. "But you said Dr. Yang's daughters were on the *Trakis Two.*"

"Not anymore."

"Oh, poor Dr. Yang. Have you told her?"

"Not yet. We just found out. Not sure if we're going to tell her. We might need her help at some point in the not-too-distant future and offering to get her family for her might make all the difference."

"But that's…"

"That's what?"

He turned again so he could see her face; she had a cute little furrow between her brows. "I don't know. It seems bad, but really it won't make any difference to Dr. Yang's daughters. And not much to Dr. Yang. Except put off her feeling horrible."

She was amazing. A few days ago, she had seemed so naive. But it had only been ignorance and already she was coming up with her own version of morality.

"But won't she find out?" she asked. "Won't she be expecting them to join her?"

"Right now, Kinross has put a lockdown on the other ships waking up any of the Chosen Ones or family members. And most of the people are happy to follow his leadership."

"People like to be led."

"Yeah. My guess is some of them, including the retired crew rotations, will never be woken. He'd have a mutiny on his hands if they ever work out what happened to their families. Your Dr. Yang was an exception. She must have been woken for a reason." And he was guessing that had something to do with Destiny. But what?

They came to another junction. "Right again," Destiny said.

"How do you know?"

"I'm not sure. But I think I have a good sense of direction and I can sort of visualize in my head where we are in relation to the building." They walked on. "So Kinross is not a good man?"

"He's using child labor to build a goddamn church."

"That's not good. You don't believe in God? I read the Bible and the *Book of Everlasting Life*. I think they are as much fiction as *Fifty Shades of Grey*."

"Probably more."

"And not nearly so…interesting."

"You like the idea of being tied up? Does pain turn you on?"

She shook her head. "I don't think so. *You* turn me on."

"Maybe that's just because you have no other options right now. Once you meet more people, that will change."

She sniffed. "I have options. Dylan said he would…fuck me if I asked him nicely. Hard."

He'd kill fucking Dylan first. He was messing with him. "Don't even think about it," he growled.

"Would you be jealous?"

"Yes."

"I knew you liked me really." Her tone held more than a hint of satisfaction. "Anyway, so what are you going to do about Kinross?"

"Nothing, except make sure he can't bother us on Trakis Two."

"What about everyone else?"

"Hey, you're mistaking me for someone who gives a fuck. That's their decision. If the assholes want to follow him, why should I give a damn?"

"But that's…" She trailed off, clearly unable to come up with a word. He decided to help her out.

"Immoral?"

She scowled. "Maybe amoral. But I was thinking more along the lines of lazy. You know he's a bad man, and he shouldn't be in charge, and you're just going to make sure you and your friends are safe and then leave everyone else to suffer. What about the poor little children?"

No one had helped him when he was a child. Except that

wasn't entirely true. Rico had taken him in. It wasn't Rico's fault that he'd been a pretty new vampire as well as a natural asshole. He'd actually made sure Milo didn't starve and had some sort of an education, if a somewhat eclectic one. "They'll survive. Children are tough." But he felt a stirring of guilt and he also realized he didn't want Destiny to think badly of him. Maybe he wanted to be her hero. Just for a little while. Maybe he'd been hoping that they would part ways *before* she realized he wasn't hero material at all.

"They shouldn't have to be tough." She stopped. "We're nearly there. We're just coming up beneath the building."

He halted and listened but could hear nothing.

He murmured a word and the light went out, leaving them in complete darkness; there was obviously no one else down here. He turned the light back on and she blinked.

"Do you know where your cell is?" he asked.

She sniffed. "My *room* you mean." She raised a hand and waved it straight ahead. "Down there, close. But this isn't the direction the men with the boxes were going in." She turned and headed a little way back, then took a fork in the tunnels. After a few minutes, she stopped again and waved a hand at a door. "My luxurious quarters."

He hadn't even recognized the place.

"They were coming from that direction," she said, waving a hand down the corridor, "and heading that way." She pointed in the opposite direction.

They didn't have to walk far until they came to a black metal door that blocked the tunnel. A newly installed door by the look of things, with a big padlock.

"It's locked," she said, sounding disappointed. He had an idea that she craved adventure.

He stepped closer, pretended to fiddle with the lock, and whispered an unlocking spell. "Not any longer," he said, then gave a shrug. "I had a somewhat misspent youth."

"Very impressive."

"I'm good with my hands," he said.

"I noticed. And I wondered how you had gotten into my cell that night. Let's see what's inside."

He pushed open the door. It led into a big chamber where the tunnel widened, maybe twenty feet by twenty feet. The room was stacked with boxes. Some big, some small. He crossed to the nearest, pulled his knife from the sheath at his waist, and forced the lid. It was full of automatic rifles. No doubt the rest would be full of weapons as well. An arsenal for Kinross's army.

"Here," Destiny said, handing him a piece of paper. "This was stuck to the wall."

It was an inventory, itemizing the location and contents of all the boxes in the room. He cast his eyes down the list: rifles, pistols, hand grenades, gas grenades, C4 and other explosives. And something marked NW. According to the inventory it was in the far corner of the room and he glanced over. A stack of twelve boxes, bigger than the rest, maybe around six feet by three feet, by two feet. He forced open the lid of the closest, then stepped back and swore.

"What is it?" Destiny asked.

"Nuclear warheads." Enough to destroy a planet at a guess. He remembered the rocket launcher he'd seen parked in the docking bay of the *Trakis Four*. Was it for launching nuclear warheads? What would the range be?

"That's not good, is it?"

"Not good at all." He needed to get back and report in. Decide on their best course of action. Maybe destroy the lot, but if they blew up the store, likely they would destroy the whole planet. Maybe they could remove some vital component, render the bombs harmless. Or he could do a spell, shift the warheads to the shuttle, take them with them. Hold them as a deterrent in case Kinross tried to come after them. But he didn't trust his magic enough on this planet. And he didn't think there was an immediate threat. They had time enough to come up with a plan and get safely away.

"I don't suppose you know how to disarm a nuclear warhead?" he asked.

"No, but we can probably find out in a book."

She was right. He'd get Rico on it. He closed the lid and knocked it back into place, then glanced at the list again. He crossed the room and came to a halt in front of another pile of boxes, smaller this time. He opened the lid and grinned. "You never know when a grenade will come in useful." He filled his backpack with as many as he could carry and then closed the lid. "Time to get out of here."

"Is this what you expected to find?" Destiny asked.

"Maybe not nukes, but weapons of some kind. People are going along with him for now, but he can't assume that will last forever. He needs to be able to back up any threats he makes."

"You need to stop him."

"I'm not a goddamn hero, Destiny. Stop mistaking me for one. It's not who I am."

She stood her ground. "I never said you were a hero. I'm not that naive anymore. But you helped me. I thought you were a decent human being."

Ha. She was way off there. Both on the decent and the human part. "Well, now you know different."

"Then maybe *I* can stop him. We have a duty—"

"Jesus, stop the duty crap. We don't have a duty to anyone here. Not to Kinross, or your Dr. Yang, or all those people sleeping in cryo, who probably bought their places and murdered the people who did win the fucking lottery. The only person you have a duty to is yourself."

She opened her mouth, no doubt to argue some more, but then she clamped her lips closed. He could almost see her brain working, going over what he'd said, her brows drawn together. Finally she muttered, "I need to read some more."

He sighed. He'd liked her naive; there had been a freshness to her. He had a feeling she was going to get difficult and stubborn and... "Come on, let's get out of here."

They left the chamber, locking the padlock behind them, and then headed back toward Destiny's cell. As they turned a corner, lights flashed on somewhere up ahead.

"Stop!" a voice called out.

"Shit," Milo said. "*Run.*"

Chapter Twenty-Four

*"…for there are two distinct sorts of ideas, those that proceed
from the head and those that emanate from the heart."*
—Alexandre Dumas, *The Count of Monte Cristo*

Milo grabbed her hand and they ran.

Behind them, the thud of booted feet sounded so close. They came to a junction and Milo hesitated, and she dragged him to the left. Then they were running again, flat-out. Her heart was racing; every cell of her body felt alive.

Milo was holding her hand. And she could still hear the people behind them. Suddenly, he tugged her to a halt and dragged her into the opening of another tunnel. He waved the torch and the light went out, then he muttered a few words and stepped back against the wall, wrapped his arms around her, and pulled her hard against him. "Quiet," he murmured. "Cloaking device."

She closed her mouth and held her breath, totally conscious of his arm around her middle, his hard body flush against her back.

Outside their tunnel, she could see an approaching light, and the sound of feet getting closer. A few seconds later, five men hurried past, not even hesitating as they ran within feet of their hiding place. Destiny hadn't come across any information on cloaking devices in all the books she had read—except science fiction. And Harry Potter. But this one clearly worked very well.

The light was disappearing and the sounds fading.

Milo put his mouth so close to her ear she could feel his breath, and a shiver ran through her. "Stay still. They'll likely come back this way."

She nodded. "How does the cloaking device work?" she asked.

"Don't worry about it."

"I'm not—" Then the words trapped in her throat as his mouth pressed against the side of her neck and the cloaking device vanished from her mind. He trailed hot kisses across her skin, and she was suddenly conscious of his hard hands splayed against her middle. She wanted to turn and face him, but he held her in place, one hand sliding over her to cup her breast, and her head fell back against him.

He squeezed gently and her nipple hardened under his touch.

His hand left her, and she opened her mouth to complain as his palm slid under her shirt and touched her bare skin.

"Oh," the word escaped her as his fingers plucked at her hard nipple.

"Shh," he whispered against her ear and a shudder ran through her.

Closing her eyes, she gave herself up to the sensations filling her. His warm breath against her ear, one hand on her breast, the other splayed over her belly, inching closer to the waistband of her jeans.

"You can breathe, though."

She gulped in air as his teeth nipped at the sensitive spot where her shoulder met her throat, and she tilted her head to the side so he could do it some more. He licked along her skin, then nibbled her ear.

Heat was building in her belly, sinking between her thighs as he massaged her breast. Then the other. Tingles ran along her nerves. She pressed herself back against him and the hard line of his erection pushed against the cleft of her bottom.

He wanted her.

His hand slid lower, over her jeans to rest at the junction of her thighs, and she pushed against him, desperate for more. Then his fingers moved between her legs, pressing upward, and pleasure shot through her. Her thighs tightened around his hand as he rubbed small circles, pressing the seam of her jeans against her swollen, sensitive flesh.

That's what it felt like.

All the reading hadn't prepared her for the sensations coursing through her. Building, the pressure rising…

Don't stop. Don't stop.

He stopped.

"They're coming back," he whispered.

If it wasn't her, then she didn't care who was coming. She wanted to come. He'd probably change his mind in a moment. She opened her mouth to protest—loudly—and his hand moved to clamp over her lips.

She gritted her teeth.

Light was filling the tunnel and now that he'd stopped tormenting her, she could hear the sound of booted feet approaching. The men went past in the opposite direction and she held herself still as the light dimmed and the footsteps faded.

"We need to go."

"I don't want to go." *I want to come.*

He turned her in his arms and a faint glow from his

"torch" lit up the tunnel, illuminating the sharp angles and planes of his beautiful face. His eyes gleamed silver as he stared down at her.

"They might come back."

She sniffed. "Don't make excuses. Just say if you don't want me."

A smile flickered across his face, then he reached down and took her hand, placed it against his chest with his palm over hers, then he pushed it downward until she reached the hard length of his erection. She could feel the heat of him through the denim of his jeans.

"Does that feel like I don't want you?"

She shook her head, then traced the shape of him, and he went totally still under her touch. He was so big, and heat flooded between her thighs.

He groaned. "But we do need to get back to the ship and put some safety measures in place."

"More cloaking devices?" she asked.

He cast her a sharp glance. "Perhaps."

"You do have some super cool devices," she said. "So many...prototypes."

"Technology is a wonderful thing. Come on."

They didn't speak on the half-hour walk back to the ship. Destiny spent the time thinking about Milo and his torch that looked like a wand and his cloaking devices that made them invisible. And about all the things he wasn't telling her.

"I made a new friend last night," she said as they walked up the ramp of the ship.

He paused and turned to her, a frown between his brows. "You met someone?"

"Not *someone* exactly. I met a dog. A really big dog." She watched him closely as she spoke, trying to gauge his reaction, but he was giving nothing away, so she continued. "It was after Dylan left. I heard barking and went to look. It was sitting outside the tunnels as though it was waiting for me. Do you think it could be an indigenous species?"

He shrugged. "I wouldn't know."

"Anyway, we went for a run and then a swim in the lake. Don't worry, I was careful—Dylan brought me this—" She lifted her arm to show him the silver bracelet. "It will flash and beep if there are any of those drone things around."

"Good. But you want to be careful of strange dogs. They can be vicious."

She started walking again. "This one seemed very friendly."

He opened his mouth but then the comm unit on his arm beeped and he raised it to his face.

. . .

"What?" Milo snapped.

"I don't want to say more now," Dylan said. "But if you're with our friend, stay there. They're watching the shuttle. Don't come back." And he ended the call before Milo had a chance to answer.

"Shit."

Something had clearly gone badly wrong. Dylan hadn't wanted to speak over the comm unit, and he hadn't mentioned Destiny by name, so he must suspect they were being monitored.

"Go inside," he said to Destiny.

For a moment, her lips tightened, and he was pretty sure she was going to refuse, then she gave a quick nod. She turned to him, stood up on tiptoes, and kissed him on the cheek. "Stay safe. I'll be waiting."

He watched the sway of her hips as she disappeared inside. She didn't look back. He had an idea she was becoming suspicious. The comment about the cloaking device had seemed…pointed. And the giant fucking dog. He was going to kill Dylan. What the hell did he think he was up to? Asshole. Dylan was the first to jump in and say they needed to eliminate anyone who suspected their real nature. So what was he doing with Destiny?

Jesus, he just wanted to take her inside and fuck her until he forgot about nuclear bombs, and politics, and the chance that Kinross had discovered that they weren't actually willing to go along with his megalomaniac plans for the future.

He wanted to be the one to show her how good it could be.

And he could because they were clearly on the same wavelength. She just wanted him for sex. Or so she said.

First, he needed to take a few safety measures, then…

After heading down the ramp, he took the same route back. He lit his wand, returned to where they had turned off the main tunnel and cast a spell. If anyone came down this way, they wouldn't even see the entrance to the tunnel.

Then he turned around and returned to the spaceship.

Looked like he wasn't going anywhere for a while. Destiny was sitting cross-legged at the top of the ramp, munching on a donut and waiting for him. He could feel the heat and intensity of her gaze as she watched him approach. He could hardly believe the change in her in only a few days.

"Are you hungry?" she asked as he halted in front of her.

He shook his head. Not for food anyway.

He studied her for a long moment. There was that hint of familiarity again, just a glimmer of something. The high cheekbones, flawless skin, the wide mouth. Dark blue eyes. He stared into them. They were the same color as Kinross's eyes. And there was a certain similarity in the shape of the bones.

Could she be related to Kinross? Was that why they wanted her back so badly? Some sort of surrogate birth on the *Trakis Four* perhaps. But why? He'd looked into Kinross's background. The man didn't have children—did that gall? That he was building an empire and had no one to hand it to? He'd been married once, but there had been no offspring and his wife had died of cancer ten years before the exodus from Earth. Maybe Destiny was meant to be the heir apparent. But why had she been locked in a cell? And she claimed she had never met Kinross. It just didn't gel.

He was betting Dr. Elvira Yang had all the answers. Maybe as soon as he found out what was going on, he would pay the doctor a visit.

"What are you thinking?" Destiny asked.

"Just wondering where you come from. Who you are."

She jumped to her feet. "Does it matter?"

"Not right now." But he had a feeling that it did matter. That it was important and that she might be the one thing that would get them off this planet alive. Because before this was over, they would need every advantage they could get. Would he use Destiny?

He didn't know. But he was betting Dylan would. The werewolf liked her—he could tell—but he very much doubted that would make a difference if Dylan's survival was at stake. Or the survival of his pack. Dylan was an alpha, so his main function in life was to protect his pack, and they would always come first.

Suddenly he felt restless, his skin too tight, his muscles jumpy. He wanted to be out of the tunnels and into the open air. He wanted to lay Destiny down under the stars and make love to her. As he admitted it to himself, the tightly wound tension inside him unraveled. Who knew what tomorrow would bring? But they had tonight. "Let's get some fresh air."

"Can we go for a swim?"

"Why not."

Chapter Twenty-Five

"Ah, lips that say one thing, while the heart thinks another,"
—Alexandre Dumas, *The Count of Monte Cristo*

They walked side by side without touching, but she could sense a resolve to him. He'd made a decision, given up the fight, and she hugged her arms around herself.

When she'd woken from cryo, all she had asked for was the chance to live a little, to experience life and love. And tonight, here and now, was more than she could have ever dreamed of. There was a niggle at the back of her mind, that this would change everything. That this would forever alter her perception of the world and where her loyalties would lie going forward. But she wouldn't think of that now.

Whatever the future held, she would have this night.

Darkness was falling as they headed out of the tunnels. She glanced around in case her new canine friend was there, but they were alone. Beside her, Milo paused and took a deep breath of air then stretched, raising his arms above his head. He was all long, lean muscle and power, and an ache started low down in her body.

Then he smiled and held out a hand, and she clasped her palm against his. They walked toward the lake. At this point, she could see the twinkling lights of the buildings on the island. They stayed in the cover of the trees, strolling along the shoreline, hand in hand like a couple from a real romance, until they could no longer see the lights. Above their heads the stars had come out.

"That's Trakis Two," Milo said, pointing up into the sky.

Most of the stars twinkled, but there was one that glowed a dull orange. A planet not a star.

"At the moment, the two planets are about as close as they ever get. Trakis Four forms an elliptical orbit around its two stars. Trakis Two orbits one of them, so every few...years they're close together. Like now."

"It's beautiful," she murmured. The stars were reflected in the smooth water of the lake.

She slipped her hand from Milo's and without another word, kicked off her boots. Then she tugged her tank top over her head and dropped it on the sand, unfastened her pants and wriggled out of them. As she stood before him naked, she could sense his eyes on her, the intensity of his gaze. She didn't look at him, just walked slowly toward the lake. The stars rippled and broke apart as she waded into the water. It was cool to the touch and she trailed her fingers over the surface. As it lapped at her belly, then her breasts, she kept walking until the water covered her, then she floated on her back, gazing at the immensity of the sky above her. The small speck of Trakis Two. Would Milo return there without her? Another night, would she float here and try to imagine him so far away? She pushed away the thought. Tonight was hers. She would worry about tomorrow...tomorrow.

She was putting off the moment, building the anticipation. Though part of her worried that it would be an anticlimax when they finally came together. She wanted this too much.

When she turned and swam back to the shoreline, he was still standing where she had left him, hands shoved into his pockets. So big and beautiful.

She waded out of the water and walked slowly toward him, the warm air teasing over her body, tightening her nipples. His gaze dropped to wander over her, his nostrils flaring, and her nipples tightened even more, a slow throb starting between her thighs.

Reaching out she rested her palm against his chest, sliding her fingers down, then gripping the hem of his T-shirt and pulling it up and over his head. She threw it down on to the pile of her clothes.

Broad shoulders tapered to a narrow waist. His skin was pale, marked by the dark ink of tattoos. A leather thong around his neck with some sort of pendant. She touched it briefly. Then stroked her fingers over the smooth swell of muscle, the rough line of some sort of scar. A shudder ran through him. She scraped her nails over his nipples and the muscles tensed. Leaning closer, she kissed his skin, breathing in the musky male scent of him as her hands dropped to his waist and she fumbled to unfasten his belt. He didn't help, just stood motionless, his hands at his sides, tension coiled inside him. While he was letting her set the pace, explore, she could sense his fierce need, and her blood heated, her nerves zinging with anticipation.

At long last, the belt was undone, and she flicked open the button of his jeans, her fingers surer now. As she lowered the zipper, he groaned, his head going back.

She hesitated for only a moment and then slipped one hand inside and found the rigid heat of him. Thick and long, the skin like satin over steel, and heat pooled in her belly, sinking lower. She was aware of her own skin, her breasts, the spot between her thighs, swollen with need.

She pushed down his pants and at last he helped, kicking off his boots and stripping off his jeans to stand before her naked.

She was filled with a mixture of emotions so strong she was almost overwhelmed, want and need and love, and she pushed that aside as well. He was like a wild animal, and if she asked too much, too quickly, he would take flight and run into the forest.

So she would take what she could get, as she always had. But some inner part of her niggled at her own restraints. All her life she'd held herself in, controlled herself and her emotions, because that was the only way to survive. She had been a prisoner both mentally and physically, and now a part of her wanted to throw off any restraints and go after what she wanted. Somehow make him care for her. Was it so much to ask?

But then she might end up with nothing.

At least this way she would have the memories of tonight. So she kept the words locked inside and vowed to show him how she felt.

"What do you want?" he murmured.

"Everything."

"Then take it. I'm yours."

For tonight.

She took a step closer, reached up, and touched her fingers to his lips. Then closer still and pressed her mouth to his skin, tasting the saltiness, breathing in his scent. She kissed his chest, flicking her tongue over his hard nipples and heard him gasp. Without thinking she sank to her knees in front of him and peered up the long line of his body.

"Destiny...?" Her name was a groan.

She leaned closer and placed a soft kiss against his hard flesh. His hands moved, and he cupped her head, his fingers tangling in the hair at her nape, but making no effort to hold her closer. She licked along the length of him, swirling her tongue around the tip, tasting the saltiness. Then she sat back on her heels and looked at him. Gilded in starlight. Her own body reacted, clenching tight, flooding with wet heat, and she pressed her thighs together, the anticipation building. She took him in her mouth, felt his body's instinctive response as his hips jerked against her. He was too big, and she wrapped her hand around him, squeezing as she sucked at the swollen head. His hips were moving in rhythm with her movements, his hand tightening around her skull.

Then his body went tense, he groaned, and hot liquid flooded her mouth. She swallowed, as it kept coming. More than she'd expected. Her hands cupped his balls and she squeezed gently, and his hips jerked against her.

Finally he stopped moving and she gave him one last kiss, sat back on her heels, and peered up at him, a big grin on her face. "It works. Just like in the books."

He laughed. Then tugged her to her feet and kissed her, his tongue pushing inside her mouth, filling her as his hard body would soon fill hers. Then he swooped her up in his arms.

"My turn."

He laid her down in the soft sand before coming down to kneel between her open thighs.

From the books she had read, she had a feeling that she should have felt shy at this moment. She didn't. Maybe her unusual upbringing had some advantages. She could feel herself yearning for him. Her sex soft and swollen and needy with the premonition of what was to come. Her hips jerked as her mind filled with the image of him coming down on her, his mouth kissing her. Tingles ran over her skin and through her body, settling between her thighs. He hadn't touched her there yet, but already she was about to explode.

His big hands reached out and stroked over her belly,

through the curls at the base and she held her breath. Long fingers stroked over her sensitive flesh, rubbing too briefly over the bundle of nerves, then lower. One finger probed at the entrance to her body, then sank inside her and she moaned softly.

So good.

Then he lowered his head and kissed her inner thigh and her body twisted beneath his touch, lifting toward him, needing more. His breath was cool against her heated skin, then his mouth was on her and all rational thought fled.

He licked long strokes over her sex, slowly, tasting her, stopping just short of where she needed him most. Then back, his tongue pushing inside her, then lapping at her, the pressure never enough, and at the same time the sensations too much for her body to contain.

She didn't want it to end, but she was striving toward something, the pressure building. She stopped thinking and concentrated on the stroke of his tongue, first so light it was only a whisper against her flesh, then harder, pushing inside her.

His hands slid beneath her to hold her up for his touch as he parted her sex with his clever fingers.

She was so close now, reaching for that elusive release, her body shaking with need. Then he sucked the throbbing bundle of nerves into his mouth, bit down gently and she shattered into a million pieces. He sucked again, and her spine arched, and she screamed, pleasure flooding her, saturating her, blowing her mind. Leaving her empty and changed forever.

Then he moved, his mouth leaving her as he came up over her body. She blinked open her dazed eyes, found him braced on his elbows above her. She stared into his face. His eyes were glowing silver, with glints of crimson in the depths, his nostrils flared. "Are you ready?" he asked.

She wasn't sure she could take anymore, but she nodded anyway, and he held her gaze as he filled the emptiness inside her with one lunge of his hard body. There was a slight moment of tension, a sharp pressure and then he went still inside her. He was so big, he stretched her, filling her, everything so sensitive after her orgasm that she gasped as he twitched inside her.

"Okay?"

She could only manage a small nod, but he obviously took it as a yes, because he pulled out of her slowly, the drag of his flesh against hers sending pleasure shuddering through her. Then back inside. As he pulled out again, her legs wrapped around him, and she drew him back into her.

"Hold on, sweetheart."

He pulled out and shoved back in hard, and it was more sensation than she had known existed in the whole world. She closed her eyes and concentrated on that place where their bodies joined. As he moved faster and harder, the feelings were too much, as though she couldn't take anymore, and the pressure was building again, until he crashed into her one last time and she exploded, shudders running through her, cracks turning into fissures, as she broke apart.

Above her, he arched his back as he found his own release. Pumping into her, his expression savage, and a wave of elation rushed through her that she could make him lose control.

Finally, he went still above her.

She was beyond words.

She wanted to cry and laugh and...

He wrapped his arms around her and rolled so he lay on his back with her sprawled on his chest, his cock still inside her, his hand on her bottom, holding her close. And she closed her eyes and felt the rhythm of his heartbeat.

What did you do after this?

How could you have this and then lose it?

She didn't want to think of what the future held. Of a life without him. It seemed impossible. She realized she felt... safe. And it was unusual. Always the world had seemed like a puzzle for which she had no answers. As though she didn't know who or what she was supposed to be. Now it didn't matter. And she closed her mind and drifted off into a light sleep.

When she woke, it was to hands moving over her skin, massaging the globes of her ass and he was hard again. She lifted herself up sleepily and stared down into his eyes, then wriggled experimentally and felt him twitch and jerk inside her. The movements sent spasms of pleasure clutching at her. She moved some more, shifted her legs so she straddled his hips. She lifted herself slowly, experimentally. It felt good. So good. Lowering herself, she ground herself against him, feeling the lovely friction against her nub. As his hands cupped her breasts and plucked at her nipples, she felt it in her sex, so her inner muscles squeezed him tight.

This time he was slow and intense, and she cried as she came, and she didn't care.

Chapter Twenty-Six

*"… in the shipwreck of life, for life is an eternal shipwreck of
our hopes, I cast into the sea my useless encumbrance, that is
all, and I remain with my own will, disposed to live perfectly
alone, and, consequently, perfectly free."*
—Alexandre Dumas, *The Count of Monte Cristo*

Milo came awake suddenly. The sun was coming up on the
other side of the lake and his arms tightened around the
woman sprawled on top of him.

Beep. Beep.

The noise sounded from the bracelet on Destiny's arm.
A tension ran through her and she pushed herself up. Sweat
stuck their bodies together. She blinked. Then her eyes
widened as she glanced at her arm.

"Drones," she whispered.

It took a moment for the word to make sense, and then he
shot to his feet, pulling her with him.

He glanced around, grabbed their clothes into a bundle
with his free hand. "Run."

He pushed her ahead of him, into the cover of the trees. Then on farther. He could hear the faint whirring of the drone now, but it was getting fainter rather than louder, and he slowed their pace. It sounded as though it was flying along the edge of the lake.

"I think we're okay," he said, halting and turning to face her. She was naked and she blinked back at him.

"That was a little abrupt," she said. She bit on her lip, a worried frown on her face. "Are they looking for me?"

"I don't know." But at a guess, yes.

His gaze wandered over her. She was beautiful: her body slender, her breasts full, her nipples hard, and blood rushed to his groin. He couldn't remember ever wanting a woman like this. They'd made love over and over again through the night, until his body was sore and still he hadn't had enough of her.

He stepped closer, meaning to kiss her and more when he heard a rustle in the bushes behind her. As he stared into the trees, he caught a flash of sable fur. A glint of golden eyes in the shadows. He exhaled and closed his eyes for a second, bringing his body under control. Then he stepped back and tossed Destiny her clothes. "We need to go back."

Disappointment flashed in her eyes, but then she nodded. "I know."

Nothing like an early morning drone chase to get things back to normal.

He pulled his clothes on quickly.

"Thank you for last night," she said. "Whatever happens, I'm glad we made love. It was beautiful."

He opened his mouth to say—what? That they hadn't made love? He didn't make love, he had sex. But he closed it again because he didn't want to dim the glow in her eyes. Not yet anyway. That would no doubt happen soon enough. He just nodded instead and bent down to tug his boots on.

When they got back to the tunnel entrance, Dylan was leaning against the wall, waiting for them, arms folded across his chest, one eyebrow raised.

Milo decided to get in first, before the wolf could make any stupid comments. He had that I'm-about-to make-a-stupid-comment look on his face. "So what's happened?"

"I got back last night, and they were watching the shuttle. And not discreetly. At least ten men, plus Silas. I presume they were there to take us in whether we wanted to go or not. Luckily, I spotted them before they spotted me and got the hell out of there. But they could be monitoring the comm frequencies."

"Crap." Had they been seen in the tunnels? Was there surveillance they didn't know about? But he didn't think so.

"Likely, they've just gotten suspicious. Maybe we're not toeing the line enough and Kinross wants to weed out any trouble, make an example of us before it escalates or gives the others ideas."

"Could be," Milo said, but there was another possibility. "Or maybe he's looked into the *Trakis Two*—followed up on that red flag we found against Rico's name. He's prepared and he has a lot of information. And if he tried to talk to Rico…"

"Let's hope *that* didn't happen," Dylan muttered.

Rico had somehow managed to do the five-hundred-year trip from Earth and still maintain secrecy. Milo could only presume that he'd had very little interaction with the rest of the fleet, because Rico had never been particularly good—actually fucking awful—at diplomacy. "Come inside," he said. "And I'll tell you what we found. It's not good."

Destiny touched his arm. "What's happening? Is it because of me?"

Actually, he didn't think so. "No. I think it's about us," he said. "But it looks like you have two house guests for a while."

Until they sorted this mess out, they weren't going anywhere without the shuttle. They couldn't even contact Rico.

A smile blossomed on her face. "That's wonderful."

"Not really. It's actually totally fucked, but we'll make the most of it."

He put a hand at her waist and steered her around, left it there as they headed back to the ship, Dylan behind them. Once inside, Destiny took the lead and they followed her not to the bridge but to the room next door, some sort of galley-cum-meeting room. There was a table and chairs for six. Whoever had built this ship had definitely been humanoid. She went to a cabinet and pulled out a bag, brought it to the table. It contained what was left of the food they'd brought her. As they sat down, she emptied the contents onto the table and picked out a chocolate muffin. They would need to find an alternative source of food from somewhere soon, if the shuttle wasn't available.

His stomach rumbled and he grabbed a bread roll and started eating. It was slightly stale. He glanced up and caught her gaze as her tongue flicked out to lick a crumb from her lips. He had a vivid memory of those lips around his dick last night and he shifted in his chair.

"Have you two been working up an appetite?" Dylan asked.

Milo was quite aware that Dylan had seen them in the forest. Without any clothes on, so he didn't bother answering.

Dylan grinned, then pulled a bottle out of his bag. "We have to get onto the shuttle," he said. "This is the last bottle I have with me."

"Probably Silas and his men are drinking it right now."

A shudder ran through the werewolf. "Don't say that."

He took a swallow and passed it to Destiny; she took a big gulp and handed it to him. Milo relaxed back in his chair. No one had said this was going to be easy. Time to break the good news to Dylan. "Kinross has enough nuclear weapons to take out a planet," he said.

Dylan raised a brow. "Well, that's not good news. But nothing we weren't expecting. He had to have something to back up his plan."

"Right. But shit, nuclear? Christ, it's the same old crap, but in more concentrated form. We need to decide what we're going to do next, but we can't do that until we discover what's going on. Why the surveillance? How much crap are we in?"

"A lot," Dylan said, grabbing back the bottle. "I think as a priority we need to find a way to contact Rico."

"The captain of the *Trakis Two*?" Destiny asked.

"And your boyfriend's uncle. He's the one who sent us here."

She turned to him, her eyes wide. "You have an uncle?"

"No." He shrugged. "Maybe. He was married to my mother's sister. A long time ago."

"How lovely." He had an idea that Destiny had some strong feelings about family. And he really didn't want to get into a discussion about his relationship with Rico right now.

"We need to get the comm unit from the shuttle. Or at least decide if that's going to be a possibility. If not, then we need to steal a unit from one of the other ships or from Kinross's headquarters." That might be easier than trying to get back to the shuttle as it wouldn't be watched so closely. But there were other things he'd like to collect from the shuttle. Not least the supply of whiskey, plus some personal stuff that might come in handy. "I think we go take a look at the shuttle first and then decide. I suppose you could cause a diversion and I could go in there." With a cloaking spell he could likely get in and out without too much bother as long as their attention was directed another way.

"Will it be dangerous?" Destiny asked.

"No," he said.

"Can I come with you?"

"No," he said again, without even thinking about it.

She was watching him, with knowledge in her eyes. She had come so far. She clearly understood that this was the beginning of the end for them. That he would be leaving soon. A sharp pang of unease hit him somewhere in his chest—he wasn't willing to narrow the area down further than that—at the thought of leaving her behind.

Would she come with them if he asked?

A few days ago, he would have said a categoric no. That her belief in Dr. Yang and her "duty" were instilled so deep that she would never turn her back on them. Now he wasn't so sure. And that wasn't just down to their great chemistry. Which was pretty fucking great. He figured her beliefs were changing as her knowledge of the world increased. She might be the most intelligent person he had ever met, and he'd met a lot of people. She read phenomenally fast. Not only that but she assimilated the knowledge. She'd taken a few physics books and gotten an alien spaceship to work. Okay, maybe she'd just pressed the red button out of curiosity, but still impressive. She had courage as well as brains.

He supposed the question he should be asking himself was—would he ask her to go with them? Hell, did he want her to?

Already, she was insinuating herself in his life. He had an idea that she would tighten the bonds if she could. And he was a loner. Plus, he'd promised himself he would never risk caring for anyone again.

That last image of Maria flashed in front of his mind. Her blackened and still smoking body dead on the altar, with the church burning around her. She'd wanted to save his soul. Hell, he was pretty sure he didn't have a soul to save. Her betrayal had broken him, and it had taken years to put himself back together. To come to terms with what he was.

Now the memory brought no pain. Maria had been a product of her times and beliefs.

If Destiny didn't go with them, then what would happen to her? He was still no closer to understanding who and what she was. Would she be safe here? She was clearly important to Kinross, so likely she would be looked after. Safe. But he couldn't dispel the niggle of worry.

Maybe if he could prove to himself conclusively that she would be safe on Trakis Four, then leaving her would be easier.

There was also the fact that she didn't know their true nature, and he wasn't about to tell her. Rico had a strict policy about what happened to outsiders who discovered what they were, and it usually involved death.

"I could keep watch when you go in," she said, dragging him from his thoughts. "I want to be useful." Her chin took on a stubborn tilt.

He thought about his answer carefully. "It will be more dangerous with you along," he said. "I'll worry about you and that will make me careless. Likely I could get killed."

Dylan smirked and raised the bottle of whiskey in his direction.

Milo cast him a dirty look that said keep out of this conversation.

Her eyes narrowed and he braced himself for an argument. But in the end, she smiled sweetly and nodded. "Okay. I'll stay here."

A feeling of unease ran through him, not helped by the fact that Dylan snorted another laugh.

How had his life gotten so complicated?

Chapter Twenty-Seven

"Yet man will never be perfect until he learns to create and destroy; he does know how to destroy, and that is half the battle."
—Alexandre Dumas, *The Count of Monte Cristo*

They left in the late afternoon.

Milo was already distancing himself, though Destiny was aware that he still wanted her. Occasionally, she would glance up and find his gaze on her, his eyes heavy with desire. But he didn't touch her. And when they left, he didn't kiss her goodbye or anything.

She held herself firmly in place, clutching the arms of her seat while every atom of her body screamed to go to him. Cling to him. Men hated clingy women, and she suspected Milo more than most.

Besides, she knew what they were doing was dangerous, and she wouldn't beg to be allowed to go along. She didn't want to be a distraction. They were only leaving her for her own protection.

She huffed. Why did *that* sound familiar?

Deep inside her, the old familiar anger stirred. She waited for it to sink back down as she had taught herself. Anger had never gotten her anywhere. Instead it grew, swelling and rising to the surface. She gritted her teeth. The truth was she didn't want to be fucking protected. She didn't need protecting. She was strong and she was fast, and she could shoot a gun... probably.

As the door slid closed behind them, she hurled her ereader across the room.

Then jumped to her feet and picked it up and heaved a sigh of relief that it wasn't damaged. She loved her ereader. Plus, she needed the information on there. It occurred to her that in some ways Dr. Yang was right; anger didn't solve anything and could make you act stupidly. Like throwing your ereader across the room.

She was still going through the engineering books. It had occurred to her that what they needed most from their shuttle was the communication system so they could contact their captain, Rico. Maybe if she got the comms system working on this ship, she could somehow rework it so they could use it to contact the *Trakis Two*. She couldn't see why not. In principle. She hadn't mentioned what she was doing to Milo or Dylan. She hadn't wanted them to tell her not to press buttons.

She'd read through the part of the books that covered the comm system on the Trakis ships, but so far, she hadn't found anything that looked the same or even similar. Now she was going through the various consoles on the bridge, eliminating anything that obviously wasn't a comm unit. She was left with two possible areas. Both almost bare except for a panel, like the ones that opened the doors, so she deduced they were activated by pressing her palm to them.

She couldn't decide between the two and in the end, she

picked at random. She pressed her palm to the panel. For a moment nothing happened, and then the screen straight in front of her came to life. It took her a moment to realize what she was looking at. The view from the back of the ship. There wasn't a lot to see, though. The light was dim, but she could just make out the entrance to the tunnel, then as she watched, Milo and Dylan came into sight, Milo holding his "torch" in front of them. They were of a similar height and both moved with an easy grace.

Dylan said something, but she didn't have sound and so couldn't pick it up. Whatever it was, Milo didn't like it. He snarled and walked on, ignoring the other man. They disappeared into the tunnel and were gone, taking the light with them.

She swiped her hand over the screen, and it broke up into smaller screens. Some showed the view from outside, others the various parts of the ship, the galley, the sleeping quarters, the engine room, which was directly below the bridge.

Useful, but not the comm unit.

She turned to the second console, held her breath as she placed her palm on the panel. At first it seemed like nothing had happened. Then lines formed on the console. Two button shapes and some sort of dial. She ran her fingers over it. Nothing. She tapped one of the buttons and heard a faint continuous crackle.

Next, she pressed the dial. No change. She sat back and studied the shape, then moved her fingers in a circular motion. The crackling got louder, and her heart rate sped up. She turned some more, and it got fainter. She frowned. Then experimented with different movements. Swirling, stabbing, zigzagging. At one point she lost the static completely. After a few minutes of experimenting, she surmised that tapping the button moved between big areas of frequencies. The dial then narrowed it down. She tapped until she got a crackle, then rotated her finger slowly around the dial.

Finally, at last the crackle morphed into words.

"Yes, sir. We're leaving now. We'll maintain a perimeter but let them through if they approach. The shuttle is set to blow."

"Good. Report in if there's any change."

She sat, staring at the console. *The shuttle was set to blow?* Could it be a different shuttle? Maybe. But she couldn't take that chance.

How long had they been gone? Over an hour.

She needed to warn them.

Her gaze settled on the pile of grenades Milo had pinched from the weapons room. She shoved a couple into her pockets and then she was off and running.

Chapter Twenty-Eight

*"That is a dream also; only he has remained asleep, while
you have awakened; and who knows which of you is the
most fortunate?"*
—Alexandre Dumas, *The Count of Monte Cristo*

"I think they've gone," Dylan said.

They were standing in the cover of a small cluster of trees
about half a mile from the shuttle. They'd been watching for
an hour now, and as far as he could see, whoever had been
guarding it was gone. In fact, he hadn't seen anyone move the
whole time. No work crews. No one coming or going from
the *Trakis Four*, which loomed close to the shuttle. The lack
of movement was unnatural. Milo didn't like it. "But why?"

Dylan shrugged. "Maybe they got bored. Or changed
their minds or... Who the hell knows? Let's just get what we
need and get out of here before they decide to come back."

Milo thought for a moment, but the truth was, there was
no more risk than if there had been a guard set. Less. There
had always been the chance that Dylan's diversion wouldn't

have worked. Or not totally. And he'd been prepared to take out any guards who were left. This was better. Though there could be someone left inside, but he'd deal with them if he had to. "We probably don't need the diversion. Better not to risk it. You stay here."

Dylan nodded, his gaze still on the shuttle.

Milo pulled his wand from his belt and cast the cloaking spell.

"Impressive," Dylan said.

He didn't answer, just headed across the open space to the shuttle. He saw no one and nothing moved. If he listened carefully, he could hear some sort of banging in the distance from the direction of the new Church building, but nothing else.

He hesitated outside the shuttle, listened, but could hear nothing from the inside. The door was shut, but when he pressed his palm to the panel, it slid open. He frowned. He'd been expecting this to be harder and the ease was niggling at him. He glanced around before he entered but could see nothing suspicious, and he stepped inside.

• • •

How was she supposed to find them? Destiny ran through the forest. At one point, the bracelet on her arm beeped and she dived for the cover of a fallen log, holding her breath until the drone disappeared.

Then up and running again.

Her heart was racing and her mouth dry.

What if she couldn't find them? What if she was too late? She couldn't bear the thought of anything happening to Milo. If she couldn't find them, she'd stand in front of the shuttle and jump up and down. To hell with being caught. She had to save him.

She was sobbing for breath by the time she came to the

edge of the forest. She stopped for a moment.

A stone landed beside her and she let out a squeak. Then searched the tree line, spotted Dylan peering out from behind the trunk of a tree, and sped over.

"What are you doing here?" he asked.

"Where is he?" she gasped. "Where's Milo?"

"In the shuttle—"

"You need to get him out of there. Now."

"It's okay," he said. "There's no one there. He's safe."

"He's not safe. The shuttle is going to explode. He's going to die. Get him out of there."

Shock flashed across his face, but he didn't argue anymore, just raised his wrist to his face and spoke into the comm unit. "Milo, get the hell out of there now. The shuttle is set to blow."

She stared at the shuttle willing him to appear. The door was open, but nothing happened, and every muscle clenched up tight.

"Where is he?"

"Don't worry, he's—"

Dylan's words were cut off as the shuttle exploded into a ball of fire.

"No!" The word was ripped from her throat and she ran forward.

Dylan grabbed her by the arm, and she fought him, trying to break away, but he was amazingly strong.

"Wait," he said. "Look. He's out."

The words didn't make sense. He wasn't out. She would have seen him. He was dead and a wail rose up inside her.

"There," Dylan said.

She followed the direction of his pointed finger. About twenty feet from where the shuttle burned, a figure lay on the ground. She recognized Milo and her brain scrambled for an explanation.

"Lazy bastard," Dylan muttered. "Now is not the time to sleep. Come on. Get up."

Milo still didn't move. Was he even alive? Had the force of the blast killed him? She wouldn't believe it.

Dylan sighed. "Let's go get him and get the hell out of here."

As they ran forward, Destiny could feel the heat from the burning shuttle. Milo lay flat-out, face down, and she crouched down beside him. Reaching out with a trembling hand, she touched her finger to the warm skin of his throat, felt the slow steady throb of his pulse and almost collapsed with relief. "He's alive."

"Of course he's alive. It would take more than that to kill a..." He trailed off and gave a shrug, then hunkered down beside her and prodded Milo in the ribs.

"Wake up," he said, adding another prod but with zero response.

Destiny stroked her hand over his cheek and through his hair. It was sticky with blood at the side. "He must have hit it when he..." When he what? Materialized out of nothing. He must have been blown out here by the force of the explosion. But why hadn't she seen it? His mysterious cloaking device?

They needed to carry him back. She looked around for something to help and caught movement at the edge of her vision. Men in dark green jumpsuits heading their way.

"Dylan, we have a problem."

He glanced up and followed her gaze. "Bloody hell. Milo, wake the fuck up." He shook Milo's arm, but nothing happened. "Crap."

He got to his feet. Was he going to leave them? She wouldn't be able to move Milo on her own. But Dylan reached down, clasped Milo by the upper arms and tossed him over his shoulder. "Grab the bag," Dylan said.

She snatched up the black duffel bag, which had been

hidden under Milo's body, and then they were running.

Dylan moved incredibly fast, hardly slowed by the big man slung over his shoulder, but all the same, a quick glance over her shoulder and she could tell they weren't losing their pursuers.

Something whizzed past her ear and she flinched. They were shooting at them. Luckily, the shot went wide. Then at last they were in the forest, the going slower as they weaved between the tree trunks. They just had to make it to the tunnels, and they'd be hidden. Unless their pursuers were close enough to see them when they entered. They needed to get some distance.

More bullets whizzed past and, up ahead, Dylan stumbled and almost crashed to the ground. He swore and righted himself and was running again, but she could see that he was in trouble. He must have taken a bullet in the leg. Could he make it? He'd have to. But she had to think of a way to give him more time.

Suddenly she remembered the grenades. Skidding to a halt, she pressed her back against a tree trunk. Up ahead, Dylan glanced back over his shoulder, he slowed, and she waved a hand urging him to go on. Then raised the other so he could see the grenade she held. For a moment, he held her gaze, then he nodded and stumbled on.

Destiny stood, back against the tree trunk, slowing her breathing. She peered around; she could see the flash of green through the vegetation; they weren't far behind now.

I can do this.

She didn't want to kill anyone, but they'd been shooting. What choice did she have? Taking a deep breath, she pulled the pin from the grenade and counted to three, then she turned, stepped out from behind the tree and hurled it into the group of men. Ducking back behind the tree, she put her hands over her ears.

She heard the muted roar of the explosion, and the men crash and blunder. She took a second grenade from her pocket and pulled the pin, counted to three and then tossed it after the first.

Then she was running again, pelting headlong toward the tunnel. Dylan and Milo must have reached safety by now. She just had to get there as well. She was going to make it. She couldn't hear anything behind her. Yet.

She stopped abruptly. The two men were sprawled on the ground feet from the entrance. She moved closer. Milo was still unconscious, his eyes closed, his face pale. Dylan looked no better, though when she touched him, he groaned. He tried to push himself to his feet, but his leg collapsed beneath him. He stared up at her with golden eyes that gleamed feral in a face that was blurring.

"Sorry, sweetheart, this is going to come as something of a shock."

The air around her rippled with something strange, and then Dylan was gone, and a huge shaggy dog lay in front of her. Her mouth dropped open as it pushed itself to its feet, staggered, then straightened and gave a growl and a shake. He looked at her and then at Milo, took his shirt in his teeth and pulled. Then let go and growled.

She shook her head, trying to get her mind to work. The bracelet on her arm was beeping and flashing. Drones were coming.

She hooked her hands beneath Milo's arms and dragged him, inch by inch to the tunnel entrance.

She could hear the whir of the drone now. Heading in their direction and she sobbed with the effort. He was so big and heavy, but she was nearly there.

The dog disappeared inside the tunnel and at last she was there. One last heave and they were both inside. She collapsed to the floor and then crawled closer to the entrance so she could peer outside.

A drone was weaving between the trees, low down, zigzagging the area. Could it find them?

Dylan, the dog lay just behind her, licking at the wound on his leg. He raised his head and stared at her, then gave a nod and continued his licking. She'd think about that later.

As the last of her strength seeped away, she sighed and dragged herself backward to sit, leaning against the rock wall, her legs stretched out. She closed her eyes. She'd never felt so terrified in her life.

Milo's bag was still slung over her shoulder, and she pulled it around and peered inside. No comm unit. There were a couple of bottles of whiskey, though—nice to see he'd gotten his priorities sorted.

She pulled a bottle from the bag, unscrewed the top, and took a deep swallow. Behind her, the dog growled. She glanced across; he was staring at the bottle, tongue hanging out.

"Not for dogs," she muttered, hugging the bottle to her chest.

He growled again. She ignored him and took another swallow, closed her eyes, and felt the warmth spread through her.

Opening her eyes, she peered out the entrance. Nothing moved. Had they lost them? Or had she actually killed them all with her grenades? She tried to feel guilty. But they'd shot first. Whatever. There was no movement in the forest and darkness was falling. Another swallow. Her head swam. It felt good.

Beside her, Milo stirred at last. He blinked open his eyes; they glowed crimson.

What?

But she couldn't get worked up. At least he was still human and not a dog.

Then he blinked and his eyes were back to normal. "What the hell happened?"

Chapter Twenty-Nine

"Great is the truth, fire cannot burn, nor water can drown it!"
—Alexandre Dumas, *The Count of Monte Cristo*

She didn't answer, and Milo shifted a little, then groaned.

He felt like he had been hit over the head with a big, solid object. He tried to sit up, but it hurt too much, and he collapsed back and just twisted his head to the side.

They were back in the tunnels. How the hell had that happened? Destiny was beside him, slumped against the wall, cradling a bottle of whiskey. She appeared undamaged, if a little dazed. Beyond her, lay a big black wolf. It regarded him out of golden eyes. Dylan had shifted. That wasn't good.

Then again, Destiny wasn't screaming.

He tried to remember back. He'd grabbed some clothes and other personal stuff and a couple of bottles of whiskey, and he'd been about to start work dismantling the comm unit when Dylan had commed him. He'd made a dash for the door and had been halfway down the ramp when the shuttle

exploded. It had hurled him out into the air and after that—
nothing.

"Destiny?"

She jumped a little. "Sorry, I was just…" She drank some
more whiskey. There was a slightly glazed look in her eyes,
but then the bottle was half empty, so it was hardly surprising.

"What happened?" he asked.

"I got the comm unit working in the spaceship. I thought
if I got it working, then you wouldn't need to go to the shuttle
and put yourself in danger. Then I picked up this comm and
it said they had set the shuttle to explode. And so I had to go
and warn you. Except I was too late."

"Not too late. I still seem to be here."

She sniffed. "I thought you were dead. You wouldn't wake
up. And then the guards came, and Dylan had to carry you
and then they shot him. And he changed into a dog. Again. It
was him the other night; I know that now." She looked at him
out of enormous blue eyes. "He's a weredog, isn't he?"

On the other side of her the "weredog" snarled and Milo
had to bite back a laugh. "Yeah, he's a weredog." The snarl
turned to a full-on growl. Milo ignored it. "Go on."

"You were still unconscious, and they were still following
us, and I had to stop them so I threw a grenade and I think I
might have killed them all."

"Good job."

A shudder ran through her. "I've never killed anyone
before."

He couldn't even remember the first person he'd killed.
Well, not on purpose anyway. The first person he had killed
was the priest who'd been trying to burn him at the stake—
burn the devil out of him. But that had been an accident. He
hadn't been in control of his powers at that point. In fact, he
hadn't even known they existed. The man had spontaneously
combusted. Along with half his congregation, including the

woman Milo had loved.

"You did what you had to do," he said. "They were bad men."

She cast him a look that said she wasn't entirely sure of that argument, but then shrugged. "Then a drone came, and I had to drag you into the tunnels because Dylan had turned into a dog. And you're heavy, and I thought I wasn't going to make it and…" She sniffed, took a gulp of whiskey, and sniffed again.

Milo tried to sit up again, and this time he managed to ignore the shooting pain in his head. He leaned back against the wall and sighed, then held out his hand. She placed the bottle in it and he took a long pull.

Dylan growled again and Milo grinned, raised the bottle to the wolf, and drank.

They'd tried to kill him. There had been no warning. A few seconds later and he would have been at the center of the blast. Of course it might not have actually killed him—he was pretty much impervious to fire as his friend the priest had discovered. But the explosion would likely have blown him into little pieces if he'd been in the enclosed space of the shuttle, and that would have been very messy. He took another drink and realized he was glad to be alive.

He cast a sideways glace at Destiny. She looked drained and exhausted and probably half-drunk as well. It sounded like she had saved his life.

"Thank you," he murmured.

"I didn't want you to die."

He shifted closer and wrapped an arm around her shoulder, pulled her close, and shut his eyes. "I didn't want to die, either." She rested her head on his shoulder and he felt the tension drain from her. Then she sat up straight and he opened his eyes reluctantly. "What?"

"You can't change into a dog as well, can you?"

He snorted. "No. Only one dog here."

The weredog in question rose to his feet, shook his body, then cast them a dirty look. He peered around, then crossed to where Milo's bag lay on the floor, grabbed it in his teeth, and stalked into the tunnels. Milo chuckled and pulled Destiny closer again. Soon he would have to get up and think about what to do next. They needed to contact Rico. Could Destiny really work the comm unit on the spaceship? And could it be made to reach out as far as the *Trakis Two*? It was worth a try. If not, they were going to have to steal something from one of the other ships. Or from Camelot. Kinross was clearly communicating with the other planets.

That was for later. Now, he just wanted to sit here and think of nothing except how good Destiny felt in his arms. He shifted again and pulled her onto his lap, held her cradled against him, all warm and soft.

He tugged at her so she straddled his hips and he buried his face in the curve of her throat, breathing her in. He licked her skin and tasted the saltiness of sweat. Her eyes were closed, and he stroked his thumb over her lower lip, then kissed her. She tasted of whiskey and warm woman, and his cock stirred in his pants.

He didn't want to think.

She was kissing him back, her tongue pushing inside his mouth, her hands in his hair, and he winced as pain shot through his head. He didn't stop her, though. He could put up with a little pain. She pressed down against him, rubbing herself against his growing erection, small moans emerging from her throat as she tried to get closer.

Someone cleared their throat directly above them, and Destiny went still on him, pulling away slightly and staring into his eyes. Her lower lip coming out.

He lifted his gaze to Dylan. "Fuck off."

"Sorry, I don't like to spoil your fun, but we have things

to do. Important things." He didn't sound at all sorry. He turned his attention to Destiny. "And I'm a were-fucking-*wolf* thank you very much," Dylan said. "Never call me a dog again."

He was pulling a T-shirt over his head. One of Milo's. He'd obviously trashed his clothes when he'd shifted and helped himself to Milo's stuff. Probably taken the last bottle of whiskey as well.

Destiny sighed but pushed herself to her feet and held out a hand to him. He took it and stood up, running his free hand over the lump at the back of his head and trying not to flinch.

"Does it hurt?" Destiny asked. She sounded as though she cared.

"I'll live."

"I'll take a look at it when we get to the ship. I read a book on first aid."

"What about me?" Dylan asked. "I got shot."

"You look all right to me," Milo said. He was quite aware that once the werewolf had shifted, he would have healed the bullet wound. So he could stop whining and trying to get sympathy. Though he supposed Dylan had carried him most of the way back from the shuttle.

"Thank you," he said.

Dylan grinned. "That didn't hurt a bit, did it?"

Milo ignored him, just turned around and strode back along the corridor to the spaceship. He headed for the galley and sank down into one of the chairs.

Destiny got a cloth and a bowl of water from somewhere and he bent his head forward obediently so she could dab at the lump on his head while she murmured soothing words. The touch of her fingers felt so good.

He glanced up to meet Dylan's amused stare.

"Is there anything left to eat?" Dylan asked.

Destiny shook her head. "No. I'm sorry, we finished the

last of the food this morning."

"Once we've had a little chat about what happens next, I'll head out and see if I can find us something."

"Like an animal? Will you turn into a wolf and hunt us some food?" Destiny sounded intrigued by the idea. He hoped she wasn't impressed by the whole changing into a dog thing.

"I was thinking more along the lines of pinching something from one of the other ships."

"Oh." She placed her water and cloth onto the table and sat down next to Milo, but she was staring at Dylan. "Does it hurt, changing into a do—" She pursed her lips. "Into a wolf?"

"The first few times. Not now." He raised his arm and Milo sensed the shiver of magic in the air. Claws extended and black fur sprouted over his knuckles as Dylan's hand changed into a vicious wolf's paw.

Destiny grinned, clearly entranced. Hell, he was only a big dog. Though the partial shifting was pretty impressive— only the strongest of shifters could do it. All the same, Destiny didn't know that—there was no reason to look so impressed. She reached out and stroked her finger over the black fur.

She showed no fear at the werewolf thing. The average human would probably have been running and screaming by now. But Destiny was far from average. He was also a little concerned about the ultimate outcome of this. Secrecy was the way they survived. Would Dylan be happy to leave her here with the knowledge that she was aware of what he really was? While Dylan came across as quite affable, Milo was aware that wasn't who or what he was. He didn't think Dylan would kill Destiny without giving her a choice. There were other ways to ensure her cooperation. He was aware that Dylan had changed Logan Farrell—if not by force—then he had made him an offer the other man couldn't refuse.

Be changed or be killed. Would he force the same offer on Destiny? Or would he just kill her? Not if Milo had any say in the matter, but he had yet to work out the best alternative.

And right now, that was the least of their worries. If they couldn't find a way to contact Rico, then they were on their own and had to somehow find a route off planet. Or they were stuck here. And that was not an option.

"Stop showing off," he muttered. "I thought we had important things to do."

Dylan shrugged, but his hand returned to normal. "They want us dead."

"It certainly seems that way. That was no warning." He still didn't understand why, though. Why had things escalated so fast?

"How safe are we here?" Dylan asked.

"Pretty safe. The wards will hold. I think."

"You think?" Dylan frowned. "That doesn't fill me with a whole load of confidence."

"Things don't work exactly the same here. But we're good for now."

"What are you?" Destiny asked suddenly, and he turned to look at her. He'd been expecting the question but at the same time hoping to put off answering a little longer. He didn't know why he was reluctant. Maybe because the last woman he told had promptly handed him over to the Spanish Inquisition. To save his soul—she had told him. And Maria had loved him.

Across from him, Dylan sat back in his chair, arms folded across his chest, with that amused half smile still on his face.

"Are you a wizard?" she asked Milo. "You have a wand and you can make things disappear and move things like…" She hesitated as if not wanting to put it into words.

"I think the word you're looking for is magic," Dylan said.

Milo cast him a cold look. "No. I'm not a wizard." Fucking Harry Potter had a lot to answer for. People were seeing wizards everywhere. Pick up a stick and suddenly you were a goddamn wizard. He'd met a few in his time and they were invariably assholes.

He tapped his fingers on the table, then looked at Destiny. She was watching him, a small frown between her eyes. She gave him a weak smile. As though to say it was all right if he didn't want to talk about it. That made him feel guilty, though he wasn't ashamed of what he was—even if a lot of people did consider him a close relation to the devil.

"I'm a warlock," he muttered.

"What?" Dylan said. "Speak up, we didn't quite hear that."

"Piss off," he growled.

Dylan laughed.

"What is a warlock?" Destiny asked. "Isn't that another name for a wizard?"

"No."

Dylan laughed again. "Aw, he's gone all shy. I don't think he likes talking about himself. So I'll fill you in, shall I?"

Destiny rested a hand on his arm. "If you don't want me to know…"

He shrugged. "Why not?"

She might as well know the worst. At least there weren't any handy priests around to hand him over to if she decided to try and burn the devil out of him. For his own good, of course. Though he supposed Captain Aaron Sekongo would probably take on the job if she asked him nicely. The thing was, though, he didn't think Destiny would do anything like that. He wasn't sure what her thoughts on God and the devil were—though she hadn't seemed too impressed with the Bible—and he had an idea that religion hadn't played a huge part in her education. Dr. Yang was a scientist, and science and religion didn't tend to go hand in hand.

"A warlock," Dylan said, "is the offspring of a witch or wizard—they're human with little powers of their own—and a demon."

"You're half demon?" she asked.

He forced himself to look at her, reluctant to read her expression. Her eyes were wide, her hand still rested on his arm, but she didn't look horrified. More intrigued.

"Demons can vary in strength and powers," Dylan continued, without giving him a chance to answer. "Minor demons have few powers, but then you have an increasing scale going all the way up to the top where you find the seven Princes of Hell, and then well, it's fair to say that the sky's the limit. Scary stuff." He held Milo's gaze. "Do you know who your father is?"

His mother had handed him to Rico to keep his safe from his father. Demons could be a little unpredictable where unwanted and unasked for offspring were concerned. His mother had played a dangerous game with the demon, she'd been desperate to gain power and get revenge on the people who had killed her sister. And she'd paid the ultimate price. His father had hunted her down and slaughtered her. And Milo would never forgive him.

"I know."

"And are you going to share?"

Milo blew out his breath. "Malpheas."

"Really?" Dylan looked at him through narrowed eyes. "You're kidding?" He let out a laugh, though for once, he didn't actually sound particularly amused.

Yeah, Milo was kidding. Not. "You've met him?"

"Hell, no. I'm not sure anyone has met him and lived to tell the tale. Have you?"

Oh yeah. He'd spent ten long years as a guest in the halls of his father's castle deep in the Abyss. That was down to fucking Rico. Again for his own good. Why was it all the people who were supposed to care for him made really fucking dubious decisions when it came to that care? His mother had given him into the guardianship of a vampire. Maria had handed him to the Inquisition. And then Rico had delivered him to his father. All for his own good. "We've spent some time together. It was…interesting."

"I bet."

Actually, without that time, Milo doubted that he would have survived. After the whole Spanish Inquisition thing, his life had gotten pretty crazy. Before that, they'd decided that most of his father's powers had passed him by. It had been a relief. In fact, the powers had been lying dormant, just waiting for something to awaken them. Nothing like being tied to a stake and set on fire to wake the sleeping demon. He'd been out of control. Angry, heartbroken—he'd loved Maria despite her betrayal—the powers had raged; he'd nearly destroyed Rico, put all their existences at risk. So Rico had made a deal with his father. Ten years of Milo's life in servitude to the demon in exchange for teaching him control.

It was fair to say that they would never be close—he would always blame his father for the death of his mother and much of Milo's time and energy had been spent seeking ways to make his father pay. But Malpheas had taught Milo about who and what he was, how to channel his powers, how to keep them contained within himself. How to hide what he was. He'd gotten the tattoos in that time—demon tattoos to harness the demon fire in his blood.

After the ten years was up, his father had offered him a home—no fucking way. Besides, Milo had been brought up in the human world and it called to him. He was half human as well as half demon and he had gone back to live among men. Well, men and vampires, among other things.

"Who is Malpheas?" Destiny asked.

"He's one of the seven Princes of Hell," Dylan replied.

"Some say the most powerful of the most powerful group of demons in existence. Shit." He jumped to his feet and paced the small room. "Does Rico know?"

"He knows."

"Shit," Dylan said again.

Milo grinned. "Sorry you came along now?"

"I'm not sure." He sat down again, studied Milo as though he were some dangerous wild animal who might… spontaneously combust them all at any moment. "Is he dead?" he asked.

That was something Milo didn't know. What had happened back on Earth? And had whatever happened extended to the other dimensions? Was Hell still in existence? Maybe he'd never know. But one thing was for sure, his father was beyond Milo's reach. "I don't know."

He cast Destiny a sideways glance. What was she thinking? Did she believe him to be evil?

"What happened to your mother?" she asked.

He touched the amulet at his throat—the last gift his mother had given him. "My father killed her."

"Oh. That's so sad."

"She used him, and she knew the risks." He gave a shrug. "Enough—that's all a long time ago and far, far away."

"Well, just remind me every so often never to really piss you off," Dylan said.

"Good plan, but too late."

Chapter Thirty

*"In politics, my dear fellow, you know, as well as I do, there
are no men, but ideas - no feelings, but interests; in politics
we do not kill a man, we only remove an obstacle, that is
all."*
—Alexandre Dumas, *The Count of Monte Cristo*

Milo wasn't human. Or not totally human.

Her head ached slightly. She analyzed the feeling and
came to the conclusion that it was probably from all the
whiskey she had drunk. She'd read about hangovers. Likely,
she was suffering from her first. She pressed her fingers to the
spot between her eyes as she sat down at the console.

Milo and Dylan had followed her to the cockpit and now
took up position behind her seat.

Dylan wasn't human, either. Though she supposed he
had been at one point. Before he was bitten.

She pushed the thoughts from her mind because she
needed to concentrate. She was going to try and contact
Milo's uncle. Who apparently wasn't a blood relative and so

not related to any demons. More than that she didn't know. But he would help Milo and Dylan leave the planet and her.

She didn't want them to go. Just thinking about them flying away and leaving her behind made an ache start in her chest. At the same time, she knew they had to leave—it was dangerous for them to stay. She relived that moment when she'd thought Milo was dead. She never wanted to live through that again. She'd rather he was away from her and safe. Actually, she'd rather he stayed with her and was safe, but right now that didn't seem to be an option.

And he'd made no mention of taking her with him.

Would she go if he asked?

She wanted to so badly, but at the same time—how could she? How could she abandon everything she had been brought up to believe? Duty. Responsibility to the rest of the human race.

At least now she understood a little of why Milo didn't feel the same sense of responsibility. Because he wasn't human. Though he didn't seem to be too fond of demons, either.

She'd always known he was a loner.

She just wished she understood more. What her role was. She knew then that she had to find a way to contact Dr. Yang. She had to discover what she was supposed to do that was so important.

"Destiny?" Milo spoke from behind her. She'd been lost in thought. Now she gave herself a little shake. One thing at a time.

She blew out her breath and placed her palm on the panel. The console came to life. Immediately, she heard the crackle of static, then silence. "This is the frequency I heard the message on." It was all quiet now.

"Can you make a note of that?" Milo asked. "It might be useful to be able to keep track of what's going on."

"I'm sure there's a way to get it to store the frequency, but I don't know how right now."

"Okay, we'll just have to find it again."

She had gotten the frequency for the comm unit on the *Trakis Two* from one of the engineering books on the fleet—it had the frequencies for all the ships, and she sat chewing on her lower lip. It was totally different from the local frequencies, and she suspected she wouldn't get there by just turning the dial. She had to somehow flick the machine to a different level. She studied the console. Tapping the button had seemed to move between big areas of frequencies. The dial then narrowed it down. She tapped the button, then ran her finger around the dial. Nothing. Not even any crackle. She tapped again. Same thing. The third time, though, she heard the faint crackle of static. She turned her finger very slowly around the dial and the crackle got louder, then cleared.

"This is the *Trakis Seven,* we are receiving you. Go ahead."

She looked up at Milo, and he shook his head, clearly he didn't want to talk to the *Trakis Seven*.

"Hello, can you identify yourself?"

She turned the dial again and the voice faded. Her finger moved around.

"This is the *Trakis Ten,* we are receiving you. Go ahead."

She thought for a moment, then waved a hand to her ereader. "Can you pass me that?" she asked.

Dylan handed it to her, and she swiped through the pages. She'd highlighted where the frequencies were and she looked up the other ships, comparing them to the *Trakis Two*.

She grinned, then reached out and turned her finger the other way. She moved quite quickly, until a red light flashed on the console, and she stopped. Then started slowly turning back the opposite way.

"*Trakis Two* here and this better be fucking important."

She'd got it. She was good. She tapped the button next to the screen and it lit up. She blinked a couple of times. A man appeared. Black hair pulled into a ponytail, olive skin, and eyes so dark brown they were almost black. He was stunning.

"Who the hell are you?" he asked.

"I'm Destiny."

He raised a brow. "Of course you are."

Milo gave her a nudge and she stood up and moved to the side so he could sit down. Dylan gave her a thumbs-up and a grin. "You are good, baby."

"Is that Rico?" She mouthed the words, not wanting him to hear, and Dylan gave a quick nod then turned his attention to the screen.

"Milo, where the hell have you been? I've been trying to contact the shuttle and nothing."

"That's because the shuttle is no more."

"What the hell? That bastard…"

"What happened?" Milo asked.

Rico's eyes had gone cold, his face turned to stone, and a shiver ran through her. There was something seriously scary about Milo's uncle. Milo had said he wasn't a demon. Destiny wasn't sure she believed him.

"Luther Kinross contacted me twenty-four hours ago. He wanted me to hand over the release codes for the *Trakis Two*. I told him to go fuck himself."

"What are the release codes?" Milo asked.

"They give access to all the primary systems on the ship," Destiny said. "I read about them. If he has the codes, he can control anything from the life support systems to the cryotubes."

"Yeah," Rico growled. "He gave me a long talk about how he knew there was something off on my ship. How I wasn't one of the captains, and I could fall in line or he'd make sure the whole fleet knew about it."

"And what did you tell him?" Milo asked.

"*Mierda*! What do you think I told the fucker? That he could go fuck himself twice. He told me he'd be sending me a message. I guess this is it."

"Christ, he nearly killed me. Some message."

At the memory, Destiny rested her hand on his shoulder and squeezed.

Rico just grinned. "I wouldn't have sent you if I didn't think you could look after yourself."

"I'm guessing he set motion sensors. The shuttle exploded five minutes after I entered. He wanted one or both of us dead."

"And they blew up the whiskey," Dylan said.

"Bastards. Well, I'm glad you didn't give the fucker what he wanted. Now tell me what's going on down there. How much shit have you gotten us into?"

"A lot of shit," Milo said. "Kinross had this all set up. He couldn't have known the *Trakis One* would be destroyed, but likely everything else he had organized from before the fleet left Earth. He has an army, and he has the rest of the Council eating out of his hands. He's also got the Church of Everlasting Life on his side. He's ruthless and he's willing to kill to get what he wants, or just to make a point. Plus, he's got an arsenal of weapons under his castle including enough nukes to blow up a planet."

That did sound bad.

"*Dios*, you're right," Rico said. "That's a lot of shit. And it also makes sense of something else he said—that we needn't think we were safe just because we were on a different planet. The bastard. So what are you going to do about it?"

Destiny held her breath while she waited for Milo's answer.

"You're the captain," Milo muttered. "You tell us."

"This was much easier when everyone was asleep." Rico

thought for a minute, a frown forming between his eyes. "Hey, how are you making this call if the shuttle is gone? For that matter, it came up as caller unknown."

"We found an alien spaceship," Milo said. "And Destiny got the comm unit working."

Rico glanced toward her, and she shivered.

"Cool," he said. "Any aliens?"

"Nope."

"Can't you fly back on that?"

"It's a fucking alien spaceship. We don't actually know how to fly it."

"You got the comms system working. How much harder can it be to fly the thing?"

Destiny could feel the muscles of Milo's shoulders bunching. Then he took a deep breath. "What are the alternatives?"

"Sardi is working on extending the distance of the other shuttle. We might be able to get there and back. If not, we're going to have to come and get you on the *Trakis Two*. And that will be a pain in the arse. So tell me you have a better plan."

"We could steal a shuttle, but we might have problems with the verification system—they work on biometrics."

"I'll get Sardi looking into overrides," Rico said. "In the meantime, you need to find a way to remove those nukes from the picture. My suggestion would be to set them to blow once you're safely away and solve the Kinross problem once and for all."

Destiny frowned. He couldn't mean that. It would kill everyone on the planet. That was hardly fair. "What about all the people?" she said.

Rico ignored her question and asked one of his own. "Who's the woman?"

"This is Milo's new girlfriend," Dylan said, and Milo tensed beneath her hand.

"Pretty. How much does she know?"

"Everything," Milo said.

Rico sighed. "Have I taught you nothing?"

"She did just save Milo's life," Dylan put in. "And she got the comms unit working."

"Is she going to be a problem?" Rico asked.

Destiny opened her mouth to answer that yes, she was going to be a problem if they decided to blow up the whole planet. That would make them as bad or worse than Kinross. But Dylan grabbed her hand and squeezed. She looked into his face and he gave a little shake of his head, so she clamped her lips shut on her instinctive response.

"No, she's not going to be a problem," Milo said.

"Make sure she's not." On the screen she could see Rico get up, pace a little, come back, sit down. "So we have a plan?"

"We neutralize the nuclear bombs," Milo said, "and we get the hell off this planet."

"And at the very least, we need to take Kinross out," Dylan added. "He's a dickhead."

"Might not be easy if he has an army," Rico said. "I still think that setting the nukes to blow once you're safely away is the best bet."

This time Destiny could not keep quiet. "You can't do that. You can't kill all those innocent people. It's…inhumane."

For a moment everyone was quiet. Then Rico laughed. It was a sound of genuine amusement. "I thought you said she knew *everything*." His gaze rose to where she stood behind Milo, and he grinned at her. Then the smile bled from his face. He snarled, lifting the corner of his lip to reveal one sharp, white fang. She swallowed and another shiver ran through her. "You really expect humanity from us?" Then the coldness left his face and he grinned again. "Never going to happen. Besides, most humans I know are total tossers." He studied her for a moment, and she forced herself to hold his gaze, not back down. Finally, Rico nodded and looked away, his attention back on Milo. "Where did you find her? I like her. Makes no difference, though."

What did *that* mean? Destiny had no clue, but neither Milo nor Dylan reacted, so she decided to keep quiet.

"We could steal the nukes," Dylan suggested. "Take them with us. Might come in useful."

Rico thought for a moment. "I'd rather get rid of them. Fuck. A brave new world. Maybe it's time for humanity to bow out and let the rest of us have a go."

Destiny considered the idea. It confused her. All her life, she'd been brought up believing humanity was something noble. That she had a role to play in their survival that was bigger than any individual could ever be. She'd been so sure. Now the doubts were building in her mind, coalescing into a solid mass of uncertainty.

She'd read quite a few novels now, and while she understood that they weren't true, she also realized that they were a reflection of real life. And most of it wasn't pretty and certainly wasn't noble. Mainly the stories involved a few good people fighting against a much stronger force of bad people.

And Rico talked of them as if they weren't part of humanity. Was that how Milo felt? Did he think of them all as some sort of Muggles? Lesser beings?

And more to the point—was he right?

Her head hurt.

She knew what nuclear weapons were. She'd read about them. They were evil. Indiscriminating. Rico was talking of using them, but he wasn't the one who had brought them here to their new world.

Who was this Luther Kinross? He was obviously a bad man, an evil man. But that didn't make the rest of them evil. All the people in cryo. The children. "We have to save them," she said. "The people who haven't done anything wrong. We have to save them from this man, Kinross."

"No. We don't." That was Dylan. "Most of them are dickheads anyway. They bought their places. The richest people on Earth. Which makes them the biggest dickheads."

"What about the children? They're innocent. They haven't had a chance yet. Maybe we could wake everyone up and give them a say. Everyone has a right to be heard."

"*Mierda*," Rico muttered. "Is she for real?"

Dylan grinned. "She had a sheltered upbringing."

Destiny opened her mouth to argue more, but Milo spoke before she could get a word out.

"Okay," he said, "we'll check out the other shuttles and see whether commandeering one is an option. You work on an escape plan from your end in case that doesn't pan out. And can you send us some information on nukes? How to disarm them—"

"How to set a timer," Rico added, with a sly glance in her direction.

He was winding her up. Though she also knew that didn't mean he wouldn't blow up the whole planet with her still on it. She had a feeling that it wouldn't even give him a sleepless night.

"Okay, so we know what we have to do. I'll be in touch. He gave her a last glance. "*Gracias*, for saving his life."

"*De nada*," she murmured.

Then he was gone.

As the screen went blank, the tension seeped out of her. She tightened her grip on Milo's shoulder for support as her body sagged and her legs went weak. She hadn't realized how frightened she had been. Milo's uncle was seriously scary. And intense. Milo was staring straight ahead at the blank screen. Was he contemplating blowing up everyone? Would he do it? Would he kill her?

Most of her thought...not. She believed he had some

fondness for her. But there was a little part of her that whispered that she didn't know him. He wasn't even human. He was half demon. That thought made her wonder something.

"What is he?" she asked, waving a hand at the screen.

Dylan grinned. "Can't you guess?"

Well, obviously he wasn't human, or he wouldn't speak of humanity with such disdain. She remembered the sharp, white fang. Dylan was a werewolf, but he didn't have fangs when he was in human form. So, not a werewolf. She ran her mind over the other supernatural beings she had read about. In the stories. That were supposed to be made up.

"He's a vampire, isn't he?"

"Clever girl," Dylan said.

She licked her lips. "Does he really drink human blood?" She wasn't sure she wanted to know the answer.

"Yeah, when he's not drinking whiskey."

Something occurred to her. "Well, he can't kill all us humans or what's he going to eat?"

Dylan laughed. "I'll remember to point that out to him, next time we talk. I'm going to go find us some food now. You two stay out of trouble."

Milo had been quiet since the call. As Dylan disappeared out the door, he turned his chair, wrapped his arms around her waist, and pressed his head to her stomach. They stood quietly for a moment, as she stroked her fingers through his hair. Finally, he raised his head. "Well, that went better than expected. You did good," he said. "He liked you."

"He did?" It hadn't seemed that way to her. She wondered what he would have done if he *hadn't* liked her. "What did you think was going to happen?" she asked.

He held her gaze. "I thought he would tell me to kill you."

And she couldn't quite bring herself to ask whether he would have done as his uncle ordered.

Where did Milo's loyalties ultimately lie?

Chapter Thirty-One

"Oh, mankind, race of crocodiles! How well I recognize you down there, and how worthy you are of yourselves!"
—Alexandre Dumas, *The Count of Monte Cristo*

"How are you feeling?" Elvira asked.

She glanced at the thermometer; his temperature was normal. Luther actually looked much better. He had some color and was out of bed. "I'm fine," he snapped. "Stop fussing."

She wanted to scream at him. Of course she was fussing. What did he expect? He held the life of her babies in his hands. He was a conscienceless monster. She wanted to ask about them, to beg him to reconsider.

Last night, she'd taken thirty minutes off to go visit the delegates from the *Trakis Two*, but their shuttle had been empty, and no one knew their whereabouts. And now the whole colony was buzzing with the news that the *Trakis Two* shuttle had exploded, but no one knew the details or whether anyone had been hurt or killed in the explosion, and she couldn't ask Luther. He might get suspicious.

"Where the hell is Silas?" he asked. "I told him I wanted to see him."

How was she supposed to know? She bit back the words. Her head ached and her brain felt mushy and uncooperative. She'd been watching Luther around the clock, terrified that he would die on her and then everything would have been for nothing. She clamped her lips closed and forced a smile to her face. "I'll go see if I can find out."

She needed to get away from him. The hatred was churning inside her and she was fighting the urge to scream at him, to rake her nails down his face. She'd sold her soul to a monster, but it wasn't as though she'd had a choice. It had been either that or stay on Earth and meet the inevitable end. She'd done this for her children so they would have a future, and now it was all falling apart, crumbling.

Where was Destiny?

It was as if she had vanished off the face of the planet.

Could she have been eaten by some wild indigenous animal? They hadn't actually encountered any carnivores big enough to eat a person yet, but who knew what was on the planet?

Even if that were the case, it wouldn't explain how she had gotten out of a locked cell. How nobody had seen her.

She headed to the door, but it opened before she reached it and Silas stood there.

"How is he?" he asked quietly.

"He's fine."

"Good. I have some news."

He stepped past her and she followed him back into the room.

"Do you want me to go?" she asked.

"No," Luther said. "Stay."

Damn. She wanted out of there. She wanted to find out

what was going on. Though maybe she would have a better chance of that in here. She sank down onto a chair at the edge of the room and held her hands together on her lap to stop the tremor.

"Well," Luther said. "Give me your report."

"The shuttle was set to explode using a motion sensor trigger. We had someone watching from a distance and they didn't see anyone enter. But it exploded."

"Bloody incompetents."

"Maybe. I'm not so sure. Anyway, we found no sign of any bodies, so whoever triggered the explosion got out."

"And no one has seen them?"

"Not since yesterday morning." Silas pulled a flash drive from his pocket and crossed to where a viewer sat on a small table. "Well, until now. You might want to watch this."

"What is it?"

"A recording from the head camera of one of the men who were watching the shuttle."

Elvira shifted so she could see the screen. At first, she couldn't make out what it was...something burning. The shuttle?

"This is just after the explosion," Silas said.

The scene shifted, moving away from the burning shuttle to pan out around the surrounding area. It moved slowly, then stopped, focusing on something on the ground. At first there was nothing, then a body materialized as if out of nowhere.

"What the hell?" Luther said. "Where did that come from?"

"We don't know. Some strange shit, right? We believe he was flung from the shuttle as it exploded, but no one can give an explanation as to why he wasn't seen." The camera was too far away to identify the man but was moving closer. Then two more figures appeared in the frame. Again, she couldn't make out the details. One of them picked up the unconscious figure and hauled him over his shoulder and then they were running.

"The next bit is a little boring, so we'll fast forward. It gets better, I promise." The film whirred forward. Silas stopped it and restarted. They were in the forest now and running fast from the look of it. Suddenly a figure stepped out from behind a tree and threw something toward the camera.

Elvira's breath caught in her throat and she jumped to her feet and took a step closer.

"That was a grenade she threw," Silas said. "It killed one of the men, knocked out the others. You recognize her?"

She swallowed. Her lips were dry, and she licked them. Then she nodded. It wasn't really something she could deny, however much she wanted to.

"Who the hell is it?" Luther asked, leaning forward in his seat and staring at the screen.

And she realized he'd never seen her, not even a picture.

"It's Destiny," she said.

Chapter Thirty-Two

*"Moral wounds have this peculiarity - they may be hidden,
but they never close; always painful, always ready to bleed
when touched, they remain fresh and open in the heart."*
—Alexandre Dumas, *The Count of Monte Cristo*

Destiny, please come home.

*You are in the hands of mercenaries who are working
to destroy our new colony. Whatever they have
told you, they are not who they say they are. They
murdered the Chosen Ones on the* Trakis Two *and
took their places. Now they are seeking to take control
of the Trakis system.*

They will use you for their evil purposes.

*You have a chance to do great good in the world. It
is what you were born for. Come back and help us
make the world a better, safer place for humanity.*

*If you're a prisoner, then find a way to get in touch
and we will come and rescue you.*

*I love you. You are my child as much as the children
of my body. Come home, Destiny.*

Dr. Yang's voice. The message started over again, and
Destiny sat and listened to it a second time. It was a recording,
set up on a repeat loop to play over and over. Presumably just
on the off chance that she was listening. Somehow Dr. Yang
had discovered that Destiny was with Milo.

She'd been fiddling with the comm unit since Milo had
left.

None of them had slept. Milo and Dylan had spent the
hours going over various ideas. They had come up with the
bare bones of a plan but were still waiting to hear back from
Rico.

Dylan had gone off to do a patrol of the forest. Milo
was checking his wards. Magic spells he'd set up to protect
the place. He was a warlock, half demon. She had to keep
reminding herself of that. He wasn't fully human.

At that moment, she caught sight of him on one of the
monitors, approaching the bridge, and she switched off the
message then swiveled her chair so she faced the door.

Now that she knew what he was, she couldn't quite
believe that she'd ever thought him entirely human. But then,
in her own defense, she hadn't actually met that many. He'd
only been the second, so perhaps it would have been more
peculiar if she had noticed something amiss.

A lump caught in her throat as he strode onto the bridge,
and her heart skipped a beat, then started racing. He was so
big and beautiful.

She had a flash back to the feel of his hard body, on her,
inside her. At the same time, she couldn't dismiss the nagging
sense that everything was going to fall apart any moment

now. Milo didn't love her—he'd told her so. And to make sure she understood, he'd told her that he would never love her, he was a loner. She suspected that he was protesting too much, but that also he was strong-willed and stubborn enough to stand by those beliefs.

He came to a halt in front of her, hands shoved into his pockets, his T-shirt molding the hard muscles of his chest.

She wanted him.

He opened his mouth to speak, but she gave a small shake of her head and his eyes narrowed. She rose to her feet, grabbed the hem of her tank top, and pulled it over her head. His nostrils flared and his eyelids drooped, the tell-tale signs that she had his attention. All the same, she wasn't giving him a chance to come to his senses. Kicking off her boots, she wriggled out of her pants to stand in front of him naked.

"Jesus."

He took a step toward her. Then, gripping her shoulders, he spun her around, urging her forward until her thighs hit the edge of the console in front of her and her hands reached out to balance herself. His arms wrapped around her, palms cupping her breasts, squeezing almost roughly, so her nipples hardened, and heat flooded her core.

She pressed her bottom back against him, and he ground into her so she could feel the hard length of his erection through his pants. His mouth nuzzled at the soft spot where her shoulder met her throat and tingles shot along her nerves, then he bit down hard, and her head went back. He bent her forward so her lower arms rested on the smooth metal surface; her bottom pushed out. She closed her eyes, the anticipation building. For a moment he moved away, and panic filled her, then in the silence she heard the rasp of his zipper. His foot came out and he pushed her legs apart. A hard palm slapped her backside, and she yelped and made to turn, but he held her in place with one hand splayed across her belly. Then he pushed inside with one hard thrust, filling her so she would have been forced forward if he hadn't held her tight.

He was so big, the sensation bordered on pain, then he moved slowly, and pleasure shot through her. She pressed back against him, and he must have taken that as a go-ahead, because then he was moving fast, pulling out and then shoving back in, hard and fast. The hand on her belly moved lower, questing between her thighs, fingers sliding between the folds of her sex, finding the small bundle of nerves so she gasped and widened her legs. He rubbed in circles while his cock hammered her from behind. The sensations were almost too much and her hands scrabbled to hold on, gripping the console in front of her, as he slammed into her until she lost conscious thought of everything but the feel of him, every atom focused on the point where their bodies met. Inside her, the tension was building and building. She recognized the feeling now and reached for it, desperately craving the release from the almost unbearable pressure. He pinched her clit, then circled and pinched again. The tension snapped and she exploded, her spine arching. She threw back her head and screamed as his hands grasped her hips, pumping into her hard and fast, until he came inside her, and still he couldn't seem to stop, tipping her over the edge yet again.

He went still, behind her. "What the hell...?" he said, pulling away.

She didn't want him to go, and she pressed back against him, then blinked open her eyes. Right in front of her was the red button. It took a moment for her sex-fogged brain to realize what was happening. She must have pressed it by mistake, and now the ship was rising. She shook her head and reached out and slammed her palm on the button and they dropped. As they hit the ground, Milo lost his footing. He still had hold of her, and he dragged her with him as they crashed to the floor. She landed on top of him, the air leaving her lungs in a *whoosh*.

His body was shaking beneath her and it took her a moment to realize he was laughing. And then she was laughing as well. She wriggled so she was still on top of him but facing him now and she could look down into his face. She'd never seen him laugh, and the harsh lines of his face were smoothed out. The laughter died but lingered in his silver eyes. "That was…out of this world."

"Is it always like that?" she asked.

"Sweetheart, it's never like that."

She'd had a feeling that was the case. What they had was special, and she might never find it again with another man. Except, he wasn't a man.

Lowering her head, she kissed him, her lips lingering. Then she pulled away and scrambled to her feet.

He was still fully dressed, his pants open, one hand resting behind his head as he watched her move around the room, picking up her clothes. He was so…sexy. A few days ago, she hadn't even known what the word meant, now she felt it down to her bones. He made her melt; he made her burn. Just looking at him now, her sex felt swollen and hot and more than ready for more.

He was going to break her heart.

Because she already loved him, it was too late to back off now. She'd read about love at first sight and she knew it was real because it had happened to her. That moment when he had stepped out of the shuttle and he'd been so beautiful her heart had hurt.

But she also suspected that love wasn't enough. And maybe there were more important things in the world. Like duty and honor. She didn't want to think that, really she didn't, but maybe Dr. Yang's early teachings were just too deeply impregnated into her very being.

With a sigh, she pulled on her clothes, then went and sat

at the comm console. She switched it on. The message picked up halfway through. She played it through a second time, as Milo came to stand beside her. When it was finished, she switched it off and swung around to face him.

His face was impassive. "Do you believe her?"

"Which bit? The part where you're out to destroy the Trakis system, the part where I can save humanity, or the part where she loves me?"

He shrugged, leaning against the console, arms folded over his chest. "Any of it?"

She shrugged helplessly. "I don't think she loves me, the rest I'm not sure of."

"I don't want to destroy the Trakis system," he said. "But I want the chance to live in freedom in this new world, not under the thumb of some immoral despot like Kinross."

"Are you moral?" she asked.

His expression closed off so she couldn't tell what he was thinking. "Probably not by most people's definition," he said. "But I have a code I live by, and I do my best to stick to it."

"And Rico, is he moral?"

Amusement flashed in his eyes. "Not even vaguely."

It didn't sound as though the idea bothered him, and she wondered again about the relationship between the two men. "Do you love him?"

The amusement vanished, and a frown formed between his eyes as he thought about the question he obviously hadn't been expecting. "It doesn't matter."

It mattered to her, but she didn't think she would get any more on the subject. She decided on a more oblique approach. "Have you ever been in love?"

He scrubbed a hand through his hair. Another question he wasn't willing to answer? Then he started talking.

"Once. I was in love once, a long time ago."

A burning sensation flooded her chest. Jealousy? "I

presume it didn't go well?"

He smiled then, though it wasn't reflected in his eyes, which remained wary. "I was twenty. Maria was eighteen. She was young, innocent, and so good it shone from her. I was young and not so innocent—I'd spent fourteen years living with Rico—any innocence was long gone. But she made me feel as though I could be good as well."

Why did she suspect this wasn't going to have a happy ending? "What happened?"

"Rico had warned me not to reveal my true nature to any humans, but I wanted Maria to know who and what I was. I believed she loved me enough to see past my obvious... disadvantages."

"You don't have any disadvantages," she said fiercely. "You're perfect."

He chuckled. "Of course I am. On the other hand, Maria obviously thought there was some room for improvement. She was horrified. I'm not sure she actually believed me about the half-demon thing, but rather thought I was deluded. Either way, she loved me enough to want to save my soul. She gave me up to the church. They in turn handed me to the Inquisition."

She'd read about the Inquisition in her history books. "How could she?" *Bitch.*

"She was born in a time when people truly had faith. She believed my soul was damned and it was her duty to get me back in God's graces."

Something occurred to her. This story didn't quite make sense. "How old are you, Milo?" She'd supposed he was around thirty, but obviously that was when she'd believed him to be human. His story made her think he must be much older.

"I was born in Spain in 1508."

Her mind went blank for a second while she calculated

how old that made him. Well, over a thousand, though five hundred of those had been spent in cryo. All the same, it made her feel very young. "Wow. And how long will you live?"

He shrugged. "I don't know. I'm essentially immortal, but I can be destroyed."

She stored the age thing away to worry about later, because it was huge, but right now she wanted to know the end of the Maria story. "What happened with the Inquisition? Did they let you go?"

He snorted. "No, they tried their hardest to burn me at the fucking stake. With Maria watching. It was a pivotal moment." She reached out and lightly touched the scar on the side of his neck. A burn?

"How did you get away?"

"It was...interesting. Up until then, we'd believed that my father's powers had passed me by. It happens sometimes. But clearly, they were just waiting for something to awaken them. Nothing like the thought of going up in flames with the woman you love cheering on to bring out the demon in a man."

She blinked and leaned closer. "What happened?"

"Demon fire. The whole place went up, priests spontaneously combusting, a blazing church..."

"Maria?"

Pain flashed across his face. "She burned as well. I was out of control. I wouldn't have done it if I could have stopped. I would have saved her. I loved her. I even understood why she had done what she did. Her duty to me."

"Where was Rico?"

"This all happened during the day. He's a vampire, so he was asleep. He woke up to find the whole town burning. He managed to knock me out. I woke up in a cell, and then that was burning. I had zero control. Rico did the only thing he could think of. He contacted my father. In effect he sold me into servitude for ten years. Ten years in Hell." His lips quirked. "Literally. But my father taught me how to control my powers. How to live with what I was."

"I'm glad. But I think you saw it as a betrayal by Rico."

"Hell, I was used to it by then. Everyone who loves you lets you down, usually under the guise of doing it for your own good. My mother, Maria, Rico…"

At least she could understand now why he was so wary about giving his heart. He no doubt believed she would let him down as well. And she had no clue right now whether that was the case.

A part of her suspected that if he would just commit to her, then she would give her loyalty to him wholeheartedly, and she would never, never let him down. But another part couldn't help thinking about what her role was in life, in the colony. Could she turn her back on that?

Especially if she believed Rico would destroy the planet. Could she allow that to happen to her own people? Where did her loyalties lie?

She hated that she didn't know more.

"You're thinking of going back, aren't you?" Milo asked. His words an accusation. "How can you after what you've seen of Kinross? And your Dr. Yang is deep in league with the bastard."

"Maybe she has her reasons."

He shook his head. "You really think she loves you? She's manipulating you as she has done all your life. You can't trust her."

"But I need to understand why."

"No, you don't. You *want* to understand, but you don't *need* to. You could turn your back on all this, just come with us," Milo said.

There. He'd asked her. Part of her yearned to just say yes.

Even if he would never love her, she could be with him.

"You don't owe these people anything, Destiny. Come back to Trakis Two with us. There's a new world to build there as well."

"With you?"

He looked immediately shifty. "I'll be there."

He was such a coward. Though at least she understood why now.

She jumped to her feet and walked the length of the bridge—all of ten paces. Then came back to him. "Why has she never told me why I'm here? What does she want of me? She says I can make a difference, but how?" She stamped her foot. "Who am I?"

"If we found out, then would you leave this place?"

"It depends on what I'm supposed to do. Whether I can make a difference. I just don't see how. I've thought and thought but can't come up with a reason, a purpose."

"Let me find out."

"How?"

"I'll go talk to Dr. Yang."

She bit her lip. "Won't that be dangerous?"

"No. I'll tell her I have important information about her family. That I just want to talk to her. There will be no danger."

A shiver ran through her. A premonition of something to come.

But he was already walking away.

Chapter Thirty-Three

"It is a bad habit to shout it from the rooftops when one challenges a person. Not everyone benefits from attracting attention."
—Alexandre Dumas, *The Count of Monte Cristo*

Milo strode away from the ship with a sense of failure.

He was aware of what Destiny wanted. His total capitulation.

Everything.

His soul. If he had one.

And if she got it, if he gave in and gave her his soul, then what would she do with it?

Jump up and down on it? Set it on fire? Decide that her duty to humanity was more important than him?

He should just walk away.

Leave her to her duty. But he couldn't do it.

Already he wanted her again.

It wasn't just sex, though the sex was the best ever. He liked her. Was amazed by how much she had grown and could only imagine the woman she would become if she had the time and space to grow further. He wanted to help her become that woman.

Even if he couldn't say the words that he suspected would change the whole situation.

The truth was it didn't matter if someone loved you. They all came with baggage, whether nature or nurture. Things that were fundamental to their very being or things that were drilled into them from birth. His mother wanted revenge, Maria wanted to save his soul, Rico...Rico had wanted to survive but also, he'd wanted Milo to survive as well.

He waited until he was a good distance away from the tunnel entrance and then he lifted the comm unit and punched in the code for Dr. Yang.

"Yes."

"It's Milo. We need to talk."

"You have Destiny with you?"

"No, but I know where she is."

"You need to bring her back." Her tone held a hint of panic. "Do that and Kinross will pardon you. Let you and your friend leave the planet."

Of course he would. And pardon him for what? He hadn't done anything fucking wrong. Yet. "I have news about your family."

She was silent for a moment. "And what do you want in return?"

"Just some information."

"I need proof that they are okay."

He thought for a moment. How the hell was he supposed to give her proof they were okay when they were long dead? He'd just have to come up with something. "How about the promise that you can come with us when we leave? You can be with your family on Trakis Two. If you help me, you or your family won't be safe here. I doubt you'll be safe anyway.

Kinross is not an honorable man."

Again, she was silent for a little while. "Your captain will agree to that?"

"He will." Maybe. Who knew with Rico? But he couldn't come up with anything better right now.

"I'll want confirmation from him."

"Well, I'm having a little trouble contacting him right now due to the fact that your boss blew up my shuttle."

"Then meet me at the *Trakis Four*. There's a conference room on the second level, room 206—it has a long-distance link."

And the comm went dead.

He could very well be walking into a trap. But he didn't think so. He suspected that everything Dr. Yang had done had been about her family. Probably Kinross had bought her loyalty with promises that she would be reunited with them. Promises he couldn't keep because her family was dead. Maybe she was getting suspicious. She'd likely had more than a glance into what sort of man Kinross was.

There was a risk, but he wanted to do this for Destiny.

Dr. Yang knew all the answers. She knew who Destiny was and what she would be walking into if she went back. Or maybe he just wanted to find the truth and it would convince her there was no reason to return. That she wasn't the savior of humanity. That she could come with them to Trakis Two without fear that she had condemned the human race to... what?

Total annihilation?

He had no clue.

He'd racked his brain for an answer as to why she was important to them and still came up blank.

A part of him suspected that he didn't have to do this, that if he told Destiny he loved her, that *he* needed her far more than the nameless hordes of humanity, then she would come with him and give him her loyalty.

But he wasn't sure. And he was scared. That once again he would give his heart and end up with nothing in return. Less than nothing.

Dammit, was it so much to ask just to come first for once? Obviously.

He paused at the edge of the trees. The same place they had watched the shuttle from yesterday. The remains were still smoldering. He searched the area but could see nothing to indicate anyone was paying attention. Off toward the lake, the bare bones of the new Church were visible, the central tower reaching into the sky, the army of workers scurrying around under the watchful eyes of Kinross's mercenaries. Children laboring, urged on by men with guns.

He watched for another few minutes, and then made his way across the open space in front of the *Trakis Four*. The skin of his back prickled, and he expected at any moment to hear a warning call, or more likely a bullet in the back with no warning. After all, they hadn't given any warning before they had blown the shuttle. Rico must have really pissed them off.

But nothing and no one stopped him, and some of the tension lessened as he reached the top of the ramp and entered the dim light of the ship. The cavernous docking bay was empty now and deserted of people. He crossed the room; the double doors were open, and he paused for a moment in the corridor. He had no clue of the layout of the ships. She'd said the second level, but he had no idea which level he was on now. He looked around, saw nothing of any help, and started walking. Eventually he came to a junction; there was a picture of a ramp on the right hand turning and he decided that was his best bet. He strode down the ramp, and at the bottom was a sign on the wall with a number: *1*. So he kept going up. The next was: *2* and he headed off down the corridor reading the room numbers.

He stopped outside room 206. The door was open.

Inside, Dr. Yang sat in a chair opposite the open doorway, her hands clasped on her lap, her eyes darting from side to side.

As he stepped into the room, her gaze fixed on him, then behind him. "Where is Destiny?" she asked.

"Safe."

She closed her eyes for a moment. "I never wanted any of this."

Any of what? Time to find out. "She wants to come back. You won her over with the *I love you* crap."

Her eyes flashed with anger. "I do care about her."

"You care about your family more."

She got to her feet and turned away, her hands wrapped around her middle. When she turned back, the expression was gone from her face. "You said you wanted information. What do you want to know?"

"Destiny believes she has an important role to play. I want to know what it is."

She pursed her lips. Then her glance shifted to the doorway. "I want proof first that your captain will give me sanctuary if I go against Kinross."

He had the impression that she was buying time. It occurred to him that he should get out of there fast, but he suspected he was already too late. So at least he could try and learn something.

For a second, he considered magicking them both out of there. But he really didn't have much faith in his ability to get them anywhere in one piece from inside a spaceship. Technology would have a peculiar effect on his magic. God knows where they might end up.

His ears pricked as he heard footsteps running down the corridor. He looked at Yang and she gave a helpless shrug.

"I'm sorry."

He forced his muscles to unwind. "Just tell me. Who is she? Why is she so important?"

She gave a little shake of her head, then soldiers appeared in the doorway, in full combat gear, guns drawn.

Ten of them. Seemed a little like overkill. He stood relaxed, his focus on the man at the center. Beneath the helmet and face mask he recognized Silas Wynch.

He turned back to Yang. "If they kill me, you'll never find Destiny." He waited, every muscle tense. If he needed to, he would vanish. To hell with the risk. To hell with giving himself away. He started the incantation in his mind, and his hand reached for the wand tucked in his belt.

"Don't shoot him," she said.

Her eyes flicked to the left. A second later, something hit him in the upper arm. He glanced sideways; some sort of dart stuck out of his shoulder. And then everything went black.

Chapter Thirty-Four

*"So he went down, smiling skeptically and muttering the
final word in human wisdom: 'Perhaps!'"*
—Alexandre Dumas, *The Count of Monte Cristo*

His head hurt.

Again.

Milo groaned. He tried to reach up to rub the bit that
hurt, except he couldn't because his hands were tied to the
chair he was sitting in.

Where was he?

What the hell had happened?

It came back to him slowly.

He'd totally misjudged the situation with Yang. What a
bitch. At least he wasn't dead. How long had he been out?
And what happened now?

The room was in darkness. He was on some sort of
hard, upright chair, his arms tied to the armrests, his ankles
fastened to the legs, everything held firmly in place.

He relaxed for a moment. They weren't going to kill

him, not until they knew where Destiny was. He had time. Maybe he could make some sort of bargain. But with what? He had nothing to give them but Destiny, and that wasn't happening. He was becoming more and more convinced that whatever her role was, it wasn't good. Not for Destiny at least. Otherwise, why not just tell her?

The light flicked on. He was in a windowless room, empty but for his chair and a screen on the far wall. It flashed to life and at the same time, the door opened. Kinross entered, with Silas at his shoulder, Dr. Yang behind them.

Kinross came to a halt in front of Milo. He had Milo's wand in his hand, and he tapped it against his thigh as he stared down. "What are you?" Kinross asked, eying him up. "Some sort of...wizard?"

Crap. Rico was going to be pissed.

"What are *you*?" he countered. "Totally deluded?"

Kinross didn't answer. He pursed his lips. "We'll get Dr. Yang to do some testing on you. She's an expert in genetics. We'll see just how human you are. We'll take you apart. Find out what makes you tick. First, we need some information. Where is the woman?"

"Which woman?"

Kinross nodded to Silas, and he stepped forward and swung his fist. It crashed into Milo's nose with a *crunch* of bone, and blood flooded his mouth. He swallowed and shook his head, spraying blood across Kinross's white shirt.

It was going to be a long night.

• • •

Something awoke her. Destiny had been sleeping, her cheek resting on her arms on the console in front of her. Now she lifted her head and looked toward the door, heart leaping. Was Milo back? He'd said it wasn't dangerous, and she didn't think Dr. Yang would do anything to him, but all the same she was worried.

Dylan stood in the doorway. His jaw was tense. "They have Milo."

She jumped to her feet. "What? Who has Milo?"

"I saw them carrying him off the *Trakis Four*. Your friend, Silas, and your really good friend, Dr. Yang."

"Carrying him?" Her mind went momentarily blank. She swallowed as fear swamped her. She forced herself to ask, "Is he dead?"

"I don't think so, but he was definitely unconscious. What the hell was he doing?"

She ran a hand through her hair, forcing her brain past the fear that paralyzed it. "He went to talk to Dr. Yang."

Dylan rolled his eyes. "Why? We had a plan. Reconnoiter the other shuttles, find a way to neutralize the nukes, and get the hell off this shithole planet."

She bit her lip until she tasted the sharp metallic tang of her own blood. "He went to ask her about me. About who I am and what I'm supposed to do."

"Does it matter what you're supposed to do? Can't you just decide for yourself? Bloody hell. Rico is going to be seriously pissed." He turned away, ran a hand through his hair, growled.

"How do we get him back?" she asked, and her voice sounded small and scared.

"Shit, I don't know. They were taking him to Camelot. The place is a fortress and guarded by an army. This is not good." He took a deep breath and smiled. "Well, panicking isn't going to help. We need a new plan."

Off to the side, a light flashed. The comm unit. She hurried over. Could it be Milo? Had he gotten away? She swiped her hand over the controls and the screen flashed to life. Rico stood there. "I thought we had a fucking plan," he snarled.

"Have you heard from Milo?" Destiny asked.

His eyes narrowed on her. "You are trouble," he said. "I'm thinking more trouble than you can possibly be worth. But then it appears you're worth quite a lot." He blew out his breath and scowled. "I just had that tosser Kinross on the comm. He's got Milo."

She swallowed. "Is he okay?"

"Not really. Want a look?" He didn't wait for her to answer. The screen flashed blank then a new image emerged. A dimly lit room, a chair in the center, a man tied to the chair. She gasped. His head flopped forward so she couldn't make out his features, but then his face lolled to the side, a mask of crimson. His gray T-shirt was dark with blood. His eyes were swollen shut.

"What have they done to him?" she asked. This was her fault. He'd gone back for her, and now he was a prisoner and they were torturing him. Had Dr. Yang betrayed him? She reached out a hand as though she could touch him, and the image vanished, replaced by Rico scowling.

"Nothing too drastic," he said. "Just beaten him up a little. He'll live. Or he will if we get him out of there."

"We have to get him out. We will, won't we?"

"What do they want?" Dylan asked. "I presume they want something."

"They'll swap Milo for the woman." He turned his attention to Destiny and studied her. "For some reason, they really want you back. I'm just trying to find out why."

"Join the club," Dylan muttered.

"That's why Milo went to talk to Dr. Yang," she said. "He was going to offer her information about her family in exchange for information about who I was, what they want from me." She blinked, her eyes pricking. "This is my fault, isn't it?"

"Yes," Rico snapped. "And if we don't do the swap, they'll kill Milo and then nuke Trakis Two."

She had to save Milo. "I'll give myself up. I was going back anyway. I was always going back." But she didn't want to. And now the last of her loyalty to Dr. Yang drained away. Nothing justified torture. Everything was messed up and she was going to lose Milo. But she'd be damned if he was going to die because of her. She *would* save him.

"Very noble of you," Rico said. "Unfortunately, I don't think it will be that easy. I don't trust that bastard Kinross not to keep Milo anyway and use him as a hostage against us, and that's not happening. He also hinted that he knew more about us than he was letting on. Which is bad news. For him."

"I'm going to rip his fucking head off," Dylan growled.

"Get in line."

"So what do we do?" Destiny said. "How do we get him back? We have to save him. He's hurt."

"Aw, she actually cares."

She glared at the screen. "Of course I care. Don't you?"

He pursed his lips. "I care. But if we want to get him out, we need to keep emotions out of this. And your boyfriend's tough. He's not going to die from a beating."

But she couldn't bear to think about him hurting. Alone, believing no one was coming to help him. She took a deep breath. Rico was right; she had to focus. They'd already proved they were treacherous. If she just gave herself up, then there was no guarantee they would let Milo go.

She could contact Dr. Yang and tell her that she would come back but only if Milo was released. How could she force them to do that?

Could she threaten to kill herself, hold a pistol to her head until Milo was away? But would they believe her? Would she actually do it? There had to be a better way. *Think!*

"We arrange to meet them in the forest," she said. "Dylan

can hide somewhere close by. He keeps a weapon trained on me. One of those with the red dots, and he tells them he'll shoot me if they make a move against Milo."

"Might work," Rico said. "If you set it up right. And select the right location. But are you really ready to give yourself up to them?"

"Dr. Yang won't hurt me." But did she really believe that?

"Milo will be pissed," Dylan said.

Would he? Did he care?

She hoped so. And she believed so. Not least because he would hopefully not let them nuke the whole planet if Destiny was still here. She could do that for humanity if nothing else.

"I'll contact Dr. Yang," she said.

"I'll start scoping out possible sites," Dylan added.

Rico grinned. "At least it's not boring. I'm on my way. See you soon, children."

Beside her, Dylan blew out his breath. "The shit is about to hit the fan. Kinross doesn't know what's heading his way."

"Neither do I," Destiny said. "Should I be worried?"

The glance he gave her held more than a hint of pity. "Hell, yes."

• • •

The metallic stench of blood hung on the air.

Keeping her mind as blank as she could, Elvira checked Milo's vital statistics. His head hung to his chest, but his pulse was strong, heartbeat and blood pressure normal. It was unbelievable considering…

As soon as she could, Elvira tuned away from the unconscious man and retreated to the far corner of the room. She wanted away from this place so much it was a physical pain in her chest. But Luther had ordered her to stay—probably because he could see how badly she wanted out. He had a cruel streak and an eye for a person's weakness.

"He's not going to break," Silas said, his tone reasonable.

"Everyone breaks," Luther snapped. "You just haven't found his weakness yet."

Silas shook his head. "Some people just get more stubborn. We'll lose him if we push much harder." He gave a shrug. "Maybe that doesn't matter. You were willing to blow him up in the shuttle."

"That was before we knew he had the woman." Luther jumped to his feet and paced the room. "Do whatever you need but break him."

Luther's color was high. He needed to sit down, relax. Right now, he was stable, but Elvira had no clue how long that would last.

The sick feeling in her stomach was a constant companion. She had no doubt that he'd told the truth—she'd seen enough evidence that his influence extended far beyond Trakis Four—and if he died, then her daughters were as good as dead as well. When Milo had contacted her, she'd considered going along with him, giving him what he wanted, but not for long. She didn't believe he could keep her family safe from Luther. She just couldn't risk it.

Her only hope was to find Destiny. At least now, they knew she was still alive. Or had been yesterday. How had she ended up wherever it was she was hiding? In the company of the representatives from Trakis Two, who as far as she was aware, Destiny had never even spoken to. Her mind flashed back to that morning Destiny had gone out with Silas. They'd encountered Milo. Had there been a connection?

They had people and drones searching the forests on the other side of the lake, but so far there was no sign of either Destiny or the other representative from Trakis Two.

And Milo hadn't spoken. Despite what they had done to him.

She'd known Luther was ruthless, but she could have done without seeing the evidence for herself. She wasn't sure how Milo had survived this long.

"Wake him up," Luther said, and she realized he was talking to her.

Her heart sank and she swallowed the bitter taste in her mouth. "It's dangerous. I don't think he—"

"I don't care what you think. Wake him up."

Her hands trembled as she filled the syringe. Just get through this, and she could put it all behind her. Once her daughters were with her safe, she could forget the things she had done to get them there. They were innocent and they were worth it. But a little voice whispered that maybe nothing was worth this, and while she had no religious beliefs, she suspected that if she had a soul, it was damned.

As she approached the unconscious man, he slowly raised his head. His eyes glittered silver behind his swollen lids, filled with a dark malevolence that sent ice trickling through her veins. She licked her dry lips and cleared her throat. "He's already awake," she said, backing off.

"He's a tough fucking bastard." Silas sighed.

She had an idea that he was as eager for this to end as she was, but his loyalty to Luther was firm.

As she turned away, the comm unit on her wrist beeped. She glanced down. The caller ID was unknown, but she swiped her finger to accept.

"Dr. Yang?"

Dear lord, it was Destiny. She closed her eyes for a moment and took a deep breath. Said a silent prayer to a god she didn't believe in. Everyone in the room had gone still, all attention focused on her. Including Milo and she avoided his glittering stare. "Destiny, where are you?"

"Is Milo alive?"

Her glance flickered to the bound man. He was leaning

forward in the chair listening. "He's alive."

"I want proof."

Kinross strode across and grabbed her wrist, spoke into the comm unit. "Come back right now, and he might just live. Stay away, and he's dead before the day is out."

"I want proof."

He gritted his teeth, then dropped her wrist and waved his hand toward Milo. "Give it to her."

She crossed the room and held the comm unit in front of his face.

"Destiny?"

"Milo? Are you all right? Have they hurt you? Sorry, stupid question, but I'm going to get you out of there."

He cleared his throat then spat blood onto Elvira's boots. "Destiny. This is an order. Do not fucking give yourself up."

"You don't give me orders."

"You can't trust them. I'm not worth it. Stay the fuck away."

Kinross made a cutting motion with his hand, and Elvira spoke into the comm unit. "Come home, Destiny. I love you. Just come home."

Milo made a snorting sound and cast her a burning look of such utter contempt that she took an instinctive step back.

"I want to speak to Mr. Kinross," Destiny said.

Luther moved closer. "Yes," he snapped.

"Here's how it's going to work, Mr. Kinross."

Chapter Thirty-Five

"There are two ways of seeing: with the body and with the soul. The body's sight can sometimes forget, but the soul remembers forever."
—Alexandre Dumas, *The Count of Monte Cristo*

"You know he's going to be super pissed," Dylan said.

Destiny wrapped her arms around her waist. The night was warm, but she shivered.

"And there's a good chance he's not going to cooperate once he realizes you're staying behind."

She'd been staring into the shadowy forest, but now she turned to look at him and frowned. He leaned against the trunk of a tallish tree, but the set of his shoulders was tense, and his hands fisted at the side. Not a happy wolf. "It's your job to get him away from here," she said.

She'd always known she was going back. At the start, she'd believed that it would be a conscious decision; she would go back because she wanted to. Because it was the right thing to do, the honorable thing to do. For the good of humanity.

They had tortured Milo.

There was no good in that. She hadn't realized she had the capacity for hate, but she hated this Luther Kinross with every cell in her body. And Silas, who she'd thought was so nice. She was clearly a crap judge of character. And Dr. Yang. That hurt the most. Dr. Yang had said she loved her, but Destiny knew the words were just smoke. Insubstantial. Dr. Yang had never loved her.

All the same, she would go with them, because they hadn't been able to come up with a way to get Milo back safe *and* for her to keep her freedom.

She didn't think they would harm her. After all, she was important. She could hear the sarcasm even in her thoughts.

There was also another thing to consider. She might hate a few people right now, but she couldn't bear the thought that Rico would set off a nuclear bomb that would destroy the whole planet. There were innocent people here. Thousands of them. Children and babies. And while he might not love her, she thought Milo, and even Dylan, had come to care for her a little. If they left her behind, then they might think twice about blowing her up. There were alternatives. Rico had sent all the information he could find on nuclear bombs and Destiny was sure they could be disarmed permanently. Except, she wouldn't be there. So she had highlighted the relevant bits for Dylan.

But maybe she was just hunting for silver linings; Milo probably wouldn't think twice about nuking her.

Who knew? She might survive this and one day…

Best not to think of the future. Just get through the next few hours.

"They're here," Dylan said, straightening from where he leaned against the tree and coming to stand at her shoulder. "Are you ready?"

She couldn't hear anything, but she supposed that he

had better hearing than her. She swallowed then nodded and slipped her hand into her jacket pocket, wrapping her fingers around the cool metal of the grenade.

Where were they?

It was another minute before she heard them, the sound of a group crashing through the undergrowth. Then she caught the flicker of light through the trees. Dylan edged closer. He touched her arm. "Thank you," he said. "If we can get you back, we will."

She forced a smile, her eyes pricking, but she was aware he had bigger responsibilities than her. He'd told her a little about his pack through the hours they had waited for this meeting. How fabulous to be part of something like that. Though she suspected she had spent too much time alone to ever be truly comfortable in a group. She was more of a loner. Like Milo.

After what seemed like an age, they appeared. She held herself very still. Dr Yang was leading the way, Silas beside her. And behind them, two men in green jumpsuits half carried, half dragged an unconscious figure between them.

Dylan stiffened beside her and she could sense the menace pulsing from his body. She stared at Milo, hunting for some sign of life. Fear flashed through her, and she took an involuntary step forward. Dylan stopped her with a hand on her arm. "He's alive," he said. "Just unconscious. Maybe it's better this way."

But she'd wanted to say goodbye.

The guards released their hold and Milo collapsed to the forest floor, face down. Both guards drew their weapons and aimed them at her and Dylan.

"Take them both," Silas said. "You two—hands in the air."

Destiny searched his face for some sign of the friendly man she had met only days ago, but his expression was blank.

This was the final betrayal. They couldn't even keep to their word. The proof that they had no honor. Hatred coiled tighter inside her.

She turned her attention to Dr. Yang. "You promised you would let them go."

Dr. Yang gave a helpless shrug. "It's not up to me, Destiny. I'm sorry. But they'll be all right."

She cast the other woman a look of disbelief. "You tortured him."

Dr. Yang turned away. No help there. Not even a protestation of love. But in a way, she knew Dr. Yang had done this for love. Just not love of Destiny.

"Hands up," Silas said again.

She glanced at Dylan. He smiled. "Time to do your thing, Destiny."

She tightened her hand around the grenade as she slipped it from her pocket and pulled the pin, keeping it in place with her finger. She held her hand up in front of her, saw the moment Silas recognized what she held in her fist.

"You won't do it," he said. "We'll all die. Including your friends."

She studied him; he stood on the balls of his feet, ready to jump for her if she showed any sign of weakness. "They'll likely die anyway. I saw what you did to Milo." She kept her voice firm, although she was shaking inside. If she couldn't pull this off, then Milo would die and likely Dylan as well. She turned to Dr. Yang, stared into her dark eyes. "Sometimes you have to be willing to make sacrifices for the ones you love. I'll do it."

Dr. Yang stared back at her, then gave a small nod. "She will. Let them go. It's Destiny we need."

For a moment Destiny thought Silas would ignore the order, then he also gave a nod. "Stand down," he murmured to the two guards and they lowered their weapons.

Some of the tension oozed out of her, but she held herself upright, her gaze never wavering. She had to stay strong for a few more minutes to give Dylan time to get Milo away.

The guards holstered their weapons and Dylan left her side and crossed the clearing to where Milo lay unmoving. He hunkered down and then reached out with his hand and checked his pulse. He looked up at Destiny and nodded. She tightened her lips as her eyes pricked. If he was alive and safe, she could put up with anything.

"Tell him…" She shook her head. What was she supposed to say? She forced a smile. "Tell him good luck. And you, too."

"Stay strong, Destiny." But she didn't feel strong. She felt weak and pathetic. She watched as Dylan hauled Milo over his shoulder and disappeared into the forest without looking back.

She locked gazes with Silas, lifting the grenade a little higher. "Don't move," she said.

They needed five minutes to get away. Five times sixty seconds. She counted in her head.

Were they safe?

Somewhere deep in the forest, a wolf howled. That was the signal they'd agreed upon. Once he had Milo to safety.

Silas glanced up at the sound, his eyes narrowing on her. She kept her expression blank as she dropped her arm to her side, then slid the pin into the grenade. Silas approached her, held out his hand, and she placed the grenade gently in it. "You've changed," he said, searching her face.

"I know." She'd been so naive that day when she had met Silas—sure that the world was a decent place, full of decent people. So happy just to be out in the sunshine. It might have been better if she'd never left the cell, not gone with Milo that night, then she would never have known this terrible sense of loss.

"Turn around."

She turned and he patted her down, found her ereader in her back pocket and handed it to Dr. Yang.

"Hold out your arms," he said.

She clamped her lips together to stop the wobble and he fastened silver cuffs onto her wrists.

"Is that necessary?" Dr. Yang asked.

"Yes," he replied, not even looking at the other woman. "Come on, let's get the hell away from here. I don't trust those bastards."

"I gave him enough tranquilizer to drug a horse," Dr. Yang said. "He won't be waking up any time soon."

"I'll still be happier back at headquarters. Move." He waved a hand in the direction they had arrived from, and Destiny gave one last glance where Dylan and Milo had disappeared and started walking.

Dr. Yang fell in beside her. Destiny stared ahead.

"You've done the right thing, Destiny," Dr. Yang said.

"Have I?" Actually, they'd done the only thing they could think of to get Milo free. If she could have found another way then she wouldn't have come back. She'd seen what these people—including Dr. Yang—were like, the measures they would go to get what they wanted. They weren't moral people. Suddenly she needed to know. "Why?" she asked, turning sideways so she could see the other woman's face. "Why do you want me back? Who am I? Why am I so important?"

Dr. Yang's face took on the closed expression Destiny knew so well. "You'll know everything soon," she said. "You must be patient just a little while longer."

She gritted her teeth and stopped walking. "Why do I have to be patient? Why not now? Why can't you tell me now?"

Dr. Yang's mouth tightened, but then Silas poked her from behind. She turned around and snarled.

He grinned at her. "You've definitely changed. I like it."

She didn't care whether he liked it or not. He was the enemy. He'd tortured Milo. She hated him.

She swung back around and marched on. She could sense Dr. Yang beside her; the other woman wasn't happy. That was hardly Destiny's fault. If she didn't know the doctor better she would have said she felt guilty and maybe she did. She *should* feel guilty.

No one spoke again as they walked. They came out of the forest and she looked around. She couldn't believe how much the place had changed in the days she'd been gone. A new road cut a swath through the dock and beyond to the bulk of the *Trakis Four* and beside it, the blackened shape of the burned-out shuttle.

They walked along the road, past a new building. Under floodlights people still worked on the walls. She looked closer and saw that they were children. The first she had ever seen. Working under the supervision of more soldiers in green jumpsuits.

A brave new world.

She turned and looked at Silas with accusing eyes. "They're children," she said. "How could you?"

Something flickered in his eyes. Maybe he wasn't entirely happy with this, either. But not enough to do anything about it. In some ways that made him even worse. "Move."

This time she didn't take Silas's hand as she stepped into the boat. It would have been awkward anyway with the cuffs. She jumped lightly in and moved to the side, then stared straight ahead as they sped across the water. It was a beautiful night, starlight reflecting on dark water. How was Milo? Had he woken up yet? Was he just a little bit upset that she wasn't there? Part of her hoped so. But another part wanted him to be happy.

Soldiers stood to attention at the front of the building.

That was new. Maybe Kinross had some unhappy residents in his new colony. As they climbed the stairs, she glanced up. A figure stood in the window above her. She couldn't make out the details; the room was dark behind him. Was this Luther Kinross?

Then they were entering the building. Her heart sank as they headed across the hallway to the doorway that led down to the underground. Her eyes pricked, but she blinked away the tears.

The walls seemed to close in on her. But she kept her head held high. She wouldn't give them the satisfaction. They put her in the same cell.

She stood in the center of the room while Silas unfastened the cuffs. She just had to hold it together until they were gone.

Finally, they turned away, but at the last moment, Dr. Yang came back and pressed the ereader into Destiny's hands. "I'm sorry."

Then she was gone, and the door clicked shut behind them. And Destiny was alone.

I have a role to play. I'm special. Important.

I'm not a prisoner. They're just keeping me safe.

Chapter Thirty-Six

"Hatred is blind; rage carries you away; and he who pours out vengeance runs the risk of tasting a bitter draught."
—Alexandre Dumas, *The Count of Monte Cristo*

Everything hurt.

Milo wasn't sure he wanted to actually wake up. At the same time, he had this nagging feeling that there was something important he needed to do.

He pried his eyes open and tried to work out—without actually moving anything—where he was. Nope. No clue. He closed them again.

"Wakey, wakey," an annoyingly cheerful voice said. "I've checked you over, and while you look like shit, there's nothing seriously wrong with you."

Somehow, he doubted that was true. He distinctly remembered the crack of breaking bones. And his hand was one throbbing lump of pain.

"Well, apart from a couple of broken ribs, a broken nose, and three snapped fingers. But you'll recover."

"Piss off," he murmured. He exhaled, opened his eyes, and tried to sit up. The first attempt was a total failure, his body just didn't respond to the commands of his brain. He gritted his teeth and forced himself to turn his head in the direction of the voice. Dylan was seated on a chair beside the bed. "Fuck."

"Welcome back," Dylan said with a grin. "I thought we'd lost you there. And that would have been a real pity, considering."

He thought about asking "considering what?" But maybe he didn't want to know. Then he thought about sitting up and decided he didn't want to attempt it again just yet. Because he'd hate to look like a complete wimp in front of Dylan.

"Destiny?"

"At a guess, back in her old quarters underneath Camelot."

"Fuck." He might as well have told the fuckers where she was and saved himself a hell of a lot of pain.

"Aw, it was sweet really. She cares about you, and I'm betting that doesn't happen a lot."

"We have to get her back."

"No. We don't have to do anything. But if you're nice to me, then I might help you get her back anyway. Because I like her." He rubbed his chin as if contemplating what to say next. "But perhaps you should consider the idea that she's safer where she is. She's obviously important to them. She might be better off there."

"Why?"

Dylan frowned. "Why what?"

"Why is she important to them? We still have no clue, and I don't fucking like it."

"How bad can it be?"

The truth was he had no idea. But he imagined pretty bad. They were evil people. He wouldn't leave her with them.

"She saved my life. We get her back."

Dylan pursed his lips and then nodded. "Okay. We get her back. But right now, you need to heal, or you'll be no good to anyone."

"My wand?"

"Lost. Actually, I presume Kinross has it. But hopefully, he won't have a clue what to do with it."

"Damn." He might have been able to heal the broken bones with his wand. He was powerless without it. "How long have I been out?"

"You've been unconscious twenty-eight hours."

Jesus, anything could have happened in that time. He tried to push himself up, but pain shot from his hand up his arm and it collapsed under him.

"Just relax," Dylan snapped. "You're no good to anybody like this." He stood up, hands in his pockets. "Rico will be here soon."

"Great," he muttered. As long as the vampire didn't stand in Milo's way.

"I thought you'd be pleased."

"How long?"

"He'll be arriving in orbit any moment. I'm going to meet him, bring him back here. You rest. Then we'll work out a plan. And we'll get her back." He picked up a glass from the table beside the bed. "Here, drink this."

"What is it?"

"Painkillers."

That sounded like a really good idea right now.

He closed his eyes as Dylan left the room. Maybe she didn't want to be with him. After all, right from the start, she'd told him that she planned to go back. To do her duty. Maybe he should just leave her there.

But part of him knew he was being unfair. She'd changed beyond belief, even in a few days. She had grown. Started to question everything about her world. She would no longer walk in blindly and do her "duty."

She'd given herself up to save him. And he hadn't even had the guts to tell her he cared. And now, he had a really bad feeling that he wasn't going to get the chance. And what would he say anyway?

He was suddenly filled with a sense of urgency. He had to go get her. He tried to get up, pushing through the pain and rising on his elbows. But the strength went out of him and he collapsed back on the bed. His brain was filling with mist, clouding, going dark.

When he opened his eyes again, he had no idea how much time had passed. Except he felt better, so probably a considerable amount.

He glanced at the empty glass on the table, then rolled his head to the side and found Dylan standing over him. A slow growl trickled from Milo's mouth. "You fucking drugged me."

"Admit it," Dylan said. "If I hadn't drugged you, you would have tried to go after her, and now you would be dead."

He couldn't deny it—that had been his plan. So he kept quiet.

"And then you know what," Dylan said, "I would be dead. And not only that, but the rest of my pack as well. Because that's what your *Uncle* Rico told me when we headed off on this little adventure together. Bring you back alive, or we all pay the price."

Milo's gaze flicked from Dylan to the man behind him. Rico shrugged. "What can I say? I promised your mother." Rico pulled something from his boot and handed it to Milo. "Here. You look like shit. Maybe this will help."

Milo took the wand and felt the strength and power flow through him. He closed his eyes and channeled that power through his blood, along his nerves, felt the bones knit together and the pain recede.

He opened his eyes, everything looked clearer.

Pushing himself up, he swung his legs over the side of the bed and sat for a moment taking stock. "I'm hungry."

"I brought food from the shuttle," Dylan said, handing him a bag.

He opened it, pulled out a bread roll, and bit into it. His brain was sharper now, and he searched his mind for the best way forward.

He was guessing that if Destiny was back in the cells beneath Camelot, then this time she would be well guarded. There were only three of them. Kinross had an army. But he figured the three of them were an even match for an army if they played it right. He just wasn't sure the others would agree.

How far could he rely on Rico for help?

The vampire had come for him. He could have just left them to their fate. But while Rico was ruthless, he rewarded loyalty. And deep down he had always known that Rico cared. Yes, he had taken him on from a sense of responsibility. He had totally failed his wife, hadn't even been there when the Inquisition had come for her. She had already been dead by the time he had returned. Reduced to nothing but ashes. So he'd taken Milo, his wife's sister's child, from a sense of guilt.

But he'd come to care. Even when he'd handed Milo over to his father, it had been because he could see no other way forward. Milo would have destroyed himself and probably everyone around him. Milo hadn't seen it like that at the time, but now with a few centuries' hindsight he could understand that it had been the only route to take. Without those years training with his father, he likely wouldn't have survived.

Rico cared for him. Milo needed to play on that. Because the vampire felt nothing for Destiny.

Somehow Milo had to make him believe that saving Destiny was the only option. He could go down the "I care for her" route. Or he could go on the offensive. He'd try the latter first.

"This is all your fucking fault," he said, glaring at Rico.

Rico raised a brow. "And how do you work that out?"

"You suggested we nuke the whole planet."

"So." He gave a casual shrug. "It's a perfectly valid solution to the problem."

"Only if you're an asshole. Destiny grew up believing it was her destiny to save the human race. She gave herself up because you suggested we blow up a big portion of what's left. So I would guess she doesn't agree with the valid-solution thing."

"How does giving herself up have any effect on that?"

"She thinks if she's here, then maybe I won't let you nuke the planet."

Rico folded his arms across his chest. "Let's pretend for the moment that you could actually stop me if I wanted to—is she right?"

"Hell, yes. I wouldn't do it anyway. Not even to kill Kinross. But I guess she doesn't know me that well."

Rico sighed. Loudly. He sat down on the chair by the bed, his long legs stretched out in front of him, and scowled. "So what do we do next?"

Milo considered the options. There weren't many. The one thing he did have on his side was that Dr. Yang believed her family was alive and that Kinross could give them back to her. Milo was about to tell her that wouldn't happen. That her family was dead, and that Kinross was responsible. At that point, any loyalty she felt to Kinross would evaporate.

She could confirm where Destiny was and maybe even

get them in.

"I get her out. We disarm the nukes. We kill Kinross and anyone else who gets in our way. And we get the hell off this shit planet."

Rico gave a lazy smile, revealing the tip of one sharp, white fang. "Sounds like a plan."

. . .

Elvira tried to keep her mind totally blank as she cleared up her laboratory on the *Trakis Four*. Soon she would be free to leave, but she was finding it harder and harder to keep the doubts from crowding her thoughts.

Destiny's face kept flashing before her mind.

Her expression as they'd left her in the cell.

She couldn't believe the change that had taken place in only a few days. Despite the fact that she'd always known Destiny's IQ was off the charts, she always came across as innocent, naive, and that had made it far easier to treat her as something…less. Now that was impossible.

The fact was she was more. More intelligent, stronger, faster. Superior in just about every way.

She cleared her mind and forced herself to concentrate on her daughters, making their faces superimpose on the image of Destiny. Just keep the endgame in mind.

Once she had her daughters back, then she would request a transfer to one of the other planets. She would move far away from here so she would never have to see Kinross again. And she would forget.

All the same, her eyes pricked, and she blinked as she worked automatically. At least she wasn't doing the operation—it wasn't her specialty. She wasn't sure she could have done it.

Just as she was finishing up, her comm unit buzzed. She

glanced down but the caller ID was blank. She considered ignoring it; she couldn't think of anyone she wanted to talk to. But in the end, she swiped a finger over the screen to accept the call.

"Dr. Yang?" At first, she didn't recognize the voice. Then she realized it was Milo. What could he want? She nearly ended the call, but he preempted her.

"I have important information for you about your family."

She went still. Was he going to threaten her daughters? Would he harm them if she didn't help him? What did he want?

But perhaps Milo could get her family to safety. Out of range of Kinross's men. She realized that the hope had been hovering in the back of her mind. That maybe she could contact him, tell him she would—what? Help him in some way if he would promise the safety of her family?

The problem was she didn't think she could get Destiny out. She was too well guarded now. So if that was what he wanted, then she couldn't help him. And then what?

God, how did things get so complicated?

"What information?" There was a wobble in her voice that she couldn't eliminate. "Tell me you won't harm them. I only did what I did to keep them safe. Luther said he would—" She broke off, unable to put it into words.

"Your daughters are dead."

For a moment the words didn't make any sense. She scrambled to get her brain to work. "You killed my family?" They couldn't be dead. She wouldn't believe it. It was a mistake. Why would they? It made no sense.

"*I* didn't kill them. They never made it onto the *Trakis Two.*"

Her legs were shaking, and she sank down onto the chair behind her. "I don't understand."

"It's quite simple. Luther Kinross stole your children's

cryotubes, along with those of most crew member families, and filled them with his own men."

"I don't believe you."

"Where do you think Luther Kinross got his army from? All the crew families on the *Trakis Two* have been replaced, and I imagine it's the same on the other ships."

Her mind was refusing to accept the information. "My daughters…"

"Never left Earth. I'm sorry."

A scream was rising inside her. She couldn't focus; black spots danced in front of her eyes. Her head felt light, and she swayed on the chair and then crashed to the floor.

When Elvira came to, she had no clue how long she had been out. It didn't matter. The comm unit was silent.

Kinross had lied to her all this time. She had no doubt he was capable of it. Had she believed she was so important to him that she was exempt from his ruthlessness?

Yes.

How could he get away with it? The only way was if the old crews were never woken from cryo. That would be no loss as far as Kinross was concerned. Most of the crew members were old, too old to be of any use.

And what did he plan to do to her once she had completed what she had been brought along to do?

She doubted she would survive much longer.

What had happened to her daughters? Had they really been left back on Earth? But she knew that Kinross couldn't have risked leaving anyone alive. The ships had still been in contact with Earth for a number of years. If Luther had left them alive, then there was a good chance his actions would have been uncovered and the information sent to the fleet.

So he'd murdered her daughters. They'd been dead for five hundred years. Had they suffered?

Was there any chance that Milo had lied? Except she couldn't think why. If her family had been alive, he could have used them to force her hand. If they were dead, how did he benefit by telling her? Perhaps he just meant to turn her against Luther.

She forced herself to breathe slowly, to push down the panic.

First, she needed proof.

She heaved herself up from the floor. Her hands were shaking. Swallowing, she steadied herself and then crossed to the computer terminal. She lowered her head to the retinal scan and the screen flared to life. She worked quickly, accessing the ship's backup files. She flicked through the cryotube records, filtered them for crew family, then found what she needed.

The family of the second-in-command of the *Trakis Three*, fourth rotation, consisted of his wife and two sons aged five and six. She took a note of the numbers and then hurried out.

She tried to work out how many men Luther had. She figured around fifty. That would mean the vast majority were still in cryo. Each ship must carry around nine hundred crew family. She headed to the cryotube chamber.

While she had no religious beliefs, as she walked the rows of tubes, glancing at the faces, she said a silent prayer. She wanted so badly to find the little boys sleeping peacefully. That would at least give her some hope that her daughters might still be alive. That Milo had been lying for whatever reasons.

She counted off the numbers, her feet slowing as she got close. She had to force herself to look down at the tube that should have contained five-year-old Benjamin Peters.

Something broke inside her as she stared at the figure inside the cryotube. It was no five-year-old boy but a fully grown male. Perhaps the numbers were wrong. Perhaps the boy was in a different tube. But she knew she was fooling herself, and a sob caught in her throat.

She leaned against the cryotube, as everything she had worked toward crumbled and disintegrated, leaving her broken and empty.

They were dead. All dead. And had been for centuries.

As she accepted it, a rage started to build inside her. She'd done everything he asked, and he'd killed her babies.

She would make him pay. For a second, she considered contacting Milo. She presumed that he wanted to get Destiny out, and she could help with that. But she couldn't be sure that Luther wouldn't get her back. He had the resources. Hundreds of loyal men at his disposal. At the thought, a new wave of rage washed through her, filling the emptiness.

He would die for this. A slow death, and every minute of it he would know exactly why.

She headed back to her lab, searched for something she could use as a weapon. She found a knife, with a long blade and slid it down her boot where it wouldn't be seen.

Then she headed off the ship. A boat was leaving the dock as she approached and she got a lift, staring straight ahead as the small vessel crossed the water. There were guards on the door, but they let her through without a word. They knew her well. Another guard stood at the doorway to the underground passages, he nodded and held the door open for her.

Once through she paused a moment, slowing her breathing.

Then she headed to Destiny's cell.

Chapter Thirty-Seven

*"The heart breaks when it has swelled too much in the warm
breath of hope, then finds itself enclosed in cold reality."*
—Alexandre Dumas, *The Count of Monte Cristo*

Destiny sat on the small cot bed, her arms wrapped around
her knees, chin resting on her hands. She'd just finished
reading *The Count of Monte Cristo* again, searching for
comfort in the familiar words, and was contemplating how
long it would take her to tunnel her way out of her cell. Too
long, at a guess. Could she pretend to be dead and they would
take out her body and…?

Probably with her luck she'd end up buried alive. Or
cremated.

She just wished she knew what was happening. And
whether Milo was okay. He hadn't looked okay.

She was filled with a sense of longing, just to see him.
Okay, to touch him as well. Would she ever see him again?
They still had to disarm the nuclear warheads. Maybe right
now he was close by.

That was unless Rico had persuaded him to blow up the whole planet. But she didn't think Milo would do that. He wasn't a bad...person. She wouldn't fall in love with a bad person. She had far too much taste. There, she'd admitted it to herself. She loved him. She loved Milo.

And it hurt. So bad.

The lock clicked, and she jumped to her feet.

At last something was happening. The door opened and Dr. Yang stood there. She stared at Destiny for what seemed like a long time, and Destiny could feel a frown forming between her eyes. "What is it?"

Dr. Yang ignored the question as she stepped into the cell. She turned abruptly. "You can go," she snapped at the guard who had followed her inside. Her voice sounded strange. Different, sort of jagged as though she'd swallowed something sharp.

"I'm not supposed to leave the prisoner alone with anyone, ma'am."

They were calling her a prisoner now—Destiny couldn't even give herself the illusion that this was for her own safety anymore.

"I hardly think that refers to me," Dr. Yang said. "I'm her doctor. I'm here to do an examination." She shrugged. "Check with your boss but give us some privacy while you do it."

He looked a little uncertain. Dr. Yang glared, and he gave a nod. "I'll be just outside the door. Call if you need me."

Did they think she was going to attack Dr. Yang? Though, she had threatened them with a grenade. Maybe they thought she was dangerous. She quite liked the idea.

Something was definitely wrong. Dr. Yang had never been a relaxed person, but right now, she looked as though she might shatter at any moment. Every muscle locked tight. Her face completely devoid of expression.

Destiny took a step forward and reached out, then let her hand drop to her side. Dr. Yang would not appreciate the gesture. "What's happened?" she asked.

Clearly something had.

Her jaw clenched and her eyes narrowed, and Destiny realized that she'd been wrong. There was a whole load of emotion there. Dr. Yang was angry. It burned in her eyes.

She swallowed, suddenly nervous, though she didn't know why.

Dr. Yang bent down and pulled something from her boot. The silver of a blade glinted in her hand.

"I have to do this," Dr. Yang said. "You understand that, don't you?"

No, she didn't understand anything. Her gaze fixed on the knife. Unblinking. "Why?"

"He killed them. He killed my babies."

Oh God, she'd found out that her daughters were dead. But that didn't explain why she was here, brandishing a knife at Destiny. She hadn't killed Dr. Yang's babies. And she couldn't see how Dr. Yang could blame her. She hadn't even been born when they had died.

"He has to suffer. I have to take what he needs most."

She wasn't making a lot of sense. Suddenly, the other woman lunged forward, her arm raised, the blade aiming for Destiny's heart.

She put up her arms to protect herself, shock slowing her down.

At the last moment she kicked out, catching Dr. Yang in the stomach, but she didn't seem to even feel the blow. She backed away. And Dr. Yang kept coming. Destiny warded her off with her arms, but she seemed to possess inhuman strength. The tip of the blade touched her just above her heart, and she went still.

"Why?"

Then behind her, the door flew open, and two men rushed in. They grabbed Dr. Yang from behind and ripped her away. She screamed as she was dragged backward, fury possessing her, her eyes wild.

Destiny rubbed at her chest. The tip of the knife had drawn blood and she stared at her hand.

She'd accepted that Dr. Yang didn't love her, but this? It was beyond reason. She shook her head. They had the doctor cuffed now and she was hanging from the guards' hold, sobbing.

A third man entered the cell, and Destiny recognized Silas. He wasn't smiling. "It's time to go," he said. He wouldn't look her in the face, and a sick feeling roiled in her stomach.

"Go where?"

"It doesn't matter. Turn around."

"Why?"

"Don't ask questions, Destiny. Do as you're told, and this will go easier."

She didn't want to do as she was told. She wanted to know what was happening. She wanted to know why Dr. Yang had tried to kill her and why Silas wouldn't look her in the eyes.

"Turn around," he snapped.

"Please tell me what's happening."

"Why don't you tell her, Silas?"

Destiny glanced around as Dr. Yang spoke. Her words dripped with venom, but as she opened her mouth to say more, one of the guards shoved a gag into it, and she just glared her hatred.

Silas grabbed her hands and pulled them behind her back, and Destiny felt the cool metal of cuffs against her wrists. She wanted to fight, but she'd already spotted two more guards outside the door. No way could she win this. She had no choice but to go where they took her.

And she didn't want to.

She was scared. Fear was like a live thing writhing inside her. She wanted Milo with a desperation she hadn't believed possible. Just to see his beautiful face one more time.

She clamped her lips together to stop herself from begging, because she knew it would have no more effect now than it had with Dr. Yang. Silas clearly wasn't happy with what he was doing, but she had no doubt he would see it through and nothing she could say would deter him. Kinross had too strong of a hold on all of them.

Silas took hold of her elbow and guided her out of the cell. She glanced back over her shoulder and caught Dr. Yang's gaze. The anger had faded to be replaced by sadness and despair.

Then Destiny was led away. She'd wanted out of that cell so badly, but now she would do anything to be locked up safe inside.

Silas led her along the corridor, then up the stairs and across the hallway to a set of metal doors. He pressed his palm to the panel, and they slid open to reveal a small metal room. He ushered her inside, the guards following, and the door slid closed. Then they were rising. They were in an elevator.

It only took a few seconds, and then it stopped and the doors opened. In front of them was another set of double doors with a sign on the door. Medical center.

That couldn't be so bad, could it? They were maybe going to do some tests on her. Dr. Yang had done a lot of tests. Some unpleasant, but none had done her any harm. The only problem was she didn't believe it. Because the world was going crazy. Dr. Yang had tried to kill her, and Silas wouldn't look at her or talk to her or tell her anything.

She stood still; her feet locked in place until someone pushed her from behind. She was going through those doors one way or another. She held her head up high and cast Silas a look of scorn.

The doors led into a corridor, they passed other doors but continued on until they reached the end and a final door. Silas rapped on the metal and it opened from the inside.

A dark-skinned man stood there in pale blue medical scrubs, a mask on his face.

Silas was unlocking the cuffs from one wrist. He refastened them in front of her and then gave her a push forward toward the other man.

"I'm Dr. Michaels," he said, his voice muffled through the mask. "I'll be performing your procedure today. Come this way."

She didn't want to. She looked back at Silas.

"I'm sorry," he said. Then he turned and was gone.

The two guards remained in place. She didn't have anywhere to go. "What procedure?" she asked, but the doctor had already turned away. She peered down the corridor, but one of the guards drew his weapon and pointed at the door, and she took the last steps through.

At least she might find out what this was all about.

Inside was some sort of reception room. Two more men in scrubs approached her, and before she could move, one took her arm and the other stabbed her with a needle, injecting something.

For a few seconds she felt nothing, then a fog crept over her brain, dulling her senses. From then on, the world took on a distant feel as though she were outside her body looking on.

They undressed her, then put on a pale blue gown that tied at the front before leading her through another door into a bigger room. There were two gurneys, and a lot of equipment. She knew what this was, but her brain wouldn't cooperate and come up with the word.

A man lay on one of the gurneys. He was already anesthetized. His eyes closed, a breathing mask over his face. Dr. Michaels leaned over him, doing something with the needle leading into his arm. He didn't look up as Destiny came in.

They led her to the second gurney and pushed her down, straightened her limbs. She wanted to get up and run, but she didn't think she could even if they would let her.

Then Dr. Michaels was leaning over her. "Count backwards from ten," he said.

And the word came to her. She was in an operating theater. They were going to operate on her.

Then it was too late to think anymore. She breathed in and the gas flooded her mind and the darkness closed in. Then nothing.

Chapter Thirty-Eight

"I can assure you of one thing, — the more men you see die, the easier it becomes to die yourself; and in my opinion, death may be a torture, but it is not an expiration."
—Alexandre Dumas, *The Count of Monte Cristo*

"Dr. Yang?"

Where the hell was the woman? The comm link was still open, but she wasn't answering.

"Dr. Yang?" Milo could sense the panic rising inside him and he didn't know why. There was no reason to believe they would harm Destiny, so why couldn't he shake the sense of foreboding?

"What's happening?" Rico appeared in the doorway, a bottle of whiskey dangling from one hand. He wandered into the room and sprawled on a chair. "Did you get hold of this doctor?"

"She was there and now she's fucking gone. Or not answering."

"You told her?" Dylan asked, coming in behind Rico.

"Yeah, I told her."

"She understood what you were saying?"

"Of course she fucking understood." He took a deep breath and forced his mind to calm down. But that sense of foreboding sat in his belly like a weight.

"We need to move," Rico said. "We have a limited time frame here, and it's running out."

"We can't go without Destiny."

Rico studied him through narrowed eyes, and Milo resisted the urge to snarl or hurl a fire bolt at the smug bastard vampire. He took another deep breath. "She gave herself up for me." Rico understood loyalty and paying debts.

"*Mierda*," Rico said, shaking his head. "This is a really bad time to fall in love."

Milo did snarl then. He did not need lecturing about love from a fucking cold-hearted vampire. Rico had never been in love. He hadn't loved his wife—that was what had made him feel so guilty about her death. He hadn't been there for her. But Milo doubted that argument would get him very far. "I have not fallen in love. I don't believe in love." Even as he said the words, he sensed the lie. He believed in love, he always had, he'd just decided that he would never give in to it again because it always ended badly.

But he cared about Destiny; he had almost from the start. She pulled at something deep inside him, something he'd believed lost centuries ago. She made him believe he could be a good person. Just like Maria. "She saved my life. I owe her. That's all it is." Dylan snorted, and Milo swung around to face the werewolf. "She saved your life as well. You owe her, too."

"She always said she was going back. They're her people. Likely, she's not in any real danger."

Milo cast him a look of disbelief. "Do you believe that?"

Dylan held his gaze for a few seconds and then looked

away. "No. I don't know what they want with her—and I've racked my brains thinking what it could be—but I don't think it's anything good." He blew out his breath. "So how do we do this?"

Milo turned away and paced the room. He was going in anyway, but it would be much easier with the doctor's help. Right now, they didn't even know where Destiny was. He was presuming she was back in the cells below Camelot, but he would have liked confirmation. Dr. Yang could also give them information on the number and position of the guards. Help them from the inside.

"How much time do we have?"

"We have a twenty-four-hour window. After that, the shuttle won't get us back."

He had an urge to move quickly, a niggling doubt that poked and prodded and told him if he didn't go now, he would be too late. But he had to temper that urgency with patience. Destiny's life depended on this. If he barged in there, she could die. She could die anyway. Hell, she could already be dead.

He turned back to the others. "One hour," he said. "We'll give the doctor one more hour, and then we're going in."

"Hey, who's captain here?" Rico asked.

"Of this particular ship—not you," Milo replied. If anyone was captain of this ship, it was Destiny. She'd discovered it, she'd got it functioning...sort of. "Dylan, you keep trying to get hold of the doctor."

"And what will you be doing?"

"Mind your own business." He stalked out of the room and headed for the bridge. He needed to be alone. And this was where he felt closest to Destiny. His bag was here; he pulled out his scrying bowl and filled it with water to form a shallow pool. Then he placed the bowl on the floor and sat cross-legged in front of it.

He gazed into the dark water, focused on an image of Destiny in his mind.

Show me.

For a moment nothing happened. He closed his eyes, pictured Destiny as she had looked lying beneath him in the forest, under the stars, after they'd made love. The look of wonder in her expression. He opened his eyes and concentrated on the water. An image formed.

Destiny's face appeared. Her eyes were closed. But she was sleeping, not dead. He tried to widen the picture, to get an idea of where she lay, but it was already wavering, and then it was gone.

At least she was alive. And it didn't look as though they had hurt her in any way.

He sat for a moment. Then he closed his eyes and concentrated on an image of Dr. Yang. When he opened his eyes, she was there, reflected in the water.

She was gagged and cuffed and lay on her side on a narrow cot. Her eyes were open, and she was staring straight ahead. Had she confronted Kinross with what Milo had told her about her family? Had Kinross had her arrested? It seemed the most likely explanation—after all, he would hardly want that information out in public. There were going to be some very unhappy people. Either way, Dr. Yang was going to be of no help to Milo.

He waved a hand over the water and the image shimmered and then disappeared.

He pushed himself to his feet. There was no point in waiting now. He might as well go in there. He would go through the tunnels and find out what he could, whether she was in her old cell, whether she was guarded. And then he'd risk magicking into the cell—he'd been there before, that always made it more accurate. He'd get Destiny and then they would go to the weapons store and neutralize that threat. Disarm the nukes and then maybe set the rest of the explosives in there to blow. Take out the whole fucking castle and Kinross in it.

There were guards everywhere in far greater numbers than Milo had previously seen. Had Kinross been waking up his sleeping army?

Two guards were stationed outside Destiny's cell, which at least meant she was likely inside. But he couldn't risk taking them out. If they got off any warning, then the place would be flooded by armed men very quickly. His best chance was to magic in and then take it from there.

He pulled his wand from his belt and whispered the spell, felt the shimmer of magic in the air, and then he was gone.

His first thought was that it had worked. His second that he had fucked up and was in the wrong cell. There was a woman on the cot, but it wasn't Destiny. Dr. Yang lay on her side just as he had seen her in the vision. She was gagged, her hands were cuffed behind her back, and her face was still, her eyes wide. Was she dead? Then she blinked.

He moved quickly, crossing to the narrow bed and tugging the gag from her mouth.

"Where's Destiny?" he asked.

She licked her lips. "How...?"

"It doesn't matter. Where the hell is Destiny?"

She sat up and turned around, presenting her cuffed wrists to him. He touched his wand to the cuffs, whispered a word, and they sprang open. She turned back, rubbing her wrists and eying the wand in his hand.

"Destiny?" he prompted.

She closed her eyes for a moment and took a deep breath. "You're too late."

Not happening. "Where the fuck is she?" He reached forward and shook her. "Tell me."

"She's upstairs, and right now, I would think they're cutting out her heart." She said the words with a total lack of expression, and they made no sense at all.

"Tell me what's happening. Now!"

"Luther Kinross has a weak heart. Actually, I suspect he doesn't have a heart at all. He brought me along on the trip to find him a cure. He promised me a future for my family if I could save his useless, worthless, treacherous life."

"So how does Destiny fit in? What has she got to do with Kinross?"

She gave him a pitying look. "Destiny is a clone. More precisely, a clone of Luther Kinross. The whole point of her existence is to provide spare parts for Luther."

The words still didn't make sense or maybe he didn't want them to. He latched on to a thought. "She can't be a clone of Kinross. She's a woman. He's a man. It isn't possible."

"It's quite possible. It just needs a little manipulation of the chromosomes." She gave a shrug. "I had plenty of time and for the first time in my life I had no limits on what I could attempt. I got creative."

"You cared for her, brought her up, and then handed her over to be slaughtered."

"I had to. I had no choice. It was the only way for my family to survive."

"They're operating now?"

"I believe so." She looked around at her surroundings. "Obviously, I'm a little out of the loop."

He couldn't be too late. He'd know if she was dead. Then he remembered the image in the scry. She'd been sleeping. Sleeping or anesthetized? His skin went cold, and a shiver ran through him. Panic awoke in his gut, twisting and clawing. He had to find her. He reached forward and grabbed Dr. Yang's arm, shook her. "Where is she?"

"Upstairs, but we'll be too late. Luther always gets what he wants."

"There has to be time."

She glanced at the comm unit on her wrist. "The operation is scheduled for five minutes. We won't make it."

"Then we have to stop it." There had to be a way to stop it. They were going to cut out her fucking heart and give it to that bastard Kinross. No fucking way. *Think.* "Where's the power supply?"

She glanced at him sharply. "At the rear of the building."

Now he remembered, he'd seen the generator house while he'd been doing a recce of the place that first night. To magic or not to magic? If the spell went wrong, then she would die. But he didn't have time to take out the guards. He'd never make it out of the tunnels.

Without giving himself time to think it was a really bad idea, he grabbed hold of Dr. Yang's arm, raised his wand, whispered a spell, and pictured where he needed to be. They reformed outside in the open air; night had fallen. Dr. Yang stumbled and he let her fall to the ground, as he pulled his pistol from his belt. There was a guard outside the generator house. He was staring at them, blinking. Milo shot him in the chest and then ran forward. The door was locked, and he shot at the lock and kicked the door open.

The room was filled with the hum of the machines. A man sat at the control console. He glanced around as Milo entered, and he shot him in the head.

He had no clue how to turn off the power, and he didn't have the time. He stood, legs braced, and blasted a continuous stream of bullets into the console. There was a small explosion and then the whole thing went up in flames. He shot some more, and all around him the hum of the generators went silent.

He ran to the door and looked out. The building was in darkness.

Dr. Yang was still huddled on the ground. He went across and dragged her to her feet. "Take me to her."

She tried to pull away and he tightened his grip.

"I don't know what's happening," she mumbled. "Who are you? *What* are you?"

"We don't have time for this. Where is Destiny?" He gave her a little shake. "Do you know?"

She licked her lips and then nodded. "She'll be in the medical center. It's on the third floor."

He pushed her in front of him. "Lead the way." This place was going to be swarming with guards any moment now, and he'd rather be gone before they got there. He needed to find Destiny. What if he was too late and they'd already started the operation? And he'd cut the power and she was lying cut open on an operating table.

He blanked the graphic picture from his mind. He'd taken a calculated risk. He had to believe she was still alive.

Already the sound of booted feet was approaching from the front of the building. He followed Dr. Yang in the opposite direction. She took him through a side door that led into a hallway and then through another doorway and into a stairwell. Inside, the darkness was complete, and he raised his wand and whispered a spell. Light flared from the tip.

She'd said the third floor. Without waiting for her to lead the way, he took the stairs two at a time. At the third floor, he found the medical center and he kicked open the door, then stood for a moment, deciding where to go. The sound of raised voices drifted down from a room at the far end and he hurried, pistol held out in front of him. Slowly, he pushed open the door. The small room inside was empty, but the voices were louder, and he crossed the room to a door in the far wall. Through the glass door he could see a dim light moving about.

He pushed open the door and raised his wand, taking in the room in a moment. Two gurneys. Three people were crowded around the closest. One of them held a torch, they were working frantically over a body. He saw immediately it was Kinross, and his heart stuttered as he forced his gaze to the other gurney, dreading what he might see.

Destiny lay on her back. She was clearly unconscious, and he forced his gaze down over her body. His legs almost gave way. They hadn't cut her open. She appeared to be in one piece, just a needle inserted into her arm, attached to an IV.

One of the men looked up. "You can't be here," he said. "This is a sterile room. You must leave."

"Fuck off," he growled.

At that moment, the lights flickered on. They must have got some sort of backup system up and running. Time to get out of there. He tucked his wand into his belt, kept his pistol in his hand, and crossed the short space to Destiny. Her hands were cuffed together in front of her. He pulled the needle from her arm and then scooped her up in his arms.

He passed close to the other gurney. Kinross. They were sewing him back up. At a guess they must have just cut him open when the lights went off. Maybe he should have waited a few minutes longer until they had cut out the bastard's heart. He aimed the pistol. No way could Kinross be allowed to live. But at that moment the door opened. He swung around, raising the pistol and aiming it at the man who stood in the doorway. Silas Wynch, and his gun was trained on Milo.

For a moment, they stared into each other's eyes. Milo's finger tightened on the trigger.

Then Silas lowered his weapon. "Get out of here."

Milo cast a last look at Kinross. There would be another time. Then he hurried from the room, past Silas. Dr Yang stood by the stairwell. "Is she alive?"

He nodded.

"I'm glad. I could have loved her, you know. If I'd let myself. But sometimes you have to make hard choices."

He didn't answer, because she was right. But it didn't make him hate her any the less. He supposed he would have to take her with him. Destiny wouldn't be happy if he left her behind, but he wished he could. Right now, they needed to get under cover, and he needed to wake her up, make sure she was okay. He held her tighter.

They didn't meet anyone on the stairs and at last they were out of the building and standing in the warm night air.

He could magic her back to the spaceship. Then come back here. But he was due to meet up with Rico and Dylan to deal with the explosives soon.

"We need somewhere safe, close by. Any ideas?"

"My laboratory on the *Trakis Four*." She thought for a moment. "I need to go there anyway. I want to destroy my work. I want to make sure Kinross can't reproduce it. That no one can reproduce it."

That sounded like a good idea. What she had done would never be right or justified. "Hold my arm," he said.

She frowned but reached out and touched his arm. He whispered a spell and a moment later they materialized at the side of the great ship.

He shifted Destiny in his arms, time to wake up sleeping beauty.

At least now he could be sure she wouldn't be so eager to return and do her duty.

Chapter Thirty-Nine

"Life is a storm. One minute you will bathe under the sun and the next you will be shattered upon the rocks. That's when you shout, "'Do your worst, for I will do mine!'" and you will be remembered forever."
—Alexandre Dumas, *The Count of Monte Cristo*

Destiny felt the soft touch of lips against her own.

She blinked her eyes open. For a moment the world was blurred and then, hovering above her, Milo's face came into focus.

A sensation of warmth filled her, and she realized it was happiness. She'd never really been happy before in her life. She hadn't expected to see him again. She'd thought it was over. Now she reached up with a trembling hand and touched his cheek.

"My beautiful warlock," she murmured.

He turned his face and kissed her palm and tingles ran up her arm, along her nerves to settle in her heart. She smiled as he closed her palm around the kiss but kept hold of her hand.

"I thought you would never wake up."

She thought back. The injection, then the darkness. They'd been going to operate on her. In that moment, as she had fallen asleep, it had come to her what her role in life was. She'd wanted to scream in denial because she'd been such an idiot. She'd thought herself so important. And with that knowledge had come the realization that it was over. Finished.

Yet here she was.

And somehow it didn't matter anymore. The look in Milo's eyes was enough to banish the dark thoughts.

"You saved me," she said. Her body felt weak and lethargic, but she forced herself to sit upright and lean against the wall behind her, her gaze never leaving his face.

"Of course I saved you. Did you think I wouldn't?"

She nodded. "I thought you would fly away and leave me behind, and I'd never see you again." She blinked and a tear slipped down over her cheek. She let it fall. "I love you. I know you don't want my love, but you have it anyway."

He closed his eyes for a moment. "I thought you were dead. I thought I was too late." His eyes darkened and he closed the space between them and kissed her. Closing her eyes, she sank into the caress.

He drew back way too soon. "I never wanted to love you." He gave a rueful smile. "My experience of love has not been...something I was eager to repeat. But it was beyond my control. I think it was a lost cause from that moment you first looked at me."

As a declaration of love, it could have been improved upon, but it was enough. Milo loved her. She sighed. "It was love at first sight. Just like in the romances."

He kissed her again and afterward, she wrapped her arms around his waist and laid her head on his chest, listening to the rhythmic thud of his heart.

In a second, she would move, because she had a feeling that they weren't out of danger yet and Milo loved her, which meant she really, really didn't want to die. So she would put off discovering just how likely that was for a little while longer.

Finally, she took a deep breath and leaned away from him. Time to get real. Find out if they had a future. She glanced around and recognized immediately where she was. In her old room on the *Trakis Four*. In her old bed, and she was wearing a pale blue hospital gown that fastened at the front. "How did I get here?" she asked. "What happened?"

He looked away for a moment and she got the distinct impression that he was trying to work out what to say, and from the frown between his dark brows, he was worried about her reaction.

She reached out and rested a hand on his arm. "Tell me."

"It's not...good."

"I can take it."

He considered her; his head cocked to the side. "Yes, you can." He took a deep breath. "It seems Luther Kinross has a heart condition. He was born with it. He'd had a transplant before he left Earth, but it was already failing. Your Dr. Yang—"

"She's not mine," Destiny said. "She was never mine."

"Anyway, she was brought along to find a solution to that problem. Kinross got her taken on as a crew member and places for her daughters on the fleet. Basically, a future in the new world. All she had to do was provide him with a new heart. That's where you come in. She made you."

"I'm a clone, aren't I? Of Kinross? But he's a man."

"And you're not. For which I am immensely glad. Apparently, it can be done, something about manipulating chromosomes."

She pressed her lips together as she thought it through. "But he's...horrible."

Milo let out a startled laugh. "And again—you're not. So obviously, that can be done as well. And on the plus side, you have enhanced everything, IQ, physical strength, and some sort of weird shit anti-aging stuff that the doctor had been working on for years." He studied her some more. "Anyway, I came to rescue you. I appeared in your cell, ready to whisk you away. Except you weren't there. Dr. Yang was. Handcuffed and gagged."

"She tried to kill me. I think she wanted to cut out my heart so Kinross could never have it."

"That was my fault. I told her that her family was dead, and it was Kinross who had killed them. I wanted her help, but I guess it sent her over the edge. She told me I was too late. That you were being operated on and we couldn't reach you in time."

"But you did."

"I blew the power supply which gave us a little more time. And I got to you before…"

"Before they cut my heart out and gave it to Kinross. Thank you."

He studied her. "You don't seem as upset as I thought you would be. I expected you'd be devastated by this."

"Maybe a few days ago I would have been. Now I'm a different person. I've learned so much, come so far." She thought for a moment, trying to come up with the best way to explain. "We can't control where we come from, who our parents are, or in my case who we were cloned from, but that doesn't stop us thinking for ourselves. We can choose what we are. If we can see past the lies that other people tell us." She pressed her lips together and frowned. "That doesn't mean to say that I'm not unhappy about this. I mean, there I was thinking I was the hero in some fairy tale, a savior of humanity." She sniffed. "Instead, I'm nothing but spare parts."

"But gorgeous spare parts." His expression went serious. "You're the best person I've ever met."

His tone was fierce and warmed her inside. She grinned. "And you're the best warlock I've ever met."

"I'm the only—"

"Don't," she said, still smiling. "Just take the compliment, Milo." She blew out her breath. "So what are we going to do?"

"We're going to kill that bastard Kinross."

She thought about his words. Part of her wanted to see Kinross dead so badly it was like a pain in her insides. But the rest of her—most of her—wanted to get away from here as fast as she could. She wanted a life with Milo. That was more important than killing Kinross.

Except he needed to be stopped. He was evil and wicked and could not be left in charge. He had lied and cheated and used child labor and tried to cut out her heart. He had to die.

But was it her job to do it?

Again, she struggled to put her thoughts into words that would make sense. "You can't make your life about revenge. Maybe Kinross needs to die—but do we need to do the killing? Maybe we can just walk away. Have a life." God, she wanted that life so badly. Had never really believed she could have one and now it beckoned to her. Just put the whole thing behind her. They could go and explore this new world together.

He frowned. "You don't want him dead? I thought that would be the first thing you wanted. Because, sweetheart, right now, he is the number one threat to humanity."

And all her life, she'd been told that she had a role to play in the survival of humanity. "Before I met you, I was so idealistic. But only people who are totally isolated from the real world can stay idealistic like that. As soon as you come into contact with real people—or even fictional people in books—the charade of humanity as a whole being something worthy of saving falls apart."

"They're not all bad."

"But why should I stand up for them? Why can't they stand up for themselves?" She shook her head. "Perhaps I am a bad person. After all, I am Kinross. I am everything that makes him who he is. His genetic code is mine. We are the same."

"No, you're not. You're you. Unique." He scrubbed a hand over his head. "Christ, I don't know if God exists. Whether he does or not, there's something in us all. Call it a soul or something else, but it's there, and it's real, and you are not just some offshoot of fucking Kinross. He's evil, and you're the best person I've ever come across." He closed his eyes and breathed deeply. When he opened them, he gave her a small smile. "Sorry. I fucking hate him. I'd rip his fucking heart from his chest if I got the chance."

"Okay, if we get the chance, we rip his heart out. What else?"

"We have to deactivate the nukes. That's nonnegotiable. He's already threatened to destroy Trakis Two."

"I can do that. I researched it. Though we need to take them as well. Otherwise there's always a chance they could get them functional again."

"So we take them to the shuttle and you deactivate them. We can always ditch them in deep space." He sat back. "Rico and Dylan are meeting us in the tunnels in"—he glanced at his comm unit—"thirty-two minutes. We just have to blow the lab—"

At that moment, a figure appeared in the doorway. Destiny went still as she recognized Dr. Yang. She waited for hatred to stir inside her, but it didn't come. Milo got to his feet and she swung her legs over the edge of the cot. She was feeling stronger already, and she pushed herself up. She took a few steps toward the doctor. "I'm sorry about your family," she said. "You must have loved them very much."

Shock flared in Dr. Yang's eyes, then her face seemed to crumple. "I'm sorry about everything."

She could see now that much of Dr. Yang's coldness had been guilt. She couldn't allow herself to care for Destiny, because then she wouldn't have been able to hand her over to Kinross, and her family would have paid the price.

She smiled. "If you hadn't done as Kinross asked, then I wouldn't exist. And I'm very glad to be alive. So thank you."

Dr. Yang gave a small nod and stood up straighter. "I've set the explosives," she said. She turned to Destiny. "No one will be able to duplicate my work. This will end now. Kinross's heart will give out very soon. He's dying."

"Not quickly enough," Milo growled.

"It won't damage the rest of the ship, will it?" Destiny asked. All those people still in cryo. She couldn't bear the thought.

"No. Just the lab. Though the systems might take a hit."

"I think we should wake everyone up," Destiny said. "Just in case."

"And they'll create a distraction," Milo said. "Kinross will have to deal with them as well as us." He turned to Dr. Yang. "Can you do it?"

"Yes. I'll need to go to the tech center to access the systems, but that should be no problem."

"How long?"

"Ten minutes." She thought for a moment. "Go wait outside. I'm less likely to be questioned if I'm alone."

He nodded.

She placed her hands on Destiny's shoulders. "I always thought of you as my creation, as less than human, and I treated you badly. But it's not true. You're more human than anyone I've ever met. Good luck, Destiny."

She dropped her hold, turned, and walked away.

Milo crossed the room and picked up a bag. "We found you some clothes. Get dressed. Then we're out of here."

Destiny dressed quickly. Jeans, a black T-shirt, and boots that were a little tight but not too bad. She allowed him to usher her out of the room, then along the corridor, through the docking bay and to the ramp that led off the ship. They paused at the top while Milo did a quick check of the lay of the land. All looked quiet. She was mulling over Dr. Yang's words. They'd filled her with a sense of unease. As though the other woman was saying goodbye. Why would she say goodbye when she was meeting them here? Any moment now.

She wouldn't. Which meant she wasn't meeting them.

"We have to go back," she said.

"What—?"

But she didn't wait to hear any more. She whirled around and ran back the way they had come, with Milo close behind her. As she turned the last corner and approached the lab, she saw Dr. Yang's small figure disappearing inside. The door closed behind her.

She made to move forward, but Milo grabbed her from behind. "You can't go, the whole place is going to blow any second now."

"But we have to save her." She fought against his hold. But he was too strong, and tears streamed down her face.

"No, Destiny. It's too late. You can't save her. Besides, she doesn't want to be saved."

"I don't care."

The alarm on Milo's comm unit beeped. He went still for a moment, though he didn't release his grip. Then he turned her in his arms and hurled them both to the floor as a huge explosion erupted behind the closed door.

Chapter Forty

"…The friends we have lost do not repose under the ground…they are buried deep in our hearts. It has been thus ordained that they may always accompany us…"
—Alexandre Dumas, *The Count of Monte Cristo*

Milo covered Destiny with his body as heat washed over them.

When he peered up, flames licked at the edge of the doors. The lights went out, replaced by a flashing red glow and the continuous buzz of the fire alarm. The sprinklers came on and cold water drenched his back.

They had to get out of there. Responders would be arriving any moment now. Destiny had gone completely still beneath him, but he wasn't sure how cooperative she was going to be. Maybe best not to give her the choice. He jumped to his feet, getting a quick glimpse of her accusing eyes before he grabbed her by the waist and slung her over his shoulder and ran.

He pulled his pistol from its holster. As he raced into the

docking bay, two men in green jumpsuits entered. He shot them both in the chest and ran on. He paused at the top of the ramp and looked out. "Shit."

A group of guards were heading his way, too many to take. He reached for his wand as a sound behind him made him turn. Footsteps. Lots of them. A mass of people appeared in the doorway. In various stages of undress, they swarmed into the docking bay, all seemed dazed and confused.

They must be the people woken from cryo. No doubt they'd come around and immediately heard the alarms and panicked.

Destiny punched him on the back.

"What?" he asked.

"Let me down."

"Not yet." He turned to face the horde. "This way out!" he shouted.

They ran toward him. He waited until they were surrounded, and then he went with them, down the ramp. Through the crowd he could see the soldiers standing to the side, obviously with no clue what to do in the face of the swarming masses.

They slowed as they reached the ground, milling about, unsure what to do, where to go. Milo edged to the side of the group closest to the forest and then slipped away. He ran to the cover of the trees and kept going until the sound of voices faded. In a small clearing, lit by starlight, he placed Destiny on the ground. She blinked up at him and a tear rolled down her cheek.

She opened her mouth, but before she could speak, he lowered his head and kissed her. Dr. Yang was dead. They were alive.

She went still against him, and then she was kissing him back, fiercely, her lips hard against his, her tongue thrusting into his mouth, and his dick stiffened.

A little voice shouted in his head that they didn't have time for this. He shut it down. They might never have time for this again. He needed it, and he was guessing she needed it more. An affirmation of life in the midst of so much death.

He cupped her face in his hands, deepened the kiss, then slid his hands down her throat, over her shoulders. He kissed her neck and she moaned. Gripping the hem of her T-shirt, he dragged it over her head. Her nipples were hard and he ran his palms over them, then down over her stomach. He flicked open the buttons on her jeans and pushed them down as she kicked off her boots. And she was naked and alive and the most beautiful thing he had ever seen. And likely they were going to die.

Love never worked out well for him, but in that moment, he realized that it didn't matter. Nothing mattered but this moment of connection, this intense feeling of belonging that gripped at his heart.

He sank to his knees and kissed the soft pale skin of her belly, the blond curls at the base, and felt her hands stroke at his hair, hold him to her. He got back to his feet because his dick was hard, and he needed to be inside of her, and they were running out of time.

He kissed her again, heat filling him as her fingers fumbled at his waist. Not fast enough, and he pushed her hands aside, unfastened his pants, and his dick sprang free. He groaned as her hands clasped him and his head went back. She squeezed and he groaned again.

He nipped her neck, then licked her skin as he cupped her ass in his hands and lifted her slightly, her legs wrapping around his waist as he backed her up against the smooth bark of a tree. Staring into her eyes, he shifted her in his arms, positioning himself at the entrance to her body. Then with one sharp thrust, he filled her and for a minute he stood, still staring into her face, holding himself still, savoring the sensation of being deep inside her.

"I love you," she whispered. "Thank you."

"I love you, too."

Her eyes glowed. He moved then, and her muscles tightened around his dick, trying to hold him inside her. He tightened his grip on her ass as he pushed back in, grinding against her and her eyes widened, a shiver running through her. He pulled out, loving the drag of her tight flesh against him. Then in again, rotating his hips, and her head went back. He repeated the action, watching the pulse fluttering in her throat. He could feel the tension rising inside her, her legs gripping him as she pushed herself against him. One more time and she broke apart as shudders coursed through her body.

He released his control then. Burrowing his head in the side of her throat as he pounded into her, each thrust carrying him higher and higher, until the last one forced him over the top and he was coming, falling. He lifted his head so he could see her face as he tumbled and know that she was there to catch him.

"I love you."

For long minutes, they stood wrapped around each other, his cock still buried deep inside her, their hearts beating in time.

He lowered her gently to the ground, then kissed her softly.

"I always wanted to fly," she said. "That's better than flying."

"Much better." He kissed her again, then eased out of her and a look of sadness flashed through her eyes. "We have to go," he said.

"I know."

He fastened his pants, then leaned against the tree and watched as she pulled her clothes on. "We're already late for the rendezvous with Rico and Dylan." As she finished dressing, he held out his hand. She slid her palm into his as he drew his wand. Her eyes widened. "Hold on," he said.

And she did.

Chapter Forty-One

"Punctuality is the politeness of kings."
—Alexandre Dumas, *The Count of Monte Cristo*

They materialized in the tunnels.

Destiny blinked, her gaze settling on the two figures directly in front of them. Rico and Dylan.

Milo was getting better at controlling his magic.

Her body still throbbed from the aftermath of their lovemaking. It had been the most beautiful experience of her life. And she supposed her next thought should be that now she could die happy.

No way.

More than anything, she wanted to live. She wanted some sort of life with Milo. She didn't care where. As long as Milo was with her, she would be home. Trouble was, she didn't think it was going to be so easy.

Maybe they should forget the nukes and just run away. Hide where no one could find them. Soon Luther Kinross would die. Dr. Yang had said his heart was failing. But

Kinross wasn't dead yet and he could presumably do a lot of damage before then.

The truth was, she hadn't been born to be a savior to humanity. Just to one man. A megalomaniac who'd carried the seeds of destruction from Earth. A man she was tied to by bonds stronger than family. She *was* him. What did that even mean? She searched inside herself for some form of recognition, but she didn't even know what he looked like.

"You're late," Dylan said, stepping forward and pulling her out of her introspection.

"And the pair of you look like you just got laid," Rico added, his tone accusing. His gaze dropped to where their hands were still connected. She almost pulled away, but then tightened her grip instead and Milo squeezed in response. A smile tugged at her mouth. Rico's eyes narrowed. "*Mierda,* I can't believe I've traveled five hundred years, with no fucking problems, and then I finally get here just to be faced with this. And the two of you are shagging and holding hands as if the sky isn't fucking falling."

"What's happened?" Milo asked.

"They blew up his shuttle," Dylan said. "He's a little pissed."

"I am *seriously* pissed," Rico growled. "We're going to have to steal another. *Dios*, I'll steal the fucking *Trakis Four* if that's what's needed to get off this fucking shithole."

The vampire didn't sound happy. His eyes glowed crimson. Was that normal? She glanced up at Milo, but he didn't seem to be concerned. "We stick to the plan," he said. "We get the nukes. Take them back to the ship. Destiny can disarm them while we go take one of the other shuttles—"

"We've been through this—they work on biometrics," Dylan said. "We can't fly them."

"Then we'll take the crew if we have to." He glanced down into her face and smiled. "We're getting through this and going home."

"*Mierda*," Rico muttered. "He's in love. Brilliant timing. And do you remember how it turned out last time? I had to pick up the fucking pieces."

"Yeah, and you did that really well." Milo dropped her hand, stepped forward, and poked the vampire in the chest. "You sold me into fucking slavery for ten years."

Rico grinned and the tension seemed to ooze away. "You're still alive, aren't you? Though not for much longer at a guess." He exhaled loudly. "Okay. While I'm tempted to just leave now, I don't like the idea of some dickhead with nukes and a grudge against us. So let's go see what we can do about that."

Dylan led the way. Milo and Destiny followed with Rico bringing up the rear. The tunnels were quiet, and they met no one.

"No guards," Dylan said.

"Likely the explosion on the *Trakis Four* worked in our favor," Milo said. "They've sent everyone they had to investigate and deal with a few thousand Chosen Ones we woke up."

"Let's get this done before they come back then." Rico brushed past them and approached the door. He pushed, but it was locked, and he swore.

Milo stepped up, placed his hand on the lock, and whispered a word. He opened the door, then raised an eyebrow at Rico. He was so clever, her warlock. As he stepped into the room, Dylan came to stand beside her.

"So did you find out who you are and what this mysterious role you have to play is?"

Mind your own business. The words hovered on her lips because she wasn't sure she wanted to share. In fact, she knew she didn't. She felt a little...she wasn't sure, embarrassed maybe. Because she had been so naive. Though in her own defense she could understand why she had been the way she was. She'd had no one to believe but Dr. Yang.

"I'm a clone of Luther Kinross," she said.

Rico turned around at her words. She squirmed a little under the scrutiny. Then she took a deep breath and said the rest as fast as she could. Get it over with.

"Kinross has a weak heart. He needs a new one. Hence, I came into existence. It seems I'm nothing but spare parts."

They were all staring at her now and she scowled. "What? Have none of you ever seen a clone before?"

"Nope," Rico said, studying her closely. "Shouldn't you be a man?"

"Apparently not. Dr. Yang made a few changes. I think she was a little bored."

Dylan was studying her, his head cocked to one side. "Yeah, I can see the resemblance, now I know. I always did get the feeling you were familiar. Jesus. Are you going to start acting like him? Any ambitions to take over the world?"

"I'll let you know." She glared. "Are we doing this?"

Rico chuckled. "I like your girlfriend," he said to Milo. "Okay, move people."

Destiny hurried over to where the nukes were stacked. The wooden cases were around six feet in length, three feet wide and two feet high. She figured they could carry one between two of them. That would be six journeys.

"Can't you magic them to the ship?" she asked Milo.

"I'd rather not. Just in case…"

Rico shuddered. "No way. We carry them."

He picked up one end as though it weighed nothing, and Dylan took the other, and between them they carried it from the room.

Milo looked at her. "Are you okay to do this?"

"Of course." She hated that she wasn't as physically strong as they were. But she could manage one end of a nuke. She hoped. Milo picked up his side and she picked up hers. It was heavier than she'd expected. Milo frowned, then whispered a word and the weight vanished.

All she had to do was guide the thing, and they caught up with Rico and Dylan as they were carrying their bomb up the ramp.

Rico glanced back over his shoulder. "You know, maybe we should just get some explosive and blow up the tunnels, bring half the planet down on top of this thing. Might be easier than taking them with us."

She didn't want to blow up the alien ship, but she kept her mouth closed. She'd read about nukes. She would do anything necessary to make sure they were never used as a weapon.

"Let's decide when Destiny has had a look at them," Milo said as they dumped the box down and headed back out. "If she can disarm them, we go that route. If not..."

As they came down the ramp and stepped onto the sand, Destiny stroked the smooth metal of the ship. "I'll be sad to leave her behind," she said. "She's the first thing I ever thought of as mine." She sighed. "She needs a name."

Milo whispered a word and the illegible script on the side of the ship shimmered and reformed. *Destiny's Heart.*

She smiled. "Perfect."

They did four more journeys with no problems. But their luck couldn't last. As they were setting off on the last and final journey, lights flashed in the tunnel that led to headquarters. She heard the sound of feet on the rock floor.

"Shit," Milo muttered, pulling his wand from his belt.

In front of them Rico and Dylan came to a halt, and both of them glanced back over their shoulders. Without any warning, something whizzed over her head. It hit the tunnel wall almost directly between her and Rico, exploding with a roar and a flash of light.

For a moment she was blinded. Then Milo shoved her

to the floor, and she went down. Rocks were falling and everything was chaos, noise and dust and panic. She couldn't move. Milo was a dead weight on top of her.

Was he dead?

He couldn't be dead. She wouldn't think that.

She wriggled and he rolled off her. Pushing herself onto all fours, she shook herself. Everything was dark. Groping, she found Milo, then trailed her fingers over him until she found his throat and the steady beat of his pulse. The tight band around her chest loosened. He was alive.

But for how much longer? All around her the tunnels creaked as though they were about to crumble. They had to get out of there.

Then lights flashed on. Her gaze flew to Milo where he lay on his back close by. His eyes were closed, but she could see the rise and fall of his chest. Rocks lay all around them. One must have hit him on the head while he'd been protecting her.

She rubbed the dust out of her eyes. Rico and Dylan were nowhere in sight. Hopefully they were on the other side of the rubble and not under it. They had to get out of there. But the tunnel back to the ship was completely blocked. No getting out that way.

She shook Milo's arm. "Wake up." Nothing. She gritted her teeth and slapped his face. "Wake the fuck up, Milo."

His eyes blinked open and he focused on her. He sat up, rubbing the back of his head and looking around. "My wand?"

"There."

She pointed to where it stuck out from under a huge lump of red rock. He reached for it, tugged, but it was stuck solid. He opened his mouth, no doubt to do some clever magic thing, when a *click* sounded behind her and she turned slowly.

Silas stood there, a rifle in his hands, aimed at Milo. "You should have just gone," Silas said. "Why the hell couldn't you have just gone?" His finger tightened on the trigger.

"Hold on, baby," Milo murmured from beside her.

Her eyes widened, then she gripped his arm.

And the world disappeared.

Chapter Forty-Two

"'Farewell kindness, humanity, and gratitude! Farewell to all the feelings that expand the heart! I have been heaven's substitute to recompense the good - now the god of vengeance yields to me his power to punish the wicked!'"
—Alexandre Dumas, *The Count of Monte Cristo*

They were in the cavern beside the spaceship, Destiny gripping his arm so tight he thought his bones might snap.

The nuke lay on the sand beside them. It hadn't blown up. Thank fuck.

Unfortunately, his wand had been left behind in the rubble. *Damn.* He had an idea he would be needing it before this was over.

"We're safe," he said. For now. He wasn't sure how long that would last. As he spoke, Rico and Dylan emerged from the tunnel, still carrying the nuke between them.

Rico halted in front of them and grinned. "Impressive. Let's get these on board and then decide what to do next. Will your wards hold?"

"They should. We're safe for now."

"They're going to keep coming," Dylan said. "Any moment and the place will be crawling with Kinross's men."

Rico sniffed the air. "Well, it's too close to dawn to leave. We're going to have to sit out the day and make a run for it under cover of darkness."

"A run to where?" Milo asked.

"The shuttle from the *Trakis Five*," Dylan replied. "We checked them out and one of the representatives is sick and confined on board. He can fly the thing, so we don't need to override the biometrics. We'll be cutting it close, though. We have another twelve hours while the planets are in alignment and after that the shuttle won't make it back to Trakis Two."

They carried the last two nukes into the ship and stored them with the others. Destiny was going to attempt to disarm them. But there was no rush now. They had the whole day and he hadn't slept in…a long time. He was exhausted and his head hurt. He had an overwhelming urge to lie down on an actual bed and hold Destiny while they both slept.

She looked as tired as he felt. Shadows under her eyes.

"I'm going to go check what's happening out there," Dylan said. "You two…don't do anything I wouldn't do."

Rico snorted. He'd found some whiskey and was swigging straight from the bottle. "I'm going to see if I can contact the *Trakis Two*. We might need them before this is over." He left as well, and they were alone.

"Let's go to bed," he said, holding out his hand.

She looked at it longingly. "I have to…" She waved a hand at the nukes.

"They'll wait. And you'll work better after some rest."

With a quick nod, she slid her hand into his, then led the way, taking him to a small circular cabin on the other side of the ship. This was obviously where she had been sleeping as her clothes lay over a small stool, and the huge bed, which took up most of the cabin, was rumpled and unmade.

He undressed her slowly, then stripped off his own clothes.

This time they made love slowly and sweetly, and afterward, he pulled her naked body close and stroked her back until her breathing evened out and she slept.

Sleep eluded him, though.

Milo couldn't shake the feeling that they were making a huge mistake by leaving Kinross alive. They couldn't rely on the bastard to do the convenient thing and die. And while he was alive, he would keep coming after Destiny. She was his one hope of life. She would never be safe until Kinross was dead. Kinross would pursue them across the universe. She would spend her whole life looking over her shoulder.

She deserved a chance at a good life.

That was one thing he could give to her.

Plus, while they had taken the nukes, who knew what else Kinross had up his sleeves? He'd obviously been planning this long before they'd left Earth. He could have weapons secreted on other ships.

None of them would be safe while he was alive.

Not Destiny. Or Rico.

The people he loved.

He didn't want to die. For the first time in centuries he had something to live for. But he knew one thing: if something was truly worth living for, then it was also worth dying for. First, he had to make sure she would be safe.

Decision made, he relaxed. He could have a little while longer. Pulling her closer so she snuggled against him, he closed his eyes and slept.

He woke to the sensation of a warm mouth engulfing his hard

cock. He groaned and reached down, threading his fingers through her hair. She peered up at him, as her hands slid over his balls, cupping him, squeezing, while her mouth played its magic and the pleasure built inside him, intensifying as he tried to control the thrust of his hips. She held his gaze as she sucked on him, sliding her lips over his shaft until his spine arched and he gave up and came with her mouth still around him.

Afterward, he collapsed back on the bed, weak and lethargic, a smile on his face. She licked her lips and then kissed his cock and crawled up the bed to snuggle against his chest.

"Sorry, I didn't mean to wake you, but I couldn't resist, and it was there and…"

"It was a wonderful way to wake up. The best ever. Now, go back to sleep."

She closed her eyes and her breathing evened out. He lay for a long time, trying not to sleep again. He didn't want to waste any of this time with her.

Finally, he knew he had to go. He slipped from the bed without waking her and grabbed his clothes from the floor. At the door, he turned for one last look. She was curled on her side, her hands under her cheek, a smile curving her lips. Fixing the image in his mind, he opened the door and stepped outside. In the corridor, he dressed quickly, then headed for the bridge. He found Rico in the pilot's seat, an empty bottle in front of him and a scowl on his face.

"Did you get through?" he asked.

"No. It seems your girlfriend is the only one who can work this thing. Either that or I've broken it. What are you doing up?"

"I'm going to kill Kinross."

Rico's eyes narrowed. "I thought we'd decided that was a suicide mission."

"Not necessarily. I think I can do it." He just wished he had his wand.

"Are you sure this isn't about revenge?"

"Maybe a little."

"Your mother gave up everything—including you—for revenge. You wasted most of your life on Earth attempting to get revenge on your father. You really want to go that route again? You think Destiny will appreciate the gesture?"

"It's not only about revenge," Milo said. "He'll come after her. He can't do anything else. She's his only hope of survival. Besides, he's the sort of man who hates to be beaten. He'll come after all of us. And we don't know what else he brought from Earth. He'll have contingency plans, and I'm sure you don't want to spend the next few years looking over your shoulder."

Rico pursed his lips. "Maybe you're right. But if so, we should all go. Make sure the job is done properly."

Milo shook his head. "One man is more likely to get through and get close enough to do it. And you need to get Destiny off this shit planet. I've never asked of anything from you, and now I'm asking. Get Destiny to safety. Give her the life she deserves."

"She's not going to be happy about this."

"She'll get over it. Besides, I'm planning to make it back."

Rico gave him a long look, then shook his head. "After a thousand years, you have to fall in love again now."

He grinned. "I know. Inconvenient. But I wouldn't have it any other way."

Rico gave him another look, but this time he nodded. "Okay. But try and stay alive. I hate dealing with hysterical females. And we leave this fucking planet in three hours. No later. Make sure you're at the shuttle."

He wanted to say something but wasn't sure how. In the end he just nodded. "Thank you," he said. "For everything."

Then he turned and walked out. He met Dylan as he exited the tunnels into the forest. He was in wolf form but shifted when he caught sight of Milo.

"You're going after Kinross?"

He nodded.

"I'd offer to come along, but to be honest you're better off alone. But good luck. Put a bullet in the bastard from me."

"I will."

Dylan gave him a sly smile. "And if you don't come back, I'll look after Destiny for you."

"I'll be fucking back and leave Destiny alone." But it comforted him to know there would be someone else to look out for her.

Now, it was time to end this.

Chapter Forty-Three

"Happiness is like one of those palaces on an enchanted island, its gates guarded by dragons. One must fight to gain it."
—Alexandre Dumas, *The Count of Monte Cristo*

Destiny woke up with a feeling of well-being. It lasted for all of two seconds, which was when she realized she was alone in the bed and Milo was gone.

She sat up and looked around the room. It wasn't big and there was nowhere to hide.

His clothes were gone from the floor.

He'd probably just woken up and left her to sleep.

Except she had a bad feeling.

She jumped out of bed. She felt better, wide awake, and the dull headache that had lingered after the anesthetic had cleared was gone. But she wanted Milo. She left the clothes where she had dropped them and pulled on one of her own yellow jumpsuits. It reminded her of Dr. Yang. It was the one time the woman had given in to what she had referred to as frivolity. Then her spare pair of boots, and she headed out at a trot. Rico was on the bridge, chatting with Dylan. Milo was nowhere in sight, and her bad feeling intensified until it was a solid lump in her throat.

Rico glanced across as she entered and frowned.

She took a step closer. "Where's Milo?"

Rico shrugged. "He's just gone to see what's happening outside. Why don't you get to work on those nukes? Keep yourself busy. We'll be heading out in a couple of hours."

"You're lying."

He frowned. "Now why would you say that?"

"Because your lips are moving."

Dylan snorted a laugh. "Ha, she's got your number."

She swung around to face him. "Where is he?"

"He's gone to kill Kinross."

"Why the hell did you have to tell her that?" Rico snapped.

"Because she deserves to know the truth."

The lump expanded until it choked off her air. Why would he have done this? Why leave her behind? She was gasping for breath. The world spinning. Dylan grabbed her by the shoulders and gave her a shake. "Get a grip," he said. "Milo knows what he's doing. If anyone can get to Kinross, he can. And Milo is not so easy to kill. Don't give up on him yet."

"I'm not giving up on him at all," she snarled. "I'm going to get him."

"*Mierda*," Rico muttered. "Now look what you've done. You can't go and get him. You're a liability. And he's better off alone."

"No, he isn't. He's better off with me."

She whirled around and ran off the bridge. She needed to think this through. In some ways, she knew Rico was right. If she didn't do this properly then she was a liability and would likely get Milo killed. And Kinross would win, and he'd take her heart, and no way was that happening. Her heart belonged to Milo.

So how to do this?

In the storage area with the nukes, she paced the room a few times, but her gaze kept being drawn back to the warheads. She came to stand over the crates, then pried open the top one and stared down at the weapon. There was a detonator in a little pocket at the side of the crate, and she took it out and studied it for a minute. The bombs could be remote detonated. And if one went off, then it would set off the rest and the planet would be decimated.

Could she do that?

She realized in that moment that humanity as a whole didn't matter. It was the individuals who mattered. She wasn't ready to die for the nameless masses. But she was ready to die for Milo.

Not only that, but she was ready to kill for him.

She just hoped it wouldn't come to that.

Rico and Dylan appeared in the doorway just as she finished prepping the detonator.

"Is that what I think it is?" Dylan asked.

She nodded.

"Is that a good idea?"

"Probably not. But I can't come up with a better one. Hopefully, I won't have to use it."

"Kinross will never believe you would do it."

She smiled. "He will believe it. And you know why? Because Kinross knows exactly what I'm capable of. After all, we're the same person."

"That is scary as hell," Dylan said. "And seriously badass. You're giving me a hard-on."

She let out a laugh.

"We brought you some presents." Dylan handed her a

couple of pistols and holsters, and she strapped them around her waist. Then Rico stripped off his long leather coat and gave it to her. She shrugged into it. It reached the ground but hid the weapons and it had lots of pockets. She slid the detonator into the inside pocket, then looked around the room.

She found the small pile of grenades and slipped a couple into the side pockets and then she was ready.

Rico stepped up close. He had a comm unit in his hand; she held out her wrist and he slipped it on. "We're heading out now," he said. "I for one want to be off planet just in case the whole place goes up. We'll stay in orbit for another two hours, comm us if you get him out and we'll meet you at the rendezvous point."

"Understood." She reached up on tiptoe and kissed his cheek. "Thanks for looking after Milo all these years." Then she turned to Dylan. He kissed her on the mouth. "And thank you for…everything." She shrugged. "And good luck."

"Hey, we'll see you soon."

She hoped so, but for all her bravado she couldn't see it happening. And she doubted very much that she would set off a nuclear explosion. Only if she had no choice…and probably not even then. But at least Milo wouldn't die alone.

She gave them one last nod and headed out.

Time to save the warlock she loved.

Or die trying.

Chapter Forty-Four

"'Without reflecting that this is the only moment in which you can study character,'" said the count; "on the steps of the scaffold death tears off the mask that has been worn through life, and the real visage is disclosed."
—Alexandre Dumas, *The Count of Monte Cristo*

Milo was heading for Camelot. Hopefully, there would be a boat to take him across the water, otherwise he'd be swimming. But as he came out of the forest, his eyes were drawn toward a huge crowd congregated around the new church.

Thousands of them thronged the area, their voices raised in anger.

He moved closer. There were a number of the green-clad soldiers, all armed, but they seemed at a loss about what to do against so many. No one took any notice of him as he weaved his way through the crowd.

Aaron Sekongo stood at the front above the crowd in some sort of makeshift pulpit. He'd lost his captain's uniform and was dressed in the long black robes of a priest. Asshole. He raised his arms. "I am Aaron Sekongo, High Priest of the Church of Everlasting Life. Please be silent. This is a house of God. Your questions will all be answered in good time. Have faith in the Lord."

The words were met with a loud roar of disapproval.

Milo stopped beside an elderly man wearing a crew uniform with a blue shirt. He couldn't remember what that meant. "What's happening?" Milo asked.

"Some guy called Kinross is going to come along and tell us that. Apparently, he's our leader. What I want to know is who elected him? Not me. I've never heard of him."

At that moment, an armored vehicle drove out of the water and headed their way. It was fully dark now and the lights cut a swath through the crowd. They parted sullenly before it, and it pulled up beside the makeshift pulpit. The top opened and Kinross appeared, with Silas at his back.

Kinross did not look well. His skin was a sickly yellow and he leaned against the handrail. Milo studied him closely, looking for similarities to Destiny. They were obvious when you knew what to look for. The shape and color of his eyes, the strong chin, the straight nose. A wave of hatred washed through him. The man was pure evil. He had to die. It wasn't revenge, though. It was justice and keeping Destiny safe.

He eased his weapon from the holster at his waist but then went still. A whole troop of guards moved to surround the vehicle, their weapons pointed into the crowd. Milo would have one shot only and then he had no doubt he would be taken down. He looked around, searching for a way to improve the odds.

Kinross took a shaky step forward. He rubbed at his left shoulder and a spasm crossed his face. He was a dying man. It was clear in every small movement he made. His heart was giving out. Not at some vague point in the future. But now.

Milo eased the weapon back into his holster. He didn't have to do this after all. Clearly, for once, God was on his side and would do the job for him. At the thought, a wave of pure happiness washed through him. This wasn't the end. He could go back and fly away with Destiny and they could have a life together.

Kinross was talking now, but he didn't listen to the words. They didn't matter.

The crowd didn't like them, though; they were greeted by an angry murmur. Things were not going Kinross's way. The rabble were revolting. Milo grinned.

Then the skin of his back prickled and he turned slowly.

The crowd had parted, and she stood there. Dressed in a yellow jumpsuit, boots, and a long black leather coat. She was the most beautiful thing he had ever seen and for a moment he melted. Then he gritted his teeth. This was not supposed to happen. She was supposed to be safe, leaving the planet with Rico and Dylan and having a wonderful life. And he'd been just about to join her.

Instead she was here. Panic grabbed him and tightened around his throat. "What the hell are you doing here?"

She smiled. "I've come to save you. I choose you over humanity."

He melted again. She'd come for him. He came first. That's what she was telling him. His euphoria lasted for all of one second, then the panic was back. They were the center of attention. The spotlight found them, settled on Destiny.

Kinross screamed over the loudspeaker. "Get that woman!"

Nobody moved.

Except the guards. They pushed their way through the crowd.

Fuck.

His mind scrambled for a way out.

Destiny reached into her pocket and tossed him a grenade. He caught it as she pulled out one of her own. Except it wasn't a grenade. It was a small, square box. The crowd had gone silent as if innately sensing danger. They backed away from the two of them, leaving them standing alone in a circle of light.

The soldiers were closing in.

"Luther!" she called out. "Do you recognize what this is?"

She held up the small box.

"You won't do it," Kinross replied, but his voice was shaky, lacking in confidence. "You would destroy the whole planet."

It came to him then what she held, and he swallowed. The detonator for one of the nuclear bombs. She really had chosen him. And he wasn't sure it was a good thing. He wasn't worth all these lives.

She took a few steps closer, so she stood directly below Kinross. "You know exactly what I'm capable of. Ask yourself—what would you do in these circumstances? Would you give up your heart, would you allow someone to cut it from your living body and take it for their own? Or would you blow everyone up before you let that happen?"

Silas aimed his weapon and a small red dot appeared over her heart. She smiled and Milo shivered as a chill ran through him.

"Do you really want to take the chance?" she asked. "A bullet in the heart and my hand spasms in death and... boom." She turned back to the crowd. "This is the detonator for a nuclear device that will kill you all."

They drew a little farther away as though that would save them.

"A nuclear device brought from Earth by Luther Kinross. He believes he should be in charge, and he has an army to back him up. And a stash of nuclear weapons just in case someone decides they don't want to live in his brave new world." She looked around. "Is that what you want in a leader? You're free people. You can make the decision."

"Don't listen to her!" Kinross screamed. "She's not even human. She's nothing but a clone. And her compatriot is a monster. A creature of the devil." Spittle frothed at the corner of his mouth, and he staggered backward, pain blossoming across his face. He backed into Silas, who dropped his weapon and took hold of his shoulders.

"We need a medic!" he shouted.

Everything seemed to stop, and the crowd fell silent.

Silas lowered Kinross to the floor and started performing CPR. He glanced up after a minute. "Where's that goddamn medic?"

A man in a red shirt pushed his way through the crowd. "I'm a doctor. Let me take a look."

Milo edged closer to Destiny. They needed to get the hell out of here while the attention was on Kinross. The mood of the crowd was volatile. It wouldn't take much to turn the tide against them. Before he could speak, Silas straightened, his face expressionless. He stared at Destiny. "He's dead. You can let go of your weapon. There's no need for it now. You can go free. I've no argument with you or your friend." He turned to the guards. "Fall back," he said. "Let them go."

The soldiers drew back and lowered their weapons.

Destiny's hand dropped to her side and she slid the detonator back into her pocket. Her shoulders slumped and she blew out her breath. And Milo heaved a sigh of relief. He hadn't really believed she would destroy them all. On the other hand, she'd given a pretty convincing argument.

Time to move.

As he reached out to take her hand, a voice called out across the crowd. "Stop them!" Sekongo shouted from the pulpit. "In the name of our Everlasting Lord, stop the abominations!"

Destiny looked at him, a frown forming between her eyes. "Does he mean us?"

"I'm afraid so."

The crowd closed in behind them, and he swore.

"You heard what our great leader, Luther Kinross, said," Sekongo again. Why didn't the asshole shut up? "She's not human and he's a monster."

A murmur ran through the crowd.

"There will be a reward for anyone who captures the abominations. Come into the grace of God."

Goddamn Church. "I think we should leave," Milo murmured.

But talk of a reward had turned the tide of feeling. The muttering grew louder, and the mob shifted restlessly.

Christ, he wished he had his wand. Though he did have a grenade. He held it up. "This might not be a nuclear bomb, but it will still kill a few of you. Back off."

The people nearest backed away, pushing into the ones behind them and clearing a path. Destiny inched closer to him, and side by side they moved slowly through the press of people.

When they reached the edge of the crowd, he grabbed her hand. "Run!"

Chapter Forty-Five

*"It's necessary to have wished for death in order to know
how good it is to live."*
—Alexandre Dumas, *The Count of Monte Cristo*

What happened?

She'd thought it was all over. Kinross was dead. Didn't
that mean she was safe?

Obviously not.

She could feel the crowd behind her, a mob screaming for
her death. What had she ever done to them?

Milo all but dragged her behind him. But they were in
the trees now, weaving between the trunks and leaving their
pursuers behind. Finally, Milo pulled her behind a thick tree
trunk. He stood with his back against it, breathing hard. Then
he turned to her, lowered his head, and kissed her. "Thank
you."

"For what?" she asked breathlessly. She'd hardly done a
good job of saving him. In fact, she'd totally messed up. But
at least she hadn't nuked the whole planet.

"For putting me first," he said.

"You are first." She glanced at her comm unit. "We're only minutes from the deadline with Rico. And no way will we make it on foot. Can you magic us there?"

"Not without my wand."

That wasn't good news. She peered around the edge of the tree. Through the forest, she could see the flickering lights of torches. A cry rang out as the mob caught sight of them. And they were baying like hounds.

"*Run*," Milo said again.

He raised his wrist as they ran and spoke into the comm unit. "We're not going to make it. Get the hell out of here. We'll find another way."

She recognized where they were now. Heading toward the entrance to the tunnels. If they could just make it then they would be hidden.

They dived into the entrance and Milo stopped so abruptly she crashed into him. He turned her in his arms, pressed her against the cool rock of the wall, and kissed her.

Outside, she could hear the crowd milling about, restless. Their voices rising and falling. She wished she hadn't woken them up now. This was gratitude for you. It would teach her not to try and do good deeds in the future.

They just had to wait it out, then find a way off the planet.

Someone shouted above the crowd. She recognized the priest's voice. "There! A tunnel. They've taken to ground. Hunt them out."

"Shit," Milo said. "The wards have failed. Get to the ship."

They turned and ran through the dark tunnels. She could hear the chase behind them, see the wavering light from the torches playing on the ceiling and walls, casting shadows.

They raced into the cavern and straight up the ramp and into the ship. The doors slid shut behind them. On the bridge, she swiped her hand over the surveillance screens just as the crowd poured into the cavern. They came to an abrupt halt as they caught sight of the ship, then began to inch forward, closer and closer. There were soldiers among them, one drew his pistol and shot at the hull.

They were shooting at her beautiful ship.

She gritted her teeth as the shots ricocheted off the surface. She had to do something. Searching the room, her gaze settled on the big red button on the console. Without conscious thought, her feet moved her toward it.

"Oh hell, no," Milo muttered from behind her.

"Trust me," she said, holding out her hand to him.

He tangled his fingers with hers, closed his eyes for a moment; when they opened, they were resolute. "Always."

And she slammed her hand on the button.

She wasn't sure what she expected.

Worst case...nothing.

Or maybe the worst case was they would set off and crash into the wall of the cavern and they'd die.

Then they were rising. She waited for the ship to stop. To level out. But no, they went up and up. Faster and faster. The crowd below them was silent, their faces raised and drenched in light from the burning torches and the ship's engines.

"Can you stop this?" Milo said. "We're going to hit the roof."

Her hand hovered over the button. But if they stopped, they had nowhere to go. *Have faith.*

She could see the roof rapidly approaching through one of the screens. She tightened her hold on Milo, and he pulled her close and kissed her and she closed her eyes, and her mind, to everything but the feel of him.

They didn't crash and she opened her eyes. Above them, the roof was sliding open and she could see the stars. And then they were through. They hovered for a moment, and she held her breath. Then they shot forward so fast that they were both knocked off their feet and she crashed to the floor, Milo on top of her so the air left her in a *whoosh*.

And then she was flying.

Epilogue

"He who has felt the deepest grief is best able to experience supreme happiness."
—Alexandre Dumas, *The Count of Monte Cristo*

They'd left Trakis Four far behind, and good riddance as far as Milo was concerned.

Seated in the pilot's seat with Destiny snuggled in his lap, he was concentrating on the fact that despite their dire circumstances, he was rock hard. He pulled her closer and she squirmed against him.

"That's really impressive," she said.

It was. He was impressed himself. "Have I ever mentioned that I hate flying," he said.

She twisted on his lap so she could stare into his face. "How can you hate flying? It's wonderful."

"We're in a spaceship and neither of us knows how it works." He waved a hand at the screen. "Added to that, we're somewhere in the vastness of space with no idea where we're heading. Except we're heading there fast."

She opened her mouth to answer, but at that moment the comm unit on his wrist buzzed. He thought about ignoring it, but then Destiny's buzzed as well, and she pressed the button to accept the call.

"This is the captain of the space cruiser, *Destiny's Heart*. How can we help you?"

"Very posh," Rico said. "I take it you both got away all right."

"We did."

"I'm glad. We'll see you on Trakis Two."

And the comm ended.

"Will we?" Milo asked. "Do we even know where Trakis Two is?" It was a big goddamn sky out there.

She reached out and touched the screen with her fingertip. "There it is," she said. "Trakis Two."

He leaned closer. It just looked like another dot on the screen to him. "How do you know?"

"I studied the star charts."

"How did you get so clever?" he asked.

Her face turned serious. "Dr. Yang manipulated my genetic code to increase my IQ."

He chuckled. "It doesn't really matter how."

"I know. I'm happy with what I am. I have free will, and I can be anything I choose to be."

She was so bright. And her words filled him with a sense of infinite possibilities. The world lay before them, vast and new. He hadn't wanted to come on this journey, and he'd thought they'd reached the end many times. But it was only just beginning. And with Destiny by his side, he was happy for the journey to never end. They'd make their own world where neither of them had to hide what and who they were.

"Do you want to explore the universe with me, Destiny?"

She turned so she straddled his lap, then flung her arms around his neck. "To the end of the universe and back." She grinned. "But first we have to learn to fly this thing."

Acknowledgments

Thank you so much to my fabulous publisher, Liz Pelletier, for suggesting I write this series and revisit my Dark Desires world, albeit a few hundred years before *Break Out*, book 1 in that series, begins. And thanks to everyone at Entangled Publishing for all the support and the amazing cover, and especially my editors, Liz and Lydia Sharp, for their great work and advice.

Thanks to my marvellous critique group, Passionate Critters, for reading my stories and telling me what they really think.

And finally, thanks to Rob, my other and better half, for putting up with me constantly disappearing into worlds of my own making.

About the Author

Growing up, Nina Croft spent her time dreaming of faraway sunnier places and ponies. When she discovered both, and much more, could be found between the covers of a book, her life changed forever.

Later, she headed south, picked up a husband on the way, and together they discovered a love of travel and a dislike of 9 to 5 work. Eventually they stumbled upon the small almond farm in Spain they now call home.

Nina spends her days reading, writing, and riding under the blue Spanish skies—sunshine and ponies. Proof that dreams can come true if you want them enough.

If you'd like to learn about new releases, sign up for Nina's newsletter here.

www.ninacroft.com

the Things to Do Before You Die series

His Fantasy Girl

Her Fantasy Husband

His Fantasy Bride

the Babysitting a Billionaire series

Losing Control

Out of Control

Taking Control

the Melville Sisters series

Operation Saving Daniel

Betting on Julia

Blackmailed by the Italian Billionaire

The Spaniard's Kiss